The Park House Affair

a novel

KACIE FOOS

This is a work of fiction. The characters, organizations, and events portrayed in this novel are either products of the author's imagination or used fictitiously.

This book is dedicated to the man I love, Mike.

CHAPTER ONE

AMELIA HELD ARTHUR'S HAND SO TIGHTLY SHE COULD FEEL his heartbeat pulsing against her palm. The faint tremor in his fingers mirrored the flutter in her own chest. Beneath the vaulted arches of St. Mary's Church, the world seemed to hush in anticipation—the soft scrape of shoes on ancient stone, the faint perfume of lilies and beeswax candles, the hush of gathered breath.

Arthur leaned close, his voice a warm whisper that brushed against her ear. "You are so beautiful, my Amelia."

She met his gaze—steady, blue, filled with something that made the world tilt—and felt her cheeks flush. "You don't look so bad yourself," she murmured back, her voice half-playful, half-nervous tremor.

Before either could say more, the string quartet began to play, the first delicate notes spiraling upward through the cavernous space. The music carried like sunlight through stained glass, echoing off centuries-old walls. Above them, ten gilded angels gleamed from the rafters—serene, watchful, forever frozen in gentle smiles. As the music swelled, the angels seemed almost to glow, as if blessing the ceremony from their heavenly perch.

Amelia drew in a slow, shaky breath and smiled at Arthur. "This is it."

He released her hand, only to offer his arm instead, every gesture so effortlessly composed. "Shall we?"

She looped her arm through his, her bouquet of lilies trembling slightly as they began their walk down the aisle. Each step felt impossibly heavy, a heartbeat echoing on ancient stone. The church itself was a masterpiece—five centuries of history pressed into every pew, every sunlit mote floating through the air.

Amelia glanced around as they moved forward, taking in the familiar faces that turned toward them—smiling, whispering, watching. Some faces she knew well; others she had only met at dinner parties or through Arthur's circle. There was warmth in many of their smiles, though not all. Two young women near the center pews caught her eye, whispering behind gloved hands, giggling as their gazes lingered far too long on Arthur. The flicker of envy was sharp and surprising. She straightened her shoulders, ignored them, and clutched her bouquet tighter, the soft petals brushing her knuckles.

At the altar, the priest greeted them both with a polite nod. Charlie stood waiting, a wide grin faltering just slightly as his leg bounced with nervous energy. Amelia smiled fondly; Charlie was incapable of hiding how he felt. He looked both ecstatic and terrified—a boy on the edge of a dream he'd longed for.

When Amelia and Arthur reached him, they parted—she stepping to her place among the bridesmaids, he joining the groomsmen. The shift in space left her oddly aware of his absence beside her, of the warmth his arm had provided.

The processional continued. One by one, more bridesmaids and groomsmen made their way down the aisle, including Peter, Charlie's younger brother and best man. Peter grinned wickedly and clapped his brother on the back—a little too hard.

"Jesus Christ—" Arthur began under his breath, but the priest's raised eyebrows froze him mid-sentence. Arthur cleared his throat quickly. "—is Lord... and smiling down at us today."

A ripple of laughter moved through the guests. Charlie elbowed him discreetly in the ribs, his shoulders shaking.

"Boys," came the sharp voice of Mrs. Turner—Charlie's mother—from the front pew. "Behave."

"Yes, Mum," they both muttered in unison.

Amelia bit the inside of her cheek, trying not to laugh. She caught Arthur's eye from across the altar—the faint lift of his eyebrow, the spark of shared amusement—and nearly lost composure herself.

Then the music changed. *Mendelssohn's Wedding March* swept through the church, bold and joyous. Everyone stood.

Amelia turned toward the open doors at the back. Wendy appeared, radiant in white, her arm looped through her father's. The sunlight framed them perfectly—Wendy's veil glowing like mist, her smile trembling with tears.

Amelia's throat tightened.

She had known Wendy for less than two years, yet in that short time, she had become one of the truest friends Amelia had ever had. To see her now—so full of love and light—stirred something deep within.

Harry, Wendy's father, looked entirely transformed. Amelia had seen him countless times at the pub—jeans, a football jersey, pint in hand. But here, in a perfectly pressed suit and freshly shaven, he carried himself like a man reborn. His face lined and kind, radiated pride.

Amelia felt a pang—quiet, unexpected, and deeply familiar. She would never have this. Never walk an aisle with her father's arm steadying hers. The thought pressed against her heart, bittersweet.

As Wendy and Harry moved closer, Charlie's composure crumbled. Tears spilled freely down his cheeks, and the congregation smiled through their own. Amelia caught Wendy's glance—her best friend fighting not to cry, her lips trembling between laughter and joy.

Charlie had always been a crier. Amelia adored that about him—how unashamedly he loved, how honestly, he lived.

When the priest invited everyone to be seated, Amelia took in the sea of faces. Lady Edith sat in the second row—elegant as ever in navy silk and a matching hat that seemed to belong in a fashion editorial. Her daughter Rosie sat beside her, luminous in a floral dress Amelia guessed was straight from an Oscar de la Renta spring collection. Rosie caught Amelia's eye and waved; her smile effortless.

Amelia waved back before returning her gaze to the front.

"Who gives this woman to be married?" the priest asked.

"Her mother, Betty, and I do," Harry said proudly, his voice thick with emotion.

Betty, seated in her wheelchair, beamed up at them. The resemblance between her and Wendy was uncanny—the same dark curls, the same warm smile.

Harry kissed his daughter's cheek and guided her toward Charlie. Then, noticing his son-in-law's trembling hands, he pulled a handkerchief from his pocket. "Here, son."

Charlie laughed through a sob, taking it and pulling Harry into a hug. The crowd collectively melted. Betty threw her head back and laughed—the sound bright and pure.

Wendy giggled through her tears, her happiness radiating like sunlight.

Amelia's own eyes burned. When she glanced sideways, she found Arthur watching her instead of the ceremony, a quiet smile on his lips. Her heart lifted. For the first time all morning, she felt calm—present.

The vows came and went in a blur of words she would later remember only as emotion: the tremor in Wendy's voice, the catch in Charlie's, the way his thumb stroked her hand when she stumbled over her lines.

Then the priest's voice rose above the silence. "I now pronounce you husband and wife. You may kiss your bride."

Charlie didn't hesitate. He pulled Wendy close and kissed her as if he'd been waiting his whole life for this one breath. The church erupted in cheers. Petals rained down, bells rang, and the gilded angels in the rafters above seemed to shimmer in the light.

Arthur leaned in close enough that Amelia could feel his breath against her cheek. "You would make the most beautiful bride," he whispered.

Her pulse quickened. She turned toward him, caught in his gaze, and smiled—unable to speak.

Outside, the day was almost impossibly bright. The courtyard of St. Mary's overflowed with laughter and color—confetti swirling like tiny bursts of joy, champagne corks popping in the distance. Wendy and Charlie stood near the steps, surrounded by friends and family. Harry knelt beside Betty's chair, kissing her softly, the two of them glowing in their own private happiness.

Arthur squeezed Amelia's hand. "Let's get out of here."

She swatted him with her bouquet, laughing. "We have to go straight to the reception."

He grinned mischievously. "We could be fashionably late. There's a hotel just down the street. You look too beautiful in that dress for me not to see what's underneath it."

"Arthur!" she gasped—just as Lady Edith appeared behind him.

"Amelia, Arthur," she said smoothly, offering her cheek for her son's kiss. "Perhaps a little discretion, darling."

Arthur smiled innocently. "Of course, Mother."

Rosie rushed up then, her floral dress fluttering as she wrapped her arms around her brother. "Arthur! I've missed you."

"When did you get back?" he asked.

"Yesterday." Rosie turned to Amelia with a warm hug. "You look stunning, Amelia."

"Thank you," Amelia said, admiring her in return. "So do you. That dress is gorgeous."

"Oh, this old thing?" Rosie teased, flicking her hair over one shoulder. "Gran sent it from Milan."

Arthur chuckled. "How is Gran?"

"Still busy terrorizing her social circle," Rosie replied. "And forever chasing Barnaby through her gardens."

"Who's Barnaby?" Amelia asked.

"Our grandfather," Arthur and Rosie said in unison.

"Well—step-grandfather," Rosie corrected.

Amelia smiled. "I'm sure that's a story worth hearing."

"Not really," Rosie said breezily. "Mummy's father ran off when she was eight, then died off the coast of Italy. Gran inherited everything, then met Barnaby. Sounds like something you'd make me read, Amelia."

Amelia laughed softly. "I'll take that as a compliment."

Rosie lifted her glass toward a friend across the courtyard. "Oh, there's one of my girlfriends—I'll catch you both later." She vanished into the crowd in a swirl of floral perfume.

Amelia watched her go, struck by how much of Arthur's family still felt like a mystery.

Charlie's voice rang out suddenly. "Alright, everyone! Reception at The Park House! Follow us!"

The crowd erupted in cheers as he helped Wendy into their car. He turned, grinning like a boy, and shouted, "I'm married!" before closing the door. Cans rattled behind them as they drove away into sunlight and laughter.

Guests began dispersing toward their cars, still buzzing with joy. Arthur placed a hand on the small of Amelia's back and guided her toward their Range Rover. He opened her door with that same quiet charm and leaned in to adjust the hem of her dress. "Nice shoes," he murmured.

She caught her breath when his fingers brushed the back of her leg. "Arthur," she whispered, glancing past him. The same two girls from earlier were watching again, whispering by another car. As he walked around to the driver's side, she asked, "Do you know them?"

He followed her gaze. "Hmm? Oh—yes. That's Emma Langley. She was one of my students last year."

"She seems rather infatuated," Amelia said lightly.

He smirked as he started the engine. "Infatuated? Speaking of which..." His hand found her thigh again.

She batted it away, laughing. "Arthur!"

"Jealous?"

"Me? Never."

Outside her window, she caught sight of Harry lifting Betty into their van, cradling her in his arms as if she weighed nothing. He kissed her softly before helping her settle inside. Love like that—steadfast, unembarrassed, unshakable—struck something deep in Amelia.

Arthur followed her gaze. "Do you know why she's in a wheelchair?"

Amelia nodded slowly. "Wendy told me. A lorry hit her while she was cycling. Wendy was only three."

He exhaled. "That's awful."

"She was lucky to survive," Amelia said. "And now look at them. Still so in love."

He smiled, glancing over. "Like us."

Her heart fluttered. "Yes. Like us."

The car filled with the soft fragrance of lilies from her bouquet in the back seat.

"These lilies are strong," she said absently.

Arthur chuckled. "Wouldn't be my choice."

"Oh? And what *would* be your choice—for your wedding?" she teased.

He hesitated, a smile tugging at his lips. "I've always imagined a fall wedding. Ranunculus, maybe."

"That's very specific," she said with a grin. "You've thought about this."

He shrugged. "My mother's a horticulturist. I grew up being lectured about flowers over breakfast. I have preferences."

Amelia laid a hand on his thigh and gave it a gentle squeeze. "Ranunculus would be perfect."

He cleared his throat, as if changing the subject could steady the air between them. "I think Charlie and Wendy will be thrilled with the reception setup. I peeked inside the tent earlier."

Her eyes widened. "You weren't supposed to look!"

"Oh, come on," he said, laughing. "That wedding planner's been shouting orders since dawn."

"Cecilia," Amelia said, rolling her eyes. "Yes. She's... enthusiastic."

"Enthusiastic? She's a human megaphone."

Amelia laughed, resting her head against the window as the car turned onto the tree-lined road leading out of Nottingham. The sunlight flickered through the leaves, warm and golden, and for the first time all day, she felt her heart settle—the quiet contentment of a perfect moment beginning.

CHAPTER TWO

"THIS WAY, EVERYONE!" CECELIA'S VOICE CUT THROUGH THE late afternoon air like a trumpet blast. Wedding guests spilled from their cars into the busy valet area, shading their eyes against the golden sunlight that painted The Park House in rich, warm tones. The sprawling estate stood in all its grandeur: white tents stretched across the manicured lawns, casting long, soft shadows, and the rolling meadows of Nottinghamshire glimmered in the afternoon glow. The notes of a five-piece jazz band floated lazily through the trees, mingling with the soft hum of conversation and laughter. Every detail seemed perfectly curated—the kind of picture-postcard day that felt impossible to believe real.

Amelia intertwined her fingers with Arthur's, feeling the reassuring warmth of his hand as they approached the reception. "Look how happy they are," she murmured, nodding toward Charlie and Wendy. The two newlyweds stood at the entrance, faces lit with genuine joy as they greeted guests, their smiles wide enough to soften even the stiffest of collars and the most formal of dress shoes.

Arthur followed her gaze, lips tugging into a soft smile. "They do look happy," he agreed. "Honestly, Amelia... it suits them."

Nearby, Harry carefully guided Betty up one of the ramps specially constructed for the day. Amelia watched, admiring the small but essential details that ensured everyone could enjoy the celebration without struggle.

"I think it's wonderful," Arthur murmured, his voice low, "how you helped Wendy organize all these ramps for Betty."

Amelia shrugged modestly. "It's her daughter's wedding. Betty shouldn't have to worry about anything. Today is for joy, not stress." She felt a small thrill of pride as she spoke, the warmth of purpose settling over her.

The couple stepped into the reception proper, and Amelia's breath caught at the sight. Tables, dressed in crisp white linens, gleamed under the soft late-afternoon sun. Each centerpiece was a miniature masterpiece—blooms of blush roses, ivory peonies, and sprigs of lavender rising from delicate glass vases. Tiny butterflies hovered above the arrangements, hand-tied to thin wires so they seemed to float, as if suspended by magic. The whimsy was a reflection of Wendy herself: exuberant, joyful, and impossibly imaginative. Guests wandered among the tables, champagne flutes in hand, their laughter mixing with the soft, jazzy rhythms from the band tucked beneath the poplars. It was an almost dreamlike scene, cinematic in its perfection.

"I NEED THE BRIDE AND GROOM AND PARENTS!" Cecelia's shrill cry cracked across the lawn, startling a few birds into flight. Guests paused, mid-conversation, glancing toward her frantic figure in the parking area. **"CAN I PLEASE HAVE THE BRIDE AND GROOM AND PARENTS FOR PHOTOS!"**

Amelia bit her lip, trying not to laugh. "My God... that woman is loud."

Charlie chuckled beside her. "We're coming, Cecelia!"

Wendy's face turned a shade of crimson brighter than any flower in her bouquets as she hurried after Charlie, leaving Amelia and Arthur to watch the chaos unfold.

Arthur slid an arm around her waist, his presence grounding her amid the manic energy. "What's next?" he asked, raising an eyebrow.

Amelia guided him toward the guest book, a large, open volume set neatly beside a stack of wedding gifts. The pen rested on its edge, inviting signatures. Arthur paused, holding it out to her. "Why don't you sign it for us?"

Amelia chuckled softly and took the pen. After a moment's thought, she scrawled, *Arthur and Amelia.* She set the pen back down.

"No last names?" he teased.

"Nope," she said with a sly smile, tugging him gently toward their table.

Their path was interrupted. Rosie, energetic as ever, swooped in, grabbing Amelia's hand with surprising strength and pulling her aside.

"I need to borrow Amelia for a moment," Rosie whispered conspiratorially.

Arthur's brows knitted, but before he could say anything, Rosie whisked Amelia behind the polished oak bar. They crouched low, peeking around the corners as the bartenders paused mid-task to regard them curiously.

"What are you doing?" Amelia whispered, pressing her back against the wood.

"Hide," Rosie said, her eyes scanning the crowd.

One bartender leaned closer; voice polite. "Do you ladies need a drink?"

"No," Amelia replied quickly, her pulse beginning to quicken.

Rosie shook her head. "Yes. I need a glass of champagne."

The bartender lowered a flute to their level, and Rosie took a careful sip before turning to Amelia, her voice dropping to a conspiratorial whisper. "I just heard a rumor. Someone might have arrived... who wasn't invited."

Amelia's stomach lurched. "Okay... um, is this a stalker situation or something?"

Rosie shook her head. "Not exactly. But it's someone you don't want Arthur to notice. Promise me you won't freak out."

"Rosie, you're scaring me," Amelia admitted, her voice barely audible.

"Look." Rosie motioned subtly, nodding toward the crowd. Amelia followed her gaze.

A tall, striking woman with red hair moved with purpose through the reception. Her plain, unassuming outfit made her stand out less at first, but Amelia quickly realized this was no ordinary guest. Her eyes were fixed on Arthur, and her steps were confident, almost predatory. Cecelia had already spotted her and was yelling futilely, but the woman ignored all distractions, jogging the last few steps to Arthur and tapping him on the shoulder.

Amelia's chest tightened. "Who is that?" she asked Rosie, her voice a whisper tinged with fear.

Arthur turned, his expression instantly darkening. His eyes narrowed, jaw tight, as if a memory had been pulled from the depths of the past. Without a word, he grabbed the woman's arm and guided her toward The Park House with precise, brisk movements.

"Where is he taking her?" Rosie demanded, standing on tiptoe behind the bar.

Amelia shook her head. "Rosie, you tell me right now who that woman is."

Rosie's lips pressed into a thin line. "I... I don't think it's my place. But trust me—she's trouble. And Arthur? He's... complicated when it comes to her."

Amelia's mind spun. Who was she? Why now? And why did Arthur react as if the world had shifted on its axis?

They crouched behind the bar, hearts hammering, watching as Arthur's steps quickened, guiding the woman with a mixture of authority and concern. The redhead followed without resistance, expression unreadable, as if she understood exactly how the exchange would unfold.

Amelia's pulse thudded in her ears. The soft jazz and clinking glasses around them became background noise, irrelevant compared to the tension spiraling before her. She wanted to follow, to step forward, but some invisible force held her back.

Rosie leaned closer. "Whatever happens, stay calm. Arthur will handle it. But..." She hesitated, glancing at the redhead moving through the crowd. "...keep your eyes open."

Amelia nodded, gripping Rosie's hand for comfort. She watched as Arthur's profile remained tense, his movements measured, every step deliberate. There was no hesitation—no uncertainty—and yet, the situation alone seemed to radiate danger. Her mind raced with questions, a thousand scenarios spinning out in a dizzying blur. Who was she? What did she want? And why did she feel like a shadow from Arthur's past, pulled into the perfect moment of this wedding day?

The redhead didn't resist at all. She allowed herself to be guided, her gaze never leaving Arthur. Amelia's stomach twisted, a mixture of curiosity, jealousy, and unease.

Rosie whispered again. "Trust him. He's always in control, but... she's different. Just... be ready."

Amelia swallowed hard, nodding. She stayed crouched, hands trembling slightly as she watched Arthur lead the woman away from the reception. The sun dipped lower, brushing gold over the tents and tables, and the moment felt suspended in time. Guests continued to laugh and chat, blissfully unaware of the tension that had quietly descended.

Amelia drew in a slow breath, trying to steady herself. Somehow, she knew this was only the beginning.

CHAPTER THREE

AMELIA PRESSED HERSELF AGAINST THE POLISHED OAK OF the bar, Rosie crouched beside her like a conspiratorial shadow. The late afternoon sun cast warm golden streaks across the white tents of the reception, but beneath that perfection, Amelia felt her stomach twist into knots. The bartender slid a chilled flute of champagne into her hand, the bubbles rising like tiny, fleeting distractions. Rosie tapped the glass insistently.

"Drink that," she ordered, her voice sharp but calm.

Amelia stared at the golden liquid. The thought of sipping it seemed almost alien when her mind was spinning. "I'm not drinking anything until you tell me who that red-headed woman was—the one who just ran off with my boyfriend," she hissed, eyes wide and heart racing.

Rosie's lips pressed into a thin line, and her eyes flicked toward the steps of The Park House. "Watch," she whispered.

Amelia's gaze followed her friend, and her chest tightened. Arthur and the redhead were still standing there, engaged in what looked like a quiet but intense argument. Amelia couldn't hear the words, but the tension radiating from their gestures was unmistakable. The woman leaned in aggressively, pointing occasionally, her voice rising just enough for Amelia to make out the sharpness in her tone. Arthur's posture was rigid, almost defensive, his hands occasionally gesturing in soft protest as he kept scanning the area as if expecting someone to intervene. "I don't know what to do!" Amelia could just make out the woman raising her voice.

"What is happening?" Amelia whispered, gripping the bar so tightly her knuckles turned white.

"Shhh," Rosie cautioned, her eyes fixed like a hawk on the scene.

Amelia noticed Lady Edith moving toward them, a picture of composed elegance. Her slow, measured approach seemed to make the redhead pale further, her features going almost ghostly as she realized she was being observed. Amelia's heart beat faster. The woman handed Arthur something—a small object Amelia couldn't quite see—before storming off toward the valet, jumping into her car, and speeding away.

Amelia exhaled shakily. "Thank God she's leaving," she muttered.

Rosie grabbed her hand firmly. "Come on," she said, steering Amelia away from the crowd, the tents, and the soft chaos of the reception. They ducked behind a large oak tree a short distance from the main party, seeking shade and a moment of privacy. The late afternoon sun painted dappled patterns across their faces, but Amelia barely noticed.

Rosie set her champagne glass on a low branch, her eyes serious. "Amelia... that was Helena. Arthur's ex."

Amelia froze. "Ex?" Her voice cracked slightly, disbelief mingling with the sharp edge of betrayal. "He never talks about an ex. What ex?"

Rosie leaned closer, urgency in her tone. "Her name is Helena. They dated off and on for about a year—until they were... *engaged.*"

Amelia's stomach lurched. The word *engaged* hit her like a punch to the chest. Her mind stumbled over it. "Engaged?" she repeated, almost unable to say it.

"Yes," Rosie confirmed, her eyes steady. "They were. And now... she's back. And she made her entrance very deliberately."

Amelia lifted the glass Rosie had handed her and took a small sip. The cold liquid slid down her throat, doing little to calm the sudden tightness in her chest. "Explain," she demanded, gripping Rosie's arm for support.

"There's nothing more to explain," Rosie said gently, though the sharpness in her eyes betrayed the tension she felt.

"Yes, there is!" Amelia snapped. She could feel anger rising, tangled with confusion and a pulse of fear. "I can tell there's more. I *know* there's more."

Before Rosie could answer, a familiar voice cut through the tension. Arthur stepped up beside them, his blue eyes flashing with agitation, jaw tight, shoulders taut. "I'll take it from here, Rosie," he said, his tone firm, unyielding.

"I was just trying to—" Rosie began.

"Go save Mum. She hates being alone," Arthur interrupted. Rosie pressed her lips together and nodded, hurrying off toward Lady Edith, who was waiting by the bar with an elegant, composed expression.

Amelia turned to Arthur, her eyes searching, her emotions a storm of confusion, betrayal, and hurt. "Who is Helena?" she demanded; voice sharp but controlled. "And why have I never known you were engaged to her?"

Arthur's shoulders stiffened. He ran a hand through his hair, his movements taut with tension. "She was a coworker," he said, voice low. "We dated a long time ago. She moved away, that's all. And now... she's back in town."

"You *worked* with her?" Amelia asked, disbelief creeping into her voice.

"Yes. That's all it was—work, and then... life happened. She left, I moved on." His voice faltered slightly, betraying a hint of unease he tried hard to mask.

Amelia's stomach twisted. She had trusted him. She had believed she knew him. And now she felt the floor shift beneath her. She took a deep breath, willing herself to stay present, to stay grounded in the moment. "Listen… today is about Wendy and Charlie. I don't know what just happened, but we should return to the wedding and support our friends. We can deal with this later."

Arthur's tense features softened slightly as he reached for her hand, his thumb brushing over hers. "I agree completely. People are starting to stare," he murmured.

Amelia forced a small, polite smile. She felt the eyes on them again—the two young women from earlier, watching their every move. Arthur pressed a quick, reassuring kiss to her cheek. Together, they walked back toward the reception, every step a careful balancing act between composure and the quiet tension simmering just below the surface.

The reception continued around them as if nothing had happened. Jazz floated lazily through the tents, mingling with laughter, the faint clink of champagne glasses, and the soft hum of conversations. The air smelled of summer flowers, freshly cut grass, and champagne, a scent that usually filled Amelia with calm—but today, it seemed almost surreal, a contrast to the unease tightening in her chest.

Amelia's gaze landed on Wendy. She stood near the center of the courtyard, her dress catching the sunlight, making her glow like a painting come to life. Charlie, flushed and radiant, held a glass of champagne in one hand, raising it toward his bride. His voice, clear and steady, rang across the crowd:

"To my gorgeous bride, Wendy. Wendy, you are the great love of my life. I can't imagine a life without you. You love with all your heart, and I am so lucky—those of you here are lucky—to know someone like you. Your parents, Harry and Betty, couldn't have done better raising you. You are kind to each person you meet, and I love how fearlessly you fight for the people you love. I will fight for you always, my darling. I will fight to make you proud, fight to provide for our future, and... I will fight off any bloke who tries to get near you. Cheers!"

The crowd erupted in laughter and applause. Champagne flutes lifted in joyful celebration, and Wendy pressed a gentle kiss to Charlie's lips, eyes glistening with tears of happiness. Amelia's chest warmed despite the earlier tension. She let herself take a deep breath, trying to anchor herself in the moment, allowing the beauty and joy of the day to seep into her bones.

Arthur squeezed her hand subtly, bringing her back to the present. "Ready?" he whispered; voice low but steady. Amelia nodded, leaning slightly into him as they moved toward their table, slipping between laughing guests and the bustling servers carrying trays of champagne and canapés. The warm sun filtered through the tents, dust motes dancing lazily in the light, creating a halo effect around the wedding party.

Even as she followed him, Amelia's mind churned with questions about Helena, secrets, and the layers of Arthur's past she hadn't known. But she forced herself to push those thoughts aside, focusing instead on the celebration around her: Wendy's laughter, Charlie's smile, the clinking of glasses, and the golden glow of the late afternoon. Today was about love, joy, and the bonds of friendship. Amelia would honor that, even as her heart whispered caution.

Somewhere at the edge of her awareness, she knew this was only the beginning. Helena's return had planted a seed of uncertainty, one she would not be able to ignore. And Amelia had a sinking feeling that the coming days would force her to confront not just Arthur's past, but the depths of her own feelings for him.

CHAPTER FOUR

AMELIA STEPPED QUIETLY ACROSS THE POLISHED HALLWAY of The Park House, the smooth hardwood cold beneath her bare feet, a glass of wine clutched loosely in her hand. She craved the quiet, the stillness away from the chaos of the reception. The day had been long, glittering, and exhausting, and she welcomed the sanctuary of the study—a room of floor-to-ceiling books, leather-bound and smelling faintly of polished wood and old paper.

The muffled music from the party drifted through the walls, a distant echo mingling with bursts of laughter and the faint clinking of glasses. Sunlight filtered through the stained-glass window, painting fractured rainbows across the floor. Amelia's gaze lingered on the glass, the White Rabbit, bowler hat perched jauntily, holding Kinsey's cane, as if frozen mid-stride in perpetual motion.

Her fingers brushed the brass lion head atop Kinsey's real cane, leaning against the fireplace. "He would have loved this party... well, most of it, at least," she whispered.

"Yes, he would have," Arthur's voice answered behind her. She turned, startled, to see him standing by the door, the corners of his mouth tugged into a faint smile, though his eyes were shadowed with something heavier, something she didn't immediately recognize. Slowly, he closed the door behind him, clicking the lock into place.

"Why are you locking the door?" she asked, a nervous laugh in her voice.

"To escape the madness. With you," he replied, and there was a warmth in his tone that drew her closer.

He moved to a tray of decanters, each amber liquid catching the sunlight, and poured himself a glass of scotch. Settling into the leather chair across from her, he swirled the liquid thoughtfully before taking a careful sip. Amelia sank into the second chair, dropping her heels on the floor, the tension in her body easing with the motion. "That feels good," she murmured. "But we can only stay a few minutes. We shouldn't disappear completely."

Arthur's lips curved into a teasing smile. "Why not, Amelia? Let's disappear together."

Her fingers intertwined with his. "Are you ready to talk about Helena?"

He shook his head, gaze darkening. "There's really nothing to discuss. I had a relationship, it ended. That's it."

"Rosie told me you were *engaged*," she countered, voice sharp, though trembling slightly.

"For... about five minutes. That's all it lasted."

Amelia's chest tightened. She felt bile rise. "You... you know what? I don't want to talk about it."

"Good," he said, and for a fleeting moment, the tension eased. "Neither do I. What I do want to talk about," he added, "is how beautiful you looked today."

She arched an eyebrow, a small grin forming despite herself. She offered her hand, and he pressed a gentle kiss to her knuckles. Her laughter trembled as it escaped her lips, and then Arthur sank gracefully to his knees before her, his lips brushing over her arm, warm and deliberate. He moved slowly, until he faced her fully. His hands cupped her face tenderly, and their lips met—soft, hesitant, slow, savoring a world they had been keeping at bay.

Amelia wrapped her arms around him, but her mind protested. "Wait... we can't. We have guests."

"It's not our wedding. Let them manage," he whispered, pressing a kiss to her neck, and she shivered.

"Arthur," she murmured, resisting the pull.

He pleaded softly, "Amelia."

Suddenly, the sharp sound of glass shattering somewhere on the dance floor jolted them. Amelia's heart leapt.

"What—?"

"Don't worry," he murmured. "Someone just broke a glass."

Then came a woman's scream. Piercing, chilling, terrifying. Amelia bolted to her feet, bare feet cold on the floor. Arthur mirrored her movements, urgency etched into every line of his body.

"Arthur?" she called, panic creeping in.

"Quick! Shoes!" he barked, and Amelia scrambled to slip them on as he unlocked the door. The sounds outside grew louder: screaming, frenzied voices, and then the abrupt halt of music. Amelia's pulse raced. She ran, following him, adrenaline propelling her.

"Someone call an ambulance!" a voice yelled.

"Harry!" Betty's terrified cry cut through the chaos.

"Harry?" Amelia echoed, dread coiling in her stomach.

The dance floor was a storm of panicked movement. Harry lay motionless, Peter shaking him desperately. Amelia's stomach turned, bile rising.

Arthur was already at Harry's side. "Arthur! Please! I don't know CPR!" someone shouted.

Wendy's voice was raw, cracking with terror. "He... he just dropped his glass and collapsed!"

Arthur shed his jacket in one fluid motion, urgency lending

him focus and precision. "Stay with us, Harry!" he cried, pressing hands to his friend's chest. "Breathe, Harry! Come on!"

"IS THERE A DOCTOR?" Cecelia's voice pierced the chaos. Silence answered. Only horror-struck faces, hands over mouths, some frozen in disbelief.

Charlie held Wendy, her tears streaking her cheeks. "Charlie..." she whispered, voice breaking, and he held her tight, anchoring her.

Betty, in her wheelchair, shook with fear. "Harry... please... don't leave me. Come back..."

Amelia pushed through the crowd and knelt down next to Harry feeling something deeply cutting into her knee. She let out a loud "yelp" and Arthur looked over at her concerned, then focusing back to Harry.

She gritted her teeth, pressing her hand against the wound, blood seeping through her fingers, but she focused on Betty and Harry.

"My God, are you alright?" Betty asked through tears.

Amelia stood up and tried to not distract Betty, "I'm okay, Betty. Really."

The ambulance sirens were a shrill promise of hope. EMTs arrived, moving with professional urgency. Arthur stepped back at their arrival, exhausted, but immediately turned to Amelia. "Let me see," he gasped.

She shook her head. "Don't touch it."

"Amelia..."

"Clear!" the EMT barked, and minute's later it was over. He was pronounced dead. Everyone was in shock. Amelia felt ice cold with only the warm blood running down her leg reminding her this was all too real.

"I'm so sorry, Wendy," she whispered, voice small.

"Are you okay?" Wendy asked staring at Amelia's knee. A large piece of glass was sticking out through her dress.

"Don't worry about me," Amelia said, forcing composure. She quickly glanced down at her knee and felt a jolt of fear.

A nearby EMT approached her, "Miss, why don't we take a look at that?"

"Oh no, really I am fine."

Amelia stared at Wendy hugging her mom crying. Arthur knelt beside Betty, hands holding hers gently. "I'm sincerely sorry, Mrs. Clark. I tried my very best."

Betty's eyes, tired and filled with sorrow, met his. "I know you did, son. Thank you."

"Miss, I insist?"

Betty turned to Amelia and Arthur and said, "Go with them. That looks terrible."

Amelia reluctantly tried to follow and realized she couldn't walk. Arthur scooped her up in his arms and carried her to the ambulance. After offering to take her to the hospital Amelia insisted there was no way she would be leaving. So, the EMT reluctantly gave her lidocaine and pulled the large piece of glass out of her knee. Amelia cringed and grabbed onto Arthur's arm. Finally, her leg stitched up and bandaged, Amelia leaned into Arthur, silent, watching Wendy and Betty, grief etched into their bodies.

The coroners soon arrived, calm and precise, moving Harry onto a gurney. Amelia thought of her mother, lost in a car accident, helpless, gone in a moment. She looked at Arthur; his hand found hers again, and she clung to it as the world seemed to shrink to grief and blood.

Even after Harry was taken, the chaos lingered. Amelia, still soaked in blood from her knee watched as Cecelia lowered her loud voice and quickly managed to have everyone exit leaving Arthur and Amelia alone outside the Park House. No goodbyes, the wedding was just... over.

Amelia leaned against the bar, her knee still completely numb, sipping wine mechanically while Arthur poured himself whiskey, both silent, letting the stillness absorb them.

She shivered. Arthur noticed and retrieved his jacket from the floor, draping it around her shoulders. "Are you going to be alright?" she asked softly.

"To be honest... no. Harry was a good man," he said quietly.

"I know. You did everything you could," she replied.

"He was gone when I got to him," he admitted.

Her chest tightened. "His poor wife," she whispered.

Arthur reached for her hand. "I know," he said, voice soft.

They sat in silence, surrounded by abandoned tables and half-eaten cake. The night pressed around them like a weight, the only sounds their breaths, distant sirens, and the hum of lights.

Amelia shifted, hand brushing against Arthur's jacket pocket, and froze. There was something hard tucked inside—a small, unmistakable shape. **A ring box.**

Her heart skipped. Time seemed to stall. She quickly removed her hand from it and looked at him, breath caught in her throat. Arthur's fingers brushed hers briefly, unaware she had discovered it. She swallowed, pulse thrumming violently. The glass of wine trembled in her hand, spilling slightly.

Arthur looked down at her, concerned. "Amelia? Are you alright?"

She didn't answer immediately, every memory, every heartbeat, every unspoken question filling the space between them. The night, the grief, the chaos, and now—this. The weight of it pressed down, heavy, undeniable.

For a long moment, neither moved. Outside, the wind whispered through the trees, leaves rustling softly. Somewhere in the distance, the last lights of the reception flickered. And inside, Amelia realized that whatever came next would change everything.

She didn't speak. She didn't move. Her fingers tightened reflexively around the stem of her wine glass. The box sat there, silent, patient, and loaded with promise, possibility... and danger.

Arthur shifted slightly, still unaware she had found it, leaning back against the bar, exhaling heavily. Amelia's thoughts returned to the box, heart pounding, mind racing. One thought repeated in her head: **this changes everything.**

She took a slow, deliberate breath, trying to steady herself, trying to find calm amid the chaos. Then, ever so quietly, she slipped her hand into his jacket pocket. Fingers brushing against the smooth edges of the box, she paused, heart hammering in her chest, and for the first time, truly understood: the rest of the night, the rest of their lives, might hinge on what she chose next.

CHAPTER FIVE

AMELIA SANK ONTO THE EDGE OF THE BED, THE SOFT FABRIC of her nightgown clinging to her skin, her hand instinctively resting on her bandaged knee. The ache throbbed relentlessly, each pulse a stark reminder of Harry. Arthur emerged from the master bathroom, a glass of water in hand. He held it out to her, the gesture small but comforting.

"Here's a pain reliever," he said gently.

"Thank you," she murmured, taking the pill and washing it down in one gulp. Arthur began unbuttoning his shirt. "I'm going to take a quick shower," he added.

Amelia nodded, pulling the covers tightly around herself. Her thoughts drifted, unbidden, to the ring box she had found tucked in his jacket pocket. And then to Wendy. A knot of unease twisted in her stomach, and before she could wrestle with it, exhaustion overtook her, dragging her into a deep, almost dreamless sleep.

Her dreams, however, had other plans. She wandered through the quiet halls of the Park House, faint strains of music calling to her. She followed it, calling out for Arthur, but the melody led her to the solarium. Laughter mingled with the sharp scent of cigarette smoke. Sitting in a chair, back to her, was a bowler hat she knew instantly—Kinsey. Across from him, Harry laughed, his eyes lighting up when he saw her.

"Harry, what are you doing here?" she asked, bewildered.

Kinsey stood, a white rabbit in his hand, and smiled. "We live here now."

The dream dissolved in a gasp. Amelia woke, heart pounding, as Arthur's arm instinctively went around her. "Are you alright?" he asked.

"I—I think so," she breathed, clutching the covers as he rubbed her back soothingly.

"It's alright. You're alright," he murmured, spooning her protectively.

"What time is it?" she asked, her voice heavy with sleep.

"About eight," he replied.

Outside, Cecelia's sharp voice rang through the air: "Be careful with that table!"

"Cecelia's been at it since five this morning," Arthur muttered.

"How do you know?" she asked, puzzled.

"Because I've been awake since five," he said, a trace of bitterness in his tone.

"I'm so tired," Amelia groaned, turning to face him. He held her tightly. She let out a long, shuddering sigh. "I suppose..." she began.

"No. Don't say it," he interrupted.

"We should probably—"

"No," he said, squeezing her tighter.

"Arthur, we have to face the day," she protested.

"I refuse," he murmured, burying his face in her hair. After a moment, he exhaled a long, reluctant sigh. "Fine." He released her, and Amelia rolled out of bed, wincing as her stitches tugged.

"Ouch," she muttered.

"How is it?" he asked, concerned.

"Awesome," she said, forcing a smile.

"Awesome," he repeated, amused. "So American."

She moved slowly into the bathroom, each step deliberate,

each motion careful. She sat, letting the weight of the day settle over her as dread prickled at the edges of her mind. When she finished, she washed her hands, staring at the shower as if it were a promise of reprieve. She undressed, letting the warm water cascade over her, melting away tension and fatigue alike.

Arthur entered, glancing at her. "How are you feeling?"

"I don't really know. I'm thinking about how this day is going to go," she said.

"I think you should call Wendy first. I'll handle everything outside," he suggested, turning on the sink.

"I think I'll call Charlie instead," she replied.

Arthur nodded, accepting the choice. "Probably better."

Amelia shampooed her hair, the suds sliding over her long strands. Three years. Three years since her breast cancer diagnosis. A survivor, she marveled at the life she had now. Her fingers grazed the faint scar of the port above her right breast. *Why am I here and Harry isn't?* she thought. Betty needed him.

Arthur, finishing his teeth brushing, said, "I'll find a fresh bandage for you."

"Okay," she agreed, stepping out of the shower, wrapping herself in a towel. She sat by the window, watching the remnants of the morning's chaos. The tents remained, but tables and chairs had been cleared, Cecelia bustling with her clipboard like a small whirlwind.

Arthur returned. "Got it," he said, kneeling to remove her wet bandage.

"Ouch," Amelia said as the puffy, red skin beneath was revealed.

"This doesn't look good," Arthur observed, his voice threaded with concern.

"No, it doesn't," she admitted.

"Maybe we should head into town and have it checked properly."

She nodded. He dabbed her stitches gently and replaced the bandage. "I'll get dressed and call Charlie."

"I'll change and check on things, then we'll go," she said.

Later, Amelia descended the stairs, her long skirt draping

around her, making it easier to show her injured knee. Her phone still lay upstairs, but she paused in the kitchen, deciding coffee and toast were non-negotiable. The smell of freshly toasted bread filled the room as the front door opened.

"Charlie!" she cried.

He smiled, albeit faintly. "Good morning."

They embraced tightly, and for a moment the grief that had shadowed their lives melted into something gentler, something familiar.

Arthur entered, observing them with a faint smile. Charlie released her and gave Arthur a brotherly hug. "It's going to be alright, mate," Arthur said.

"I don't know. This is all... shit," Charlie admitted, his voice heavy.

Amelia motioned toward the kettle. "Coffee? Tea?"

"I'll have a cuppa," he said.

As Amelia busied herself, Arthur explained about the tents. "Cecelia says everything will be cleared in a couple of hours."

"How's Wendy and Betty holding up?" Amelia asked.

"A total mess," Charlie said. "They didn't sleep until almost three."

Amelia gasped. "And your honeymoon?"

"Canceled," he said quietly.

"No," she whispered, shocked. "Prague?"

"Prague can wait," Charlie said, and they shared a fleeting, sad smile.

Arthur set down her tea. "Amelia, sit. I'll get this."

Amelia did, grateful for a moment's respite. "Let us know how we can help," she said.

Charlie rubbed his eyes. "Wendy and I are moving in with Betty. She can't manage alone, and our home isn't suitable."

"But your home," Amelia said softly, "you just finished it."

"I love my wife," Charlie said, gaze steady. "I'll do anything for her and her mum. Listing our home and moving in is the only way."

Amelia squeezed his hand. "First time I've heard you say, 'my wife.'"

"I love saying it," he replied with a faint smile.

The moment was fragile, tender, a reminder of how quickly life could shift between joy and grief.

Later, at the Urgent Treatment Center, Amelia's knee was examined. The doctor frowned. "It looks infected. Any detail about the original stitch?"

"I kneeled into a large piece of glass last night," she said. "A medic pulled it out and stitched me up."

Her eyes widened. "Why a medic?"

Arthur explained quietly about Harry. The doctor nodded solemnly. "I'll prescribe antibiotics. Surgery is optional, but if the infection worsens, you must return immediately."

"I'll take antibiotics," she insisted, anxiety curling in her chest.

Arthur's face fell, but he did not argue. She could not face another invasive procedure, not after years of medical battles.

The phone rang, a distraction. Arthur's mother. "I'm with Amelia at UTC. Her knee is infected, getting antibiotics now," he explained.

Amelia collected her paperwork from a young beautiful receptionist who kept staring at Arthur who continued speaking with is mother on the phone. Amelia waved her hand in front of her and said, "I'm over here."

"Is that Arthur Bonneville you are with?"

Amelia flushed, "yes, and we are leaving now."

Arthur put his phone away and held the door for Amelia giving the receptionist a polite wave goodbye. Amelia turned back to watch her smile and wave seductively, "Come again!"

Arthur blushed and replied, "Let's hope not."

Walking to the car, Arthur revealed, "My Gran is coming today."

"Is that bad?" she asked.

"She's... set in her ways," he said, a hint of apprehension in his eyes.

"Let me guess. She's not keen on her only grandson marrying an American?"

Arthur stopped walking and grinned. "Marrying?"

Amelia blushed furiously. "I—well... I meant dating."

Arthur blushed and opened the car door for her.

She sat down and felt a teasing tension unfold over the attractive receptionist. He started the car and Amelia muttered, "That receptionist couldn't keep her eyes off you."

"Oh?"

She crossed her arms and stared out her window. He turned the car back off. "Wait? Why did you turn the car off?" A soft, electric warmth spread between them when he leaned across to kiss her. "You need to trust me," he said.

"I do," she whispered, though her pulse raced with lingering doubts.

He pulled a small tube from his jacket. ChapStick. Relief and amusement mingled as she realized the moment's intensity.

"Let's get back to the house. We will take a nap and then get changed before dinner," he said casually.

"Changed? Dinner?"

"I told you. Gran. Oak Hall. Tonight."

The weight of anticipation settled in Amelia's chest. Tonight, she would meet his family, navigate the expectations of tradition, and face the stirring currents of emotion she had tried so hard to set aside.

CHAPTER SIX

THE GRAVEL DRIVE CURVED TOWARD OAK HALL LIKE A RIBBON of moonlit silver, and Amelia's pulse matched its rhythm—quick, unsteady, full of nervous energy. She clung to Arthur's hand as they ascended the marble steps to the entrance. Her knee ached with each movement, but she kept her posture straight, chin lifted, determined not to limp in front of his family.

She had met Lady Edith. She had even survived Lady Edith. Rosie had become something close to a friend. But meeting Arthur's *grandmother*—the formidable Lady Newcroft—felt different. There was something about the way Arthur said, *Gran is... traditional,* that had made Amelia's stomach tighten ever since.

Inside, the air carried a faint sweetness of lavender polish and lemon oil. The vast hall was bathed in soft gold from a chandelier whose crystals shimmered like rain. It smelled of roast chicken and rosemary—comforting, yet formal—a scent that belonged to families who had servants and traditions that reached back centuries.

Arthur looked effortlessly elegant in his navy sport coat, the one that made his blue eyes almost dangerous. Amelia, in her soft green chiffon dress, felt out of place and aware of it—an intruder in a portrait of privilege. Still, when he smiled down at her, all her insecurities softened.

"You look beautiful," he murmured, squeezing her hand.

She smiled faintly. "You have to say that. I'm limping."

"You limp elegantly," he teased.

Before she could reply, a voice floated from down the corridor. "Is that you, darling?"

"It's us!" Arthur called back, leading her through a grand corridor lined with ancestral portraits—men in uniforms, women in pearls, their painted eyes cold and dignified.

"Good heavens," Amelia whispered. "They're all staring."

"They're family," Arthur said. "So yes, they are."

As they neared the study, the sound of a clock ticked sharply—a heartbeat that seemed to mark the end of her composure.

Lady Edith sat in a velvet chair, her glass of wine glinting by lamplight. Across from her sat an older woman, poised and still, dressed in a white suit so crisp it seemed to repel dust itself. Her silver hair was pulled back tightly into a bun, her almond-shaped eyes unblinking, her lips curved in something between politeness and disdain.

"Hello, Gran," Arthur said warmly.

Her features softened into a practiced smile. "Arthur, my darling boy. How is my favorite grandson?"

From a corner, Rosie's voice pierced the room. "He's your *only* grandson."

Arthur laughed under his breath and bent to kiss his grandmother's cheek. "You look lovely as ever."

Lady Newcroft's eyes flicked briefly toward Amelia. "Thank you, Arthur." Then, assessing her guest: "And this must be the American."

Amelia stepped forward, hand outstretched. "It's lovely to meet you, Lady Newcroft."

The older woman took Amelia's hand with only her fingertips—a gesture that said *you may approach, but do not presume familiarity.*

"Ah yes," Lady Newcroft murmured. "The American who's stolen my grandson's heart."

"She has," Arthur said, his tone protective in a way Amelia had never quite heard before.

A flicker of something—surprise, perhaps annoyance—passed across Gran's face. "When your mother told me you had broken it off with Helena, I was shocked."

Amelia's breath caught. The name hit like a cold wave. *Helena.* She looked toward Rosie, who offered only an apologetic wince.

Lady Edith, sensing the danger, rose quickly. "How are Wendy and her mother, Amelia? I told Gran about the tragedy."

"They're holding together," Amelia managed. "The funeral's in two weeks."

Gran sighed dramatically. "Two weeks? How terribly *hasty.* Mourning takes time. What is the rush to move on?"

Arthur's hand tightened around Amelia's.

"And your knee?" Lady Edith asked gently.

"It's improving, thank you."

"She's lying," Arthur said lightly. "Doctor prescribed antibiotics. Surgery was the safer option."

Gran's lips puckered. "We don't discuss medical matters before dinner. It's uncouth."

Arthur exhaled through his nose. "Then perhaps we should change the subject. Where's Barnaby?"

"Dinner is ready, Your Ladyship," a tall, stone-faced man announced from the doorway.

"Thank you, Leopold," Gran said with a dismissive wave.

"I'll fetch Barnaby," Lady Edith offered.

Amelia smiled. "May I join you?"

"Of course."

Arthur took a step, but his grandmother intercepted him. "Escort me, Arthur," she commanded, looping her arm through his. He gave Amelia an apologetic glance before obeying.

As Rosie moved to follow, Gran's icy voice cracked through

the air. "Leave your mobile here, dear. We're having *dinner*, not a circus."

Rosie groaned but obeyed. "Yes, Gran."

The moment they left the study, Gran began her quiet inquisition. "Amelia is a pretty girl," she said.

"Yes, she is."

"However," Gran continued smoothly, "such a mess."

Arthur's jaw tensed. "How do you mean?"

"Your mother told me she's been ill and has no family to her name. You really must think about these things, Arthur. You can't build a proper life with someone so fragile."

"I thought we weren't discussing medical matters," he said flatly.

Gran smiled thinly. "Illness is one thing, *mortality* another."

He stopped walking. "She's healthy. And she *does* have family—distant, but real. Her mother died in an accident, her father of cancer. She's survived things you couldn't imagine."

Gran tilted her head, her tone soft but cruel. "Survivors often carry misfortune with them. I only want you to think of your future. A man like you needs heirs, not heartbreak."

Rosie, unable to hold back, groaned. "Gran, that's vile."

"Truth often is, dear," Gran replied.

Arthur released her arm. "I think Amelia's worth any risk."

Gran didn't respond. She merely smiled that imperious smile that said she always had the last word.

Outside in the garden, Amelia followed Lady Edith into the fading light. The air was sweet with roses and the damp earth still held the day's warmth.

"Barnaby?" Lady Edith called softly.

A voice answered from behind a rose trellis. "I'm here, my dear. Just admiring your latest triumph."

Barnaby emerged, a man of round cheer and kind eyes, dressed in a cream pinstripe suit that looked almost tropical. His mustache twitched when he smiled.

"This must be the young woman I've heard so much about," he said. "Miss Levingston, isn't it? You look positively radiant in that shade of green."

"Thank you, sir."

"Barnaby Silver," Lady Edith introduced. "My stepfather."

He bowed slightly, then kissed Amelia's hand with old-fashioned grace. "The pleasure is entirely mine."

"Barnaby's been tending to my roses again," Lady Edith said, amused.

He gestured proudly to a cluster of yellow blossoms glowing in the sunset. "Would you look at this beauty? Edith's creation. A new hybrid—the first bloom tonight."

Amelia leaned closer. The petals were pale gold with edges blushed pink, luminous in the fading light. "It's exquisite."

"She's modest," Barnaby said. "But I've already insisted she enter it in the Chelsea Flower Show."

"Oh, I couldn't possibly," Lady Edith protested. "People would say it's favoritism. He's a judge."

"Not this year," Barnaby said with a twinkle. "I'm traveling."

"To India," Lady Edith sighed.

"With your wife?" Amelia teased.

Barnaby looked scandalized. "Good Lord, no. That woman and I in a confined space? I'd throw myself into the Ganges. I love dearly; however I like to travel alone. It's more of an adventure."

Amelia laughed aloud—the first real laugh she'd had since the wedding.

The laughter faded when they returned to the dining room. Gran sat at the head of the table, upright as a queen, Leopold standing behind her like a shadow. The table gleamed with silver and candlelight; every setting aligned with military precision.

Arthur pulled out Amelia's chair. Beneath the table, his hand found hers, warm and reassuring. Leopold served the first course, soup.

Gran tasted hers, set the spoon down, and announced, "This is dreadful. Far too salty."

Rosie stifled a laugh. "It's fine, Gran."

"It's *inedible.* Leopold, tell the cook to remake it."

"Chef Martin," Lady Edith corrected gently.

"As I said," Gran replied, "the cook."

Arthur's jaw flexed. Amelia focused on her bowl, willing herself invisible.

Gran eyed her granddaughter next. "You'll never marry if you eat like that, Rosie. You'll balloon."

Rosie's spoon froze mid-air. "Thank you for that, Gran. Truly invaluable insight."

Barnaby, patient as ever, sipped his wine. "Genevieve," he said mildly, "perhaps tonight we can forgo calorie commentary?"

Gran ignored him. "Arthur, tell me—what ever happened to Helena?"

The table fell silent.

Lady Edith whispered sharply, "Mother."

Gran pressed on. "I simply wonder what became of her. Such a refined girl. And now you're living *in sin* at The Park House."

Arthur's fork clattered against his plate. He stood; fury barely contained. "I think we should leave."

"Sit," Barnaby's voice boomed across the table—a deep, commanding sound that stilled everyone. "That's enough, Genevieve."

For the first time, Gran faltered.

"Barnaby, I was only—"

"I said enough." His tone left no room for argument.

Gran dabbed her lips with a napkin, then rose. "I'm suddenly not feeling well. Excuse me."

They watched her glide from the room like a ghost.

Barnaby turned to Amelia and Arthur, his voice softening. "Please, stay a while. Don't let her ruin the evening."

Amelia's heart was still pounding. "That's kind of you, sir, but I'm quite tired. My knee—"

"Of course," he said kindly. "Get some rest, my dear."

Arthur helped her up. She thanked Lady Edith, who murmured an apology, and smiled at Rosie's exaggerated wave.

Outside in the night air, Amelia exhaled. The cold wrapped around her like relief. Arthur walked beside her in silence until they reached the car. Finally, she said quietly, "She hates me."

He looked at her, his expression soft but serious. "She hates everyone. Don't take it personally."

Amelia laughed lightly, shaking her head. "That woman could freeze fire."

Arthur smiled faintly, kissing her temple. "You handled her beautifully."

She leaned against him as they walked toward the car. "Next time, remind me to bring armor."

"I'll bring the sword," he said.

And as they drove away from Oak Hall, the laughter they shared carried just enough warmth to eclipse the chill that Gran had left behind.

CHAPTER SEVEN

THE HEADLIGHTS CUT THROUGH THE NARROW COUNTRY ROAD, revealing fleeting glimpses of hedgerows and stone walls slick with evening dew. The drive from Oak Hall to The Park House wasn't long, but to Amelia, it felt longer. She felt a bit unnerved by Arthur's grandmother. Like she was starting all over again with the Bonneville's extended family. It had taken so long to have Lady Edith warm to her, she wondered if she had the energy to do this all over again.

Looking over to Arthur, his hands steady on the wheel, his jaw was tight, he seemed just as irritated. He was always so calm, so composed, even when furious. His anger didn't roar; it simmered, quiet and controlled like the hum of the engine.

"Well," he said finally, his voice breaking the silence like glass. "That wasn't... great."

Amelia gave a small laugh that sounded more like a sigh. "You think?"

He smiled faintly, but it didn't reach his eyes. "She can be... difficult."

"Difficult?" Amelia repeated, disbelief flickering across her face. "Arthur, she called me fragile. And suggested you shouldn't be with someone who might die."

He glanced at her, his expression pained. "I know. I'm sorry. She's old-fashioned—brutal, even—but she doesn't mean half of what she says."

"Then she means the other half," Amelia murmured, staring out her window. The passing trees blurred into streaks of shadow and light. "She made it very clear she doesn't approve."

"She doesn't approve of anyone," he said softly. "Not even my mother."

The weight of that truth lingered for a moment.

Then Amelia turned to him, her tone gentler but sharper, like glass under silk. "She seemed to like Helena."

"Oh no she didn't. She picked and prodded at her just like she did to you."

"To be honest, I feel very uncomfortable about not knowing about Helena, Arthur. I thought we shared everything to each other. Why didn't you tell me you were engaged?"

He exhaled slowly, his shoulders stiffening. "Because it's in the past. I was going to tell you eventually."

"But you didn't," she pressed.

His hands tightened on the steering wheel. "The past is the past, Amelia. None of it matters now."

She watched him carefully, searching for sincerity. "I think it does matter. If we're as serious about each other as I think we are, shouldn't we share everything?"

Arthur's voice dropped an octave. "Do you share everything with me?"

The question cut through her defenses. She looked away. The truth was, she didn't. There were entire parts of her life—dark, aching, unspoken—that she'd sealed away like a locked diary. He didn't know what it had been like to live with her aunt and cousin after her mother's death, how she'd survived chemo alone, or how she still sneaked off for her scans, terrified that one day she'd find the cancer had returned. She swallowed, feeling suddenly small. "When did you get engaged?"

"Only for a few weeks," he said quietly. "Up until just after Kinsey died."

Her heart dropped. "Wait. Was I here then?"

He hesitated, just long enough for her pulse to quicken. "No. Of course not. I ended it before we met."

"Why?"

His expression hardened. "Because I found out she'd been unfaithful."

"Oh." Amelia's voice was faint. "I see."

Arthur looked straight ahead, eyes on the road. "It's in the past. Let's focus on the present." He reached for her hand, but she pulled it away instinctively.

"I just don't understand why you didn't tell me," she said. "That's not something small, Arthur. You were engaged."

He sighed, his patience fraying. "Because I knew this would happen. You'd want to dissect something that doesn't matter anymore. I love you. Now, in this moment, and forever. Isn't that enough?"

The sincerity in his voice silenced her anger. It should have been enough. It *was* enough. And yet, a small voice inside her refused to quiet. She looked down at her hands. "What happened to her? Helena. Where is she now?"

Arthur hesitated, and that hesitation said more than words. "This is exactly why I didn't tell you," he said finally. "Because I knew you'd get upset."

"We're past that," she said evenly.

He sighed. "She works at the university. With me."

The words landed like stones in her stomach. *Rosie had said something like that at the wedding,* but with everything that had happened—the chaos, the heartbreak—Amelia had forgotten. Now it came flooding back.

"So, you work with her?" she asked, voice trembling slightly.

"Yes," Arthur replied. "But, I hardly see her."

"Hardly?" Amelia's tone sharpened. "Or occasionally?"

Arthur's knuckles whitened around the steering wheel. "I really don't know why we're doing this," he said, his voice clipped. "Didn't you hear me, Amelia? I love *you*. That's what matters."

Amelia sat back, feeling her anger dissolve into exhaustion. She hated confrontation. She'd spent years avoiding it—smiling through cruelty, nodding through pity, surviving through silence. Maybe he was right. Maybe some things didn't need to be said.

She stared out the window, at the moon breaking through the clouds. "I love you too, Arthur."

He relaxed slightly, glancing at her before turning on the radio. Music filled the car—soft jazz, the kind that felt like a distraction. That was his way of ending a conversation: filling the silence before it could grow teeth.

Amelia rested her head against the window. The rhythm of the road lulled her into a strange calm, but her thoughts refused to settle. She thought of Helena—what she looked like, how she spoke, how she might still walk into Arthur's office each morning, her perfume lingering in the air. She wondered if Helena knew about her, if she laughed about her in private, calling her fragile like Gran had.

Arthur reached over and touched her hand again, gently this time. "Please," he said, "let's not carry tonight into tomorrow."

She turned her hand palm up, letting him intertwine his fingers with hers. His warmth was steady, grounding. "I'm not angry," she said softly. "Just... surprised."

"I should've told you," He admitted. "I'm sorry."

The sincerity in his voice melted some of the tension. She believed him. She *wanted* to believe him.

The road ahead curved toward home. The Park House came into view—a silhouette against the moonlight, quiet and familiar. The sight brought her a measure of peace. Whatever the night had been, this was theirs. Their home.

CHAPTER EIGHT

A MELIA WAITED IN THE DARK PORTICO WHILE ARTHUR FITTED the great iron key into the Park House lock, the old brass plate cold with night. The door was stubborn as an old man with a secret; she shifted from foot to foot and hissed, "Can you please hurry up? I need to pee."

Arthur's mouth tilted. "Perhaps when you restored the home, you might have considered changing the locks to something made in this century." He pushed, the heavy bolt gave, and he stepped back to hold the door for her with a small bow. "After you, Miss Levingston."

She slipped past him, the hall's cool air swallowing her whole. The lilies in the foyer had faded into a heady sweetness, and the long corridor stretched ahead—lamps glowing low, portraits solemn and watchful. She was already moving, limping carefully toward the nearest bath, the ache in her knee sharpening to a bright sting with each step.

Inside, she shut the door and sank onto the toilet with a gust of breath. When she peeled back the bandage, her stomach turned—the skin around the stitches was an angry, furious red, heat pulsing out from it as though the wound had learned to breathe. "ohhhh shit," she whispered. She pressed the bandage back into place, washed her hands, and caught her own reflection: pale, restless eyes; hair a midnight tangle; mouth determined, tight.

He works with her.

Helena.

The name had been pretty once. Now it curdled.

She dried her hands and opened the door. "Arthur?"

"In the study," he called, voice echoing down the corridor.

She found him in the leather chair beside the fire—no fire lit yet, only the faint scent of old smoke—a crystal tumbler in his hand. He was rubbing the scruff at his jaw the way he did when he was thinking too hard. The amber liquor made his knuckles glow. She saw it all at once: the fatigue, the tension he disguised as calm, the plea he wouldn't say.

"I just want to know one thing," she said, stepping in—no preamble, no softness to cushion it.

He lifted his chin. "Why?"

"Because I'm a woman," she said simply, and he almost smiled.

"Go on."

"Do you and Helena have any kind of... relationship? Now. Do you spend time together?"

He shook his head, a clipped, frustrated motion. "No. I mean— yes, we see each other. But no, we don't *spend* time together. She's only just returned. As I mentioned in the car, she teaches in the same corridor."

"The same *hallway?*" The room tipped a little, her stomach a wash of nausea. "Arthur. How could you not tell me that?"

He winced. "I know. Every time I meant to say it, I stopped. I told myself it would only upset you."

"Why?" Her voice was soft and steady, a blade wrapped in velvet.

He set the glass down and stood, then didn't reach for her—he sank to both knees before her instead, his hands sliding to her thighs, warm through the silk of her dress. The gesture stole her breath. He looked up, eyes clear and unflinching.

"Because I love you, Amelia," he said, each word deliberate. "And what we have… this is the only thing that has felt truly right in years. I couldn't bear to bruise it with an old story that means nothing."

"Nothing's perfect," she whispered.

"Then we're perfectly imperfect," he said, mouth curving. "But I can't imagine a day without you in it."

She let the breath leave her chest slowly. On the table behind him, the glass prismed a cut of light onto the rug. She rested her hands over his. "I'm still angry you didn't tell me."

"I know." His hands moved up, slow and sure, finding her waist. "But you can trust me." He leaned in and didn't claim her mouth yet—he tested the delicate skin of her neck first, a question disguised as a kiss. She felt her resistance drain like tide water—and with it, the room's angles softened and blurred. Her eyes fell closed.

"I do," she murmured into his hair.

They kissed as though they had borrowed the night's last hour and intended to spend it to the bone. He rose, guiding her up with him, threading their fingers together. Each step up the staircase was a small rebellion against her knee, which burned and tugged and nagged. But the heat in her body ran louder than the pain, and they vanished into the dark together.

It was the pain that woke her—a blunt, relentless knock from behind the bandage, as if the wound were a locked room and something inside it wanted out. She blinked at the pale morning, at the slow lace of sunlight creeping across the ceiling. Arthur lay on his stomach, the white sheet slung low around his hips, his back bare and beautiful in that defenseless way that sleep makes of men. She slid out carefully, every movement measured, and padded to the bathroom.

Under the harsh vanity light, the red looked angrier than last night, the edges glossy with a wet sheen that made bile tickle the back of her throat. When she tugged the bandage free, a little ooze smudged the gauze. "Oh no," she breathed. She reached without thinking and touched the faint ridge at her chest where the port had been. The body remembers. Even when you're fine, it remembers.

You'll have to call. Schedule the surgery.

The thought skittered in like a cold draft.

But the morning stacked itself in front of her like a tower: the nine o'clock client at the office; notes to finalize; a site visit penciled for tomorrow; Wendy to check on; and Arthur—Arthur, who would go to the university and walk the same corridor as Helena. The name rattled like a bead in a jar.

She found the bottle of antibiotics on the counter and shook two into her palm, swallowing them with water that tasted faintly of copper. If she didn't look at the wound, it could be ordinary. If she wrapped it again, she could rewrite the morning. She cleaned it herself—alcohol biting as it bloomed across the skin, tears burning the corners of her eyes that she refused to let fall. Fresh bandage. Hands washed. Breath steadied.

Back in the bedroom, Arthur slept on, one hand under the pillow, his mouth softened. She wanted to climb beside him and let the day wait. Instead, she slipped into the closet and shut the door gently, bathing herself in the small, domestic light.

She chose an easy dress—soft slate-blue, a line that didn't argue with a bandage—and a cardigan to soften the edges. When she turned for shoes she saw it: Arthur's jacket from the wedding, hanging with its lapels in perfect alignment. The memory of the firm, square shape nestled in the pocket flooded her—the ring box she had felt in the dark like a secret heartbeat.

Don't.

But her hand was already lifting. The closet door swung open behind her. "And where do you think you're sneaking off to?"

She whirled, hand snatching back. "I'm getting dressed for work. I didn't want to wake you."

He leaned against the doorframe, hair in delicious disarray, smile crooked. "I can call in."

"Why?" She laughed, too bright. "So, we can lounge and read the paper like pensioners?"

"So, we can spend the day together," he said simply.

"I can't. I have a nine o'clock and a ledger that hates me." She tugged on her dress. "I wanted an early start."

"Then I'll drive you," he said, reaching for his shirt.

"There's no need," she said, fastening the cardigan. "Really."

He rubbed the back of his neck. "Are you running away from me Amelia Levingston?"

"Trust me," she said wryly, slipping into flats, "if I tried to run, my knee would stage a protest march." She moved toward away from him and into their bathroom. "I'm fine." she said standing in front of their mirror.

"Let me look," he said.

"I just cleaned it," she lied gently. "Don't worry."

He watched in the mirror as she twisted her hair and pinned it, the smallest of frowns between his brows. "Promise me you're alright."

"I promise." She turned and offered her mouth; he kissed her softly, but when she stepped away to brush mascara onto her lashes, he didn't leave. He lingered, hands in his pockets, rocking once on his heels like a shy schoolboy.

"What?" she asked, smiling at his reflection. "You're acting strange."

He dragged a hand through his hair, then pushed off the door and came toward her. "I'm just... nervous."

"Nervous about what?"

He stopped in front of her and opened his palm. A ring lay there—light caught and fractured in its facets as if a star had got trapped in it. For a breath she couldn't move. The room softened at the edges and slid away.

"What you're going to say," he said quietly, "when I tell you I can't let you leave this house another day without this on your finger."

The world rearranged itself—the closet, the vanity light, the hum of morning—and she did the only thing her body knew: she closed the space between them and wrapped her arms around his neck. He laughed into her hair, relief hot with joy. "Arthur," she exhaled, pulling back enough to see his face.

"Well?" He tried for lightness, but the nerves trembled at the base of his throat. "What's your answer?"

She blinked, still half-dreaming. "I'm still waiting."

"For what?"

"For you to get down on one knee, obviously." The grin broke over her then, a bright, reckless thing she hadn't felt in years.

He sank to one knee on the cool tile, the gesture both theatrical and tender, and held the ring up between them. "Will you, Amelia Jo Levingston, do me the incredible honor of being my wife?"

Her eyes flooded—too fast to stop, too sweet to hide. She nodded before the word formed, then found it, a breath and a vow. "Yes."

He slipped the ring onto her finger, the band cool, the stone a small empire of light. He stood and gathered her against him, his mouth finding hers with a relief that tasted like rain after heat. "You've just made me the happiest man in the world," he said into her hair.

She looked down. The ring was an antique emerald-cut diamond, two tapering side stones like slim shoulders, the whole setting elegant and quiet—chosen, she realized, with a tenderness that knew exactly who she was. "It's the most beautiful ring I've ever seen."

"I knew you'd love it," he said, eyes bright.

She kissed him again, and heat swept through her, and for one wild minute she almost said *to hell with the nine o'clock, to hell with everything.* But the day pressed in, stubborn and real. She swallowed the impulse. "I don't want to go to work," she admitted. "But I have to."

"Then at least let me drive you," he said. "Please."

"Fine." She laughed. "Get dressed before I change my mind."

He darted into the closet for trousers and a shirt. She followed, drawn as if by a string, and found his wedding jacket again. "I have to tell you something," she said, fingers drifting toward the pocket. "I felt this the other day." She slipped the small velvet box free and held it up, teasing—then opened it.

Another ring nestled in the black. Not hers. Something older, richer, grander—a pear-shaped diamond flanked by two blood-bright rubies, the metal a warm, time-softened gold.

Arthur froze with his shirt half-buttoned. "Oh. Give that to me."

"What is *this?*" She didn't hand it over. Her voice tried for lightness and missed. "I thought—" she glanced at her own ring—"I thought this was *the* ring."

"It is," he said quickly. "It is. That one—" He swallowed, searching for the path with the fewest thorns. "When Helena came to the wedding... she returned it."

The name sat between them like an open door.

"Returned it?" Amelia repeated. "Why did she have it?"

"Because it's a family ring," he said. "It was my mother's engagement ring. Originally my grandmother's. It was always meant to be in the family."

The rubies winked in the morning light, red as a heartbeat. Her stomach twisted—not with envy, exactly, but with something more slippery: history made metal. "And you didn't want to propose with *that* one?"

"No." He pulled a pale blue shirt from its hanger and buttoned it with hands that were steadier when stitching wounds or writing lectures or driving too fast on empty roads. "I wanted to choose something just for you." His mouth thinned, and there it was—the other truth. "And... I didn't want to ask you with a ring that belonged to Helena for a time. Even if she never wore it."

The words landed with care. They still landed.

"I see," Amelia said, because there was no gracious response that didn't wound either of them. She set the velvet box gently on the shelf as if it might break, then stepped past him, the scent of his cologne brushing her shoulder like a question.

In the corridor, she steadied herself on the banister and began the careful descent. Her knee pulsed hot; she gripped harder, willing her face to give nothing away. Arthur caught up and placed an easy hand at the small of her back—not pressing, just present.

"Breakfast?" he offered; voice neutral.

"I'd rather get to the office," she said, too quickly. Then softened it. "I'll grab something in town."

"Alright." He veered toward the study. "I need my bag and a few papers."

She opened the hall closet and reached for her purse, the leather cool under her fingers. The diamond on her hand flashed—a tiny sun—and her heart did a small, disbelieving somersault. *Engaged.* The word fit strangely and perfectly, like a coat you'd admired for months and finally slipped into.

Arthur returned, smile gentled by thought. He caught her admiring the ring and stopped in front of her. "Do you really like it?"

"I love it," she said, and meant it.

"Good." He kissed her—brief, public, domestic. "Please don't think about the other ring. Or Helena. It's all in the past."

"It's hard not to," she admitted, honest and small. "I've only known about her for two days."

He exhaled, the sound a tired prayer. "I don't know what else I can say. What's past is past. *You* are my future." He touched the band lightly, as if blessing it. "All I want is this. You and me."

She nodded. The sincerity was a balm—and yet, beneath it, the faintest grit remained, like sand you couldn't quite rinse from your palm. "Okay," she said softly.

They stepped outside into gold. Morning had laid its first light across the grass, and the Park House stood tall as a promise. In the fringe of trees, a small herd of fallow deer lifted their heads at the sound of the door, their ears twitching like silk pennants, then lowered them again to the dew-sparked meadow.

Arthur opened the car door for her with a ceremony that made her smile. She gathered her dress, slid into the seat, and let the world pause for a beat—the quiet between breaths—staring at the ring that had changed everything and nothing at once.

You're engaged, her mind said, dazed and delighted.

You're engaged, said the part of her that counted losses before wins, that catalogued thorns by instinct.

Both things could be true. Both were.

Arthur rounded the bonnet and got in, that familiar, steady presence filling the small space. He turned the key; the engine woke; the radio offered a whisper of strings. He put the car in gear, then glanced over, blue eyes intent and certain.

"Ready?"

Amelia looked from his face to the window—the drive, the day, the world sliding open—and back to the diamond burning gently on her hand. The word rose, bright and brave.

"Ready," she said.

They rolled down the lane beneath a vault of green, into the morning that waited for them both—him with his corridor at the university and whatever ghosts threaded it, her with her office and clients and a bandage that would require more than denial. Love—real love—wasn't a curtain that fell and sealed the scene. It was a door that opened and let the weather in.

She watched the sunlight pane and unpane the windshield and thought, *We will make room for all of it.* Then she gently pressed her palm over the ring, as if to settle it there, and let the day begin.

CHAPTER NINE

"**I** CAN'T HELP BUT NOTICE SOMETHING NEW ON YOUR FINGER," said Eloise Kitt, her French accent curling around each word like ribbon. She sat across from Amelia's desk, chin poised delicately on her manicured hand, gaze fixed on the diamond that glimmered under the late-morning light.

Amelia looked down, the sight still catching her off guard. "Oh," she said, smiling shyly. "Yes. My boyfriend proposed this morning."

Eloise's red-painted lips parted into a catlike grin. "*Félicitations. How très romantique.* This morning, you say? How... intriguing."

Amelia laughed softly, brushing a strand of hair from her cheek. "Thank you. It's been a bit of a whirlwind."

"So," Eloise mused, her eyes narrowing playfully, "you are to become the future Marchioness?"

Amelia blinked. "The what?"

"The wife of a Marquis, no? Lord Bonneville?" She said it like a line from a film, perfectly timed, perfectly knowing.

"I suppose so," Amelia murmured, cheeks warming. She hadn't thought of it in those terms. Not yet. It sounded absurdly grand—and not at all like her. "But let's not talk about me," she said quickly, waving her hand. "Let's talk about your project."

Eloise sighed and crossed one leg over the other, the movement elegant and dismissive all at once. She was a woman who seemed to have been born in couture. Even here, in the quiet countryside of Nottinghamshire, she managed to carry the aura of Paris Fashion Week into Amelia's small design office.

Amelia tapped a file and slid a mood board toward her. "We've confirmed DeVol for the kitchen design, which I think will be perfect—but today I'd like to revisit the master bath. I've sourced this wallpaper for you to feel. It has a hand-painted texture that will work beautifully with the Italian marble you've chosen. The copper bathtub will tie it all together."

Eloise touched the wallpaper sample with the tips of her fingers, then sighed. "I feel as if I've seen this before."

"That's because you have," Amelia replied, smiling tightly. "At our first pitch meeting."

"Hmm." Eloise's lips pursed. "It's disappointing."

She reached into her black Chanel purse, produced a silver cigarette case, and flipped it open with a snap. Amelia felt her stomach drop.

"Oh—do you mind?" she said quickly.

Eloise paused, cigarette halfway to her lips. "Do I mind *what*, exactly?"

"The smoking," Amelia said, forcing a polite tone. "Sorry, but I'd prefer you didn't. We try to keep the office air... breathable."

Eloise's brows lifted. "*Mon Dieu.* Americans and their rules." She sighed dramatically and slipped the cigarettes back into her bag. "You would be happier if you smoked. This, I promise you."

Amelia smiled thinly. "I think I'll take my chances."

To pivot the conversation, she gestured toward the copper bathtub image again. "If we pair it with these gold leaf accents, the whole room will glow—romantic, ethereal, like something from a dream."

Eloise picked up her phone, barely listening.

Amelia swallowed. Losing this client would be a disaster. Eloise Kitt wasn't just another customer—she was a brand, a walking endorsement. Getting featured in *Vogue Interiors* or *Architectural Digest* could change everything for White Rabbit Design.

"Alright," Amelia said brightly, "let me ask you something different. What do you dream about?"

Eloise's eyes flicked up. *"Excuse-moi?"*

"Your dream," Amelia said. "If you were in that bath, surrounded by bubbles, and you opened your eyes—what would you see?"

"Isn't that your job?" Eloise said dryly. "To see what I cannot?"

"Humor me," Amelia said, leaning forward, earnest now. "Just for a moment."

Eloise arched an eyebrow. "Only if I can smoke."

"Fine," Amelia groaned, waving her hand. "One cigarette."

Eloise grinned triumphantly, lit up, and exhaled a perfect stream of smoke toward the ceiling. Amelia's throat burned just watching her. It made her think of Kinsey—of the way his hands had trembled in the hospital, of the smell of stale tobacco that seemed to haunt even the cleanest rooms. She'd watched Arthur fight his own cravings for months before he finally quit. The memory made her chest tighten.

"So?" she prompted, desperate to redirect. "Your dream?"

Eloise tapped ash delicately into her coffee saucer. "I like birds," she said finally.

"Birds?" Amelia repeated, thrown off.

"Oui. Birds."

"Any particular kind?"

Eloise shrugged, already looking back down at her phone. "Surprise me. I am far too busy with the twins' lessons to think about such things."

Amelia exhaled slowly. "So, I have full creative control?"

"Of course," Eloise said, standing. "Do you know why I hired you, *chérie?*"

Amelia shook her head. "No."

"That stained glass window on your Instagram. The one with the white rabbit. I showed it to my husband, and he said, 'That woman understands beauty and artistry.' So please—don't let me down." She slipped on her sunglasses, then paused at the door. "Actually—one more thing."

Amelia braced herself. "Yes?"

"I want a live bird. In the bathroom. Imagine it, *non?* The song of a canary while I bathe. Divine." She giggled and swept out the front door, the scent of her perfume lingering like a dare.

Amelia collapsed into her chair. "A live bird," she muttered. "Wonderful." Her knee throbbed. She pulled up her skirt and peeled the bandage back—the skin was redder now, angrier. The edges glistened. "Oh, hell."

The bell over the front door jingled. Charlie stood there, hair a mess, face unshaven, his shirt wrinkled beyond redemption. He looked as though sleep had forgotten his address.

"Morning," he said, voice hoarse. "How'd it go with Eloise?"

Amelia squinted. "What are you doing here? Why aren't you with Wendy?"

"She told me to get out of the house for a while. I figured I'd come by, see how the meeting went."

"She wants a live bird in her bathroom," Amelia said flatly.

Charlie cracked a weak grin. "Of course, she does."

He slumped into his chair, the smell of stale beer and grief filling the space between them. "You, okay?" she asked softly.

"Not great." He rubbed his eyes. "Wendy's barely sleeping. Bettys worse. The house feels... wrong."

Amelia hesitated, then smiled faintly. "You look terrible."

"Thanks." He sniffed his shirt. "I smell terrible too."

"You do," she said, laughing despite herself. "I was going to check in later today, bring lunch."

"Better not. They need quiet. Betty doesn't want to see anyone."

Amelia nodded. "Who's minding Harry's pub?"

"Harry's brother, Nic. For now."

"That's kind of him," she said, and then Charlie noticed the sparkle on her hand.

"Wait a second. What is *that?*"

Amelia blushed. "Oh. This? Arthur sort of... proposed."

Charlie's eyes widened, then glistened. "Amelia! That's—bloody hell, that's amazing!" His voice cracked halfway between laughter and tears.

"Don't cry," she said, grinning.

"I'm not crying," he said, blinking rapidly. "You're crying." He turned away, fumbling for the office bathroom.

Amelia tried to follow, but her knee buckled. "Ouch."

He spun around. "Your leg again?"

"It's awful," she admitted. "I need to go back in. I think it's really infected."

"Let me see."

She hesitated, then pulled her skirt up just enough. Charlie knelt, gently peeling the bandage back. "Amelia. That's bad."

The door opened.

"What's all this?" Lady Edith's voice cut through the room like the crack of a whip.

Amelia's face went crimson. She dropped her skirt—straight over Charlie's head. "Oh!"

Charlie jumped back, hands in the air. "This isn't what it looks like!"

Lady Edith stood in the doorway, arms crossed, perfectly composed. "Your head was under my future daughter-in-law's skirt?"

Amelia flailed for words. "I was showing him my knee!"

Charlie, mortified, blurted, "It's true. I'm a married man!"

Lady Edith's expression softened into mischief. "I know, dear. I was merely testing your reflexes." Then, quite unexpectedly, she smiled. "Arthur called me this morning. He told me the good news. I came to congratulate you."

Amelia froze. "Oh—that's... kind."

And before she could think to move, Lady Edith opened her arms and *hugged her.* The world tilted. The woman who had once treated her like an interloper now smelled faintly of roses and warmth. Charlie covered his mouth, stifling a laugh at Amelia's stunned expression. When Lady Edith released her, she turned to Charlie. "And you, my dear boy." She offered *him* a hug too. He accepted without hesitation, "I'm truly sorry about Harry," she said softly. "He was a good man."

Charlie nodded, eyes damp. "Thank you, your ladyship."

"Stay strong," she said, squeezing his shoulders. "The days ahead will be hard. But you're not alone. Our family will be there for yours, as yours has always been for us."

He swallowed. "I'm sorry I left my job at Oak Hall, truly. The Bonnevilles have always looked after us."

"You never really left," she said simply. "You're working with Amelia, and soon she'll be one of us." Her smile turned genuine. "We're all connected in the end."

Charlie laughed softly. "I suppose that's right."

Lady Edith turned back to Amelia. "Now, my dear, sit. Let me see that knee."

"Are you sure?"

"I bore three children. I believe I can handle a scraped-up knee."

Amelia sank into her chair and revealed it to her. Lady Edith frowned and covered her mouth, "That knee looks dreadful. Cover it back up please."

Amelia sank back into her chair with a groan. "I know."

After collecting herself a moment, Edith took her hand, noticing the ring. "He chose beautifully. It suits you."

Amelia looked down at it, her heart softening. "He did, didn't he?"

"I am happy for you both," Edith said. "Surprised he didn't wait until the chaos settled—but that's Arthur. Once he decides, there's no stopping him."

Amelia hesitated, chewing her lip. "Can I ask you something?"

"Of course."

"It's about the ring... and Helena."

Edith sighed. "Ah. I thought that might come up."

"I didn't even know she existed until she showed up at the wedding," Amelia said. "I feel like everyone else knew."

Charlie cleared his throat. "I did. But I didn't think it was my place."

"Exactly," Amelia said, throwing her hands up. "See? Everyone knew. Except me."

Lady Edith's tone softened. "You have every right to feel that way. But believe me, there is nothing to fear. My son adores you. Whatever happened with that woman is dust and shadow now."

Amelia nodded, though her stomach still twisted. "I want to believe that."

"Do," Edith said gently. "And believe me when I say—I want us to start fresh. No more frost between us."

Amelia smiled faintly. "I'd like that."

Lady Edith stood, smoothing her coat. "Then it's settled." She turned to Charlie. "Take as much time as you need with your family. They'll say they don't want you there, but they do."

"I will," Charlie said quietly.

Edith surprised him again with another hug. "You'll be alright, dear."

He nodded, eyes glistening. "Thank you."

As he left, Edith turned back to Amelia. "I'll drive you to the doctor."

Amelia hesitated. "Actually... could you take me to the university instead? Arthurs there. I'll wait for him."

Edith frowned. "That's quite a walk from the car park."

"I'll manage."

"Very well," Edith said, with a trace of approval. "You're a strong girl."

While Amelia gathered her things, Edith wandered the office, trailing her fingers along the bookshelves. "You know," she said, "this place used to be a toy shop. Hayward's, I think it was called. Arthur was too young to remember, but Kinsey loved it. I once bought him a little stuffed lion here."

Amelia smiled softly. "Your family and your lions."

"Yes," Edith said, eyes going distant. "We do love them. My late husband and I went to Africa for our honeymoon. He fell in love with lions there. Said they reminded him of home." She chuckled faintly. "I never did see the resemblance."

They stepped outside, the afternoon bright and still. Amelia locked the office door and slid the key into her bag. The bandage under her skirt throbbed with every step, but she said nothing. Ahead, Lady Edith's car gleamed like a promise.

As they crossed to it, Amelia thought of Arthur's words that morning—*You can trust me.*

She wanted to. She truly did.

But as the ache in her knee deepened, she couldn't help but wonder which wound would heal first—the one on her leg, or the one she didn't yet have a name for.

CHAPTER TEN

THE RIDE TO THE UNIVERSITY PASSED IN A HUSH PUNCTUATED by the soft tick of Lady Edith's indicator and the murmur of mid-day traffic. Nottingham's stone and brick rose around them—orderly, self-possessed—until the gates appeared and the campus unfolded like a small, patient city. Redbrick buildings shouldered ivy and scaffolds of shade; swathes of lawn lay clipped and scholarly; bicycles leaned against railings as if dozing.

Edith eased the car to the curb near the humanities quad. "Here we are," she said, putting the gear in park. "I'll drop you at this entrance. It's the closest."

"Thank you, Lady—" Amelia stopped herself.

"Edith," she corrected gently. "I must insist."

Amelia smiled. "That will take some getting used to."

Edith studied her for a beat—Amelia's careful posture, the way she guarded her right knee. "Would you and Arthur come to Oak Hall for dinner tonight?" She added quickly, as if anticipating resistance, "I know Mother was... difficult. But perhaps we should try again. Barnaby would like to know you better. And Mother—well. You're engaged now. Family deserves familiarity at the very least."

"Let me ask Arthur," Amelia said, palms smoothing the skirt over her bandage. "We'll let you know."

"Very well," Edith said. "We have a wedding to plan, after all." Her mouth softened into something almost playful. "And lions to keep in line."

Amelia laughed, then opened the door and stepped out into a breeze that smelled faintly of old books and cut grass. She lifted a hand in farewell as Edith pulled away, the black car gliding into the stream of students.

Inside, the corridor's air shifted to academic—chalk dust, coffee, copier ink—the scent of a life arranged around thinking. She moved slowly, her knee throbbing with that hot, punitive ache. The bulletin boards were crowded with flyers for readings and recitals, announcements typed and torn in neat tabs: *Creative Writing Colloquium, Medieval Manuscripts Seminar, Poetry in the Park.* Names she didn't recognize beside names she did. She liked this feeling: the hum of a place where ideas were the traffic.

Arthur's classroom door had a rectangle of reinforced glass you could peer through—she did, and there he was, at the front, sleeves rolled to his forearms, one hand describing a shape in the air. Even from here he looked composed, precise, that controlled warmth she'd fallen in love with. A stack of students listened as if plugged into a current only he could provide. Her chest loosened at the sight of him, then tightened with a strange flicker of pride: *that's mine.*

She checked her phone: ten minutes of lecture remained. A long couch and two chairs sat in the dim end of the corridor like a little bay of waiting. She turned toward them, focusing on the rhythm of breath over the pulse of pain.

A figure detached from the flow of students and came toward her—a tall man, light-blond hair, unlined face, long strides. He looked not at her so much as into her path, as if he'd already calculated where she would stop. She glanced behind herself— no one. When she looked back, he was already smiling, a quick upward slant that didn't reach his eyes.

"Rough day?" he said.

She pretended not to hear and kept moving. *Don't invite, don't feed,* she told the part of herself that made friends with strangers on planes and baristas and buses. But his voice came again, silkier, as if he were humoring a child. "Rough day?"

She stopped because not stopping seemed ruder than she was able to be. "I hurt my knee," she said, neutral, non-committal.

He bit his lower lip as if weighing a joke. "Want me to fetch a wheelchair? I'd be happy to push you wherever you need to go."

For a second, she couldn't tell if he was mocking or sincere. Something about the offer—too ready, too intimate—made her skin tilt. So, she did what she'd learned to do when someone's energy felt wrong: she smiled, airy, disengaged. "You're very kind, but I'm fine."

She pivoted and continued to the chair. When she sat, he had already gone. She let out a breath she hadn't realized she was holding. Students streamed past in clutches, the corridor filling briefly with the noisy weather of change-over—zippers, laughter, the scrape of chair legs from inside rooms.

She pulled out her phone and typed *pet shops near me,* because Eloise's parting decree had been ridiculous and, unfortunately, a brief—the phrase *live bird in the bathroom* looping in her brain like a novelty song you can't shake. A canary? Too obvious. A finch? A wren? How did one even—wouldn't the steam be lethal? Droppings, mess, noise. She imagined Eloise soaking in copper, an indignant goldfinch correcting the acoustics. She buried her face in her hands. It was absurd, and yet... the challenge tugged.

"Are you all right?" a voice asked—soft, concerned.

Amelia lifted her head quickly, shaping the automatic smile. "I'm fine. Just—oh." She saw the hair first, a high, dark flame— then the rest of her resolved: tall, effortlessly proportioned, books balanced in the crook of one arm. Beauty that looked like it knew it and expected compliances accordingly.

"Sorry," the woman added, the apology more social than

sincere. "You had your face in your hands. I thought perhaps you were crying."

"I'm not—no." Amelia's smile held. She took in the details: the fine, almost translucent skin; the mouth curved but not yielding; the lecture notes visible beneath the top book—*Gawain and the Green Knight.* An edges-of-things kind of person, all soft glow and sharpened line. It took her a beat to understand the recognition wasn't imagined. *Her.*

Helena.

"Oh, I'm fine," Amelia said again, buying herself a second. *She doesn't know me,* Amelia thought, absurdly. *She doesn't know me at all.* "Work problem. Client wants a bird in a bathroom."

One of Helena's eyebrows flicked elegant surprise. "Are you a student?"

"No. My—" the word still felt wild in her mouth "—fiancé teaches here."

Helena's posture stilled a fraction. "Does he?" she asked, smooth as glass. "What's his name?"

Amelia paused, the moment stretching like pulled thread. *Don't be a coward,* she told herself, hot irritation at the impulse to swallow her own life. "Arthur Bonneville," she said.

A small sourness crossed Helena's face; she took half a step back, as if the air had changed temperature. Her gaze fell to Amelia's hand and snagged there, where the ring caught the corridor's pallid light and made it something else. Helena's throat moved in a quiet swallow.

"He proposed this morning," Amelia said before she could stop herself. It landed too bright, too proud. She hated herself for adding, "I'm not used to saying fiancé yet."

"I'm sure," Helena said, and the words wore a politeness that wasn't clothed enough. "I teach creative writing and medieval literature," she added, as if resuming a script in which the names had been different, the scene kinder.

"That sounds wonderful," Amelia said, because it did, because honest admiration arrived despite everything.

The classroom doors up and down the corridor bellowed open, and a river of students spilled into the hall, chattering, slinging bags, the decibel level spiking. Helena tightened her armload of books.

"I must be off," she said, then paused, almost theatrically considerate. "Congratulations... again."

"Thank you," Amelia replied, looking down at the ring because it helped steady her. As Helena turned away, Amelia surprised herself—some private, perverse nerve of courage firing. "I'm Amelia Levingston, by the way."

Helena pivoted halfway back and nodded with chilly correctness. "Helena Darling." She didn't offer her hand. She didn't need to. The corridor seemed to look at her as she moved—boys disguising glances in shamefully poor disguises, girls recalibrating posture as she passed—and then she was gone, sweeping into the classroom directly opposite Arthur's door.

Amelia's stomach rolled. Across the hall. They were opposite each other, everyday mirrors. She stood to test her balance and caught Helena watching her from behind her desk—neutral, assessing, present. The sight shot a little cold through Amelia's ribs.

Arthur's door clicked open. "Amelia?" he said, surprised, pleased, and then immediately alert. "What are you doing here?"

Three students gathering their folders looked up at her with the mild curiosity given to faculty spouses and unexpected sights. She crossed to him, the last ten steps a series of calculated tolerances.

"Hi," she managed.

"What's wrong?" he asked at once. Of course, he saw it—the sheen of sweat at her hairline, the way she favored the leg.

A flash of movement across the corridor tugged his attention. Helena had left her desk again and was visible, angled toward their doorway like a flower toward sun. Amelia didn't turn to confirm it; she felt the line of attention.

"Oh, Helena *Darling?*" she said, too casually, too loud. "We've just met."

Arthur's face shifted through surprise to wariness fast enough to leave a wake. "You didn't come here to—" He chopped the air, mortified on her behalf, protective of her dignity, both things at once.

"No," she said, stung. "It was coincidence. Well—no, it wasn't. Not coincidence. I came to see you, and now I see you work *directly across the hall* from your ex-fiancée." The last word was not so much spoken as set down between them and left.

Two students stifled laughter as they edged past. Arthur put a gentle hand on Amelia's arm. "Lower your voice," he said quietly. "Please. Come sit."

She sank into the chair behind his desk because the room tilted when she didn't. Her knee sent out throbbed commands, her body trying to claim her attention the way a child tugs a sleeve. She scrubbed the sweat from her brow with the back of her hand. "It's my knee," she said, shame mixing with pain. "I need to go back to the medic. I can't... it's worse."

He looked at his watch. "I've another class at two—hold on." He reached for his phone.

"No, I didn't realize you had Arthur, I don't want to make trouble. Could you just drive me to the clinic? I'll find a way back."

"How did you get here?"

"Your mother drove me," she said.

His eyebrows leapt, irrepressibly amused even now. "That's... new."

"I'll tell you later," she murmured. "Please."

"Of course," he said, tone already switching to the decisive one she liked best. "One minute." He stepped away from the desk and lifted the phone to his ear. "Hi—it's Arthur. Any chance you can cover my two o'clock? Family emergency. Yes. I'll send notes. Thanks." He ended the call and turned back to her, eyes softening. "You'll always come first," he said, matter-of-fact, as if reporting the weather rather than offering a vow. "Let me take care of you."

Her throat tightened. She reached for him; he folded her into himself, the corridor's noise thinning to a thread around the edges of the embrace. Over his shoulder, down the corridor, a small flash of movement: Helena again, head angled, arms crossed, watching as one might watch the perimeter of a territory.

"Arthur?" Helena's voice carried from the doorway opposite—warm in register, cool in usage. She stood there with a sheaf of papers, the pose deceptively collegial. "Do you have a moment?"

"Now isn't a great time," he said without turning, the refusal polite but firm.

Amelia released him and faced the doorway. "Hello again... Helena."

"We met just now," Helena told Arthur, eyes flicking to the ring. "Congratulations on your engagement."

For a heartbeat, Arthur might have been carved—everything stilled from the inside out, breath caught. "Thank you," he said at last.

"I didn't know you were seeing anyone," Helena observed, a historian's statement, filing facts into columns.

"That isn't anyone's business," he replied—gentle words, steel core.

"I suppose it isn't." She shifted the papers in her hand—official, white, weaponless. "This can wait, then. Another day. Pleasure to meet you again, Emily."

"Amelia," they said together, a duet that briefly, absurdly, tethered them.

"Amelia," Helena repeated, as if testing a spice she hadn't decided whether to like. She stepped back into her room, the door remaining open—a mouth not quite closed.

Amelia let her eyes close for a beat, then opened them and said, very softly, "She works across the hall from you."

"Yes," Arthur answered, as if confessing to rain.

"Of course she does," Amelia said, and stood because the

alternative was to cry in the chair. The motion pulled a sharp line of pain through her knee; she caught the desk.

"Wrong way," Arthur said gently, touching her elbow. "Car park's this side."

She followed him into the corridor, the tide of students thinned to eddies, the hum dropping a register now that rooms had swallowed bodies again. The fluorescent strip above them flickered once—an electric blink that made everything feel like a film frame.

"What changed?" he asked, walking slower to match her pace. "The pain?"

"It so much worse," she said, breath measuring itself. "And it looks angrier."

He nodded, jaw setting. "We'll go now."

They passed the opposite doorway. Amelia couldn't stop herself: she glanced in. Helena stood at her desk, not pretending not to watch. Their eyes met—the brief, unblinking click of a camera. No expression on Helena's face was large enough to be named; everything was refined down to elements: curiosity, calculation, the faint, satisfied light of someone who has correctly guessed the next move in a game.

The corridor exhaled them into a stairwell dim with old paint and an echo that turned footsteps into geology. Amelia gripped the rail; Arthur took the steps at her speed, one hand a warm, steady pressure between her shoulder blades. Outside, the wind had picked up, tugging leaves into small, frantic dances.

"Do you need me to carry you?" he asked, half-serious.

"I need you to pretend I'm not a Victorian fainting at the opera," she said. Her smile felt brittle and brave.

He opened the passenger door for her and she folded herself in, turning carefully so the bandage didn't bite. When he rounded to his side and slid in, the car was briefly a small confessional—a bubble in which only their breath existed.

"Clinic," he said, already reaching to start the engine. Then he stopped and looked at her, as if remembering there were things doctors couldn't touch. "We'll sort this," he said. "The knee. Everything."

She nodded. "Okay."

He started the car. As they pulled away from the curb, Amelia looked back once through the passenger window. On the second-floor landing, behind the glass of the corridor, a slim figure had paused at the railing—red hair caught in the light, arms folded like a ruler set against a page. The distance turned Helena from a person into a silhouette, but even silhouettes can suggest expression. She stood very still, watching the car until it turned and was gone.

Amelia faced forward. The ring on her hand threw little squares of light across her knee, butterflies of brightness that seemed almost comically at odds with the nausea and heat and the way her heart tried to wobble between love and alarm. She pressed her palm over it to steady the flashes.

"After the clinic," Arthur said, eyes on the road, "we'll go home. I'll make tea. We can decide about dinner with—" He hesitated, then said it anyway, brave. "With Gran and Barnaby."

"We'll see," she murmured, and closed her eyes for a moment because keeping them open made the world too detailed.

The university receded behind them, a redbrick permanence that didn't care about engagements or ex-fiancées or knees. The sky was chalk and silver. In the mirror, for a second, she thought she saw a pale car slide out a few lengths behind and then tuck itself back, like a thought that refuses to resolve. She looked again and it was only the ordinary arrangement of traffic, and the ordinary ache of worry being what it always is: a talented mimic.

Arthur's hand found her knee, not pressing, just resting—an old, simple kindness. She covered it with her own. The contact held.

In the rear view, the campus gates dwindled to black iron parentheses. Ahead, the road unspooled, indifferent and long. Somewhere behind on a second-floor landing, a woman leaned on a rail like a figure in a medieval illumination, bright and varnished and edged in gold leaf—the kind of image that can watch for centuries without moving.

Amelia kept her face toward the windscreen and the future it implied. She felt the watchfulness anyway, a prickle between shoulder blades that had nothing to do with cold. Not fear, exactly. Not yet. Something older and feline: the sense of being seen by something that could bide its time.

Arthur turned left toward the clinic.

Amelia gripped his hand a little tighter and let the car carry them there.

CHAPTER ELEVEN

THE SMELL OF DISINFECTANT CLUNG TO THE AIR LIKE COLD metal. Amelia sat on the paper-lined table, her hands twisting the edge of her hospital gown. The doctor peeled off her gloves with a snap that echoed far too loud in the small room.

"Well, you were smart to come back in," she said briskly. "This is not good."

Arthur, standing near the sink, straightened. His jaw tightened, that quiet, contained panic she recognized from every moment he tried to stay calm for her. "What's wrong?"

"It's very infected which makes me wonder if there are fragments of glass left in there, or perhaps it even cut into the knee cap. Either way, I want the surgeon to open this back up, clean it out properly and then we will restitch."

Amelia felt sick, "That sounds awful."

The doctor continued, already scribbling something into the chart. "I'm going to call the surgeon now and see if we can get you in first thing."

Amelia's hand rose almost unconsciously to her chest, fingers brushing the faint scar above her heart—the old port scar. "It would be... today?" she asked, voice small.

"Most likely first thing in the morning," the doctor said before sweeping out the door.

Arthur crossed to her immediately. "It will be fine," he said, but his voice was all effort, not belief.

Her phone vibrated in her lap—Wendy. Amelia snatched it up. "Wendy?"

"Can you come over tonight?" Wendy's voice trembled; she sounded hollow, stretched too thin.

"Yes, of course," Amelia said.

"Just you," Wendy added.

"Just me?" Amelia frowned. "You don't want Arthur there?"

"No. I just... I need *you*, Amelia. Please."

Before Amelia could answer, the doctor swept back in. "Good news," she said, too bright, "we can do it this afternoon if you are alright with just lidocaine. If you want to be sedated, you need to head straight there."

"Please," Wendy whispered over the phone, frantic.

Amelia's chest pulled in two directions—duty and dread. She met the doctor's gaze. "Could I schedule it for tomorrow morning instead? I—something urgent has come up."

The doctor's expression hardened. "I really think it would be best to do this today. You don't want this infection to spread."

Arthur's voice cracked with quiet urgency. "Listen to her, Amelia."

Her heart thudded. She lifted the phone back to her ear. "Wendy, listen—I have to get my knee operated on today."

There was a pause, a fragile breath. "Oh. I totally understand," Wendy said softly. "Take care of yourself."

Then the line went dead.

"She hung up," Amelia murmured, lowering the phone. "God, I feel like the worst friend in the world."

Arthur touched her shoulder. "You're doing the right thing."

The doctor nodded toward the door. "I'll leave instructions at the front desk. Go straight there. They'll be expecting you."

"I've eaten today," Amelia blurted.

"They won't use general anesthesia," the doctor assured her. "You'll be awake like I said."

Her stomach twisted. "Awake?"

"They'll make you very comfortable."

Arthur's hand tightened on hers. "Can I stay in the room with her?"

"I'm afraid not."

And that was it—the sentence that cracked her thin composure. The air felt too heavy. Her pulse rose until her ears rang.

In the car, Amelia tried to call Wendy again, but it went to voicemail. Then she called Charlie—no answer. Her fingers trembled around the phone. "Something's wrong," she whispered. "They always answer."

Arthur kept his eyes on the road. "They're grieving, love. Maybe they just need quiet."

But Amelia's gut said otherwise.

By the time she was changed into her gown, her panic had settled into a cold, clinical terror. She handed her phone to Arthur because she couldn't hold it anymore—her palms slick, her breath shallow.

"It's going to be alright," he said, kissing her forehead.

How could he know that? How could *anyone* promise safety?

As she followed the nurse into the operating suite, a memory surfaced: the fluorescent lights above her during her biopsy, the sterile chatter of unseen faces, the cold sting of the table. It was all the same choreography—the same surrender.

The nurse helped her onto the narrow bed. Machines hummed quietly. The surgeon entered, masked, gloved, efficient.

"Alright, Amelia," he said as a nurse handed her a pill and

some water, "This will help you relax. You'll stay awake, but it'll make the time pass easily. Then I'll numb the knee and clean everything out. You'll feel some pressure, but no pain."

Pressure. No pain. Lies wrapped in kindness.

Amelia nodded anyway.

The ceiling swam. Time shortened, folded, disappeared. She remembered flashes: a voice counting down, the cold tug of metal instruments, her own hand gripping the edge of the bed.

The doctor stood beside her, unmasking. "We found a piece glass lodged in the kneecap," she explained. "A decent-sized one. It was likely causing the infection. I've cleaned the area and stitched you back up—twenty-one sutures. You'll be sore for a while."

Twenty-one. Amelia repeated the number in her head like a curse.

By the time Arthur wheeled her to the car, dusk had arrived— the world tilted in gold and shadow. The pain was sharp again, the meds thinning out like tidewater. She said nothing the entire drive home.

Arthur's phone rang once—his mother. He answered, murmured apologies, explained about the surgery. When he hung up, Amelia stirred.

"Mum wishes you feel better," he took her hand.

"I just want to go to bed," she sighed.

"I'll make dinner."

"I'm not hungry."

"You really need to eat a little something Amelia."

They turned into the drive, headlights sweeping over the familiar front of The Park House—except someone was sitting on the stone step outside. Rosie, a small heap of chaos with two suitcases beside her, waving both arms.

Arthur braked. "What on earth..."

Amelia leaned forward. "Is that—Rosie?"

They parked. Rosie bounded toward them before the car even stopped, her hair wild, her expression dramatic. "Where have you *been?* I've been waiting for an hour."

"Rosie," Arthur said, climbing out, "what are you doing here?"

"I couldn't take another minute there. I'm moving in."

Amelia blinked. "You're—what?"

"Temporarily!" Rosie amended quickly, gesturing at her bags. "Gran has gone completely mad. I can't be in that house another night."

Arthur's brow furrowed. "What happened?"

"She's lost it. Just completely gone." Rosie tossed up her hands.

Amelia eased her door open, careful with her bandaged leg. Arthur rushed to her side, but Rosie's eyes widened as she saw the stiff brace under Amelia's skirt. "Good Lord, what happened to you?"

"She just had surgery," Arthur said sharply.

Rosie recoiled, then recovered. "Oh my, gross. I mean—sorry. Let me help you."

Amelia almost laughed through the pain. She took Rosie's arm and hobbled inside while Arthur carried the suitcases.

"I think I'll stay downstairs tonight," Amelia said, staring at the steep staircase.

"Nonsense." Arthur scooped her into his arms before she could protest.

Rosie clutched her chest dramatically. "My brother, the gallant knight! Where do I find one of those?" she sighed, then trudged back outside for the rest of her luggage.

Later, Rosie sat in the kitchen with a glass of wine and a pile of crackers. Arthur entered, sleeves rolled, tired but composed.

"Is she alright?" Rosie asked.

"She's resting. I'll take her some food soon." He poured himself a drink and sank into the chair across from her. "So—what happened tonight?"

Rosie snorted. "What happened to me? What about you? You're engaged!"

Arthur's mouth quirked. "I am."

She leaned forward eagerly. "Tell me *everything*."

He swirled his wine. "I surprised her this morning in the bathroom."

Rosie's face twisted. "Ew. Please don't ever start a story that way again."

He laughed softly. "It was more romantic than it sounds."

"And then she needed surgery?" Rosie frowned.

"Her knee got infected. They had to clean it out today. It's been a nightmare."

"I'll bet," she said, watching him. "But that's not what's really on your mind."

Arthur hesitated. "She met Helena."

The glass nearly slipped from Rosie's hand. "No. She didn't."

"Yes."

"Arthur!"

He sighed, rubbing his forehead. "In the hallway at the university. And then Helena walked into my classroom while Amelia was there. It was... awful."

Rosie poured him more wine. "I honestly don't understand you. Why didn't you ever tell Amelia about her?"

"It was a mistake," he admitted quietly. "I thought if I didn't talk about it, it would stay buried. I didn't want to spoil what we have."

Rosie pointed at him with her glass. "Amelia loves you. She would've understood. But now? She's probably unraveling."

He pressed his palms to his eyes. "I know."

"And you haven't told her the rest?"

He froze. "What rest?"

"The part you're dying to say but haven't yet."

Arthur sighed and dropped his voice. "Last week Helena came to my office. Said she'd broken it off with the man she left me for. He was abusive. She told me she's still in love with me."

Rosie shot out of her chair. "Arthur!"

"I know." He exhaled. "I didn't encourage her, but… she was distraught. She said he's been calling, begging her back. She's filed a restraining order."

"And you haven't told Amelia any of this?" Rosie demanded.

"No. You're the first person I've told."

"Arthur, you have to tell her."

"I can't," he said quietly. "She's already so shaken. The surgery, the stress, all of it."

Rosie crossed her arms. "Secrets are what destroy things, not truth. Trust me."

He looked up at her, weary. "I'll tell her. Just… not tonight."

Rosie dropped back into her chair, still bristling. "So. That's my brother's disaster. Now for mine."

Arthur raised an eyebrow. "Go on."

"When Mum told Gran you got engaged to Amelia, Gran went berserk. Called her a nobody. An American. Said you were throwing away your name for—" Rosie waved a hand "—romance."

Arthur groaned.

"And then she turned on me. Said I was a disappointment. That she'd cut me off unless I went back to university. I packed my bags before she could finish her rant."

"You might actually benefit from going back," Arthur said gently.

Rosie scowled into her wine. "Maybe. I just don't know what to do with myself. I feel… stuck."

"You love fashion," he reminded her. "Amelia's working with Eloise Kitt now."

Rosie's eyes widened. "You're lying. *Eloise Kitt?* I *love* her. She's brilliant."

"Speak with Amelia about it," Arthur said.

She shook her head. "What good would that do? I can't just—show up and ask to be her intern."

"Well, you can't stay here forever."

A knock cut through the kitchen's warmth—sharp, deliberate.

Arthur frowned, setting down his glass. "Now who on earth..."

He crossed the tiled floor and opened the door.

Lady Edith stood there in her trench coat, two suitcases beside her, wind pressing at her hair.

"Mum?" he said, startled. "What are you doing here?"

Her expression was composed but cold, a storm barely sheathed. "I'm no longer a guest of Oak Hall."

The words landed like the first crack of thunder before a long, inevitable storm.

CHAPTER TWELVE

"**S**AY THAT AGAIN?" ARTHUR BLINKED AT HIS MOTHER, WHO stood perfectly poised on the doorstep, the late evening wind pressing against her silk scarf.

"I said," Lady Edith repeated coolly, "I'm staying here for a little while."

"Mummy?" Rosie's voice carried from the hall, small and uncertain.

"Hello, darling," Edith replied smoothly, stepping across the threshold as though the house still belonged entirely to her. "Arthur, be a dear and fetch the rest of my bags from the car."

Arthur hesitated, his hand still on the door. "You're moving in?"

"Temporarily," she said, brushing past him. Her perfume—bergamot and something sharper, expensive—lingered in the air like a declaration.

From the staircase above, Amelia's voice floated down, weary but curious. "Who's at the door?"

Lady Edith looked up, her expression softening by a single degree. "It's just me, Amelia. Feeling any better?"

Amelia clutched the banister, trying not to wince. "I am a bit hungry."

"Wonderful," Lady Edith said, as though that were all that mattered. "Let me fix you something. I'll bring it right up."

Arthur gave Amelia a helpless look—the kind that said *I have absolutely no control over this woman*—but Amelia was already retreating upstairs, muttering something about resting. He turned back to his mother, who was now in the kitchen, opening cupboards as if she'd never left The Park House.

"Mum, what are you doing here?"

"Well, I didn't have another place to go," she replied.

Arthur ran a hand through his hair. "Why don't I handle this."

"Oh no dear, I can handle this," she said airily, already pulling cold chicken, a head of lettuce, and a jar of Dijon from the refrigerator.

Rosie appeared at the door to the cellar. "I'm going to fetch more wine. I feel this evening calls for it."

"Grab a good Burgundy while you're down there, darling," Lady Edith called, her voice rich and melodic. "And bring three glasses."

Arthur leaned against the counter, watching her slice bread. "Mum—"

She cut him off without looking up. "Gran and Barnaby are selling their London house."

Arthur froze. "Which leaves you..."

"Nowhere," she said simply, spreading mustard with surgical precision.

"Of course."

Rosie returned, arms full of bottles, her eyes already glinting with mischief. "I brought extra," she announced, setting them down with a clatter.

Lady Edith smiled faintly. "You always do." She handed Arthur a plate with the finished sandwich. "Take this up to Amelia, would you?"

"Are you hungry?" Arthur asked, but she was already reaching for more bread.

Rosie hopped onto a stool. "Mummy, make me one too. I'm *starving.*"

Arthur rolled his eyes. "Rosie, you can make your own sandwich."

Lady Edith gave him a look sharp enough to cut glass. "Oh, let her be, Arthur. She's had a dreadful day."

Rosie grinned triumphantly and poured three glasses of wine. "One for Mummy, one for me, and one for Amelia."

"What about me?" Arthur asked.

"Arthur you can fetch a glass and pour your own wine." Rosie teased.

Arthur took the extra glass with a sigh. "Thank you."

Upstairs, Amelia was waiting in bed, her leg elevated on a pillow, a faint ache pulsing beneath the clean white bandage. The smell of antiseptic still lingered on her skin.

Arthur pushed open the door, balancing the plate and glass. "I should've brought you a tray," he said softly.

"Oh no, this is fine." Amelia shifted to sit up.

"How does it feel?"

"Like it was cut open and poked with a fork," she said dryly.

He smiled despite himself and handed her the wine. "My mother made you a sandwich."

"That's different." She took a bite and sighed.

Arthur sat beside her, his shoulders relaxing for the first time all day. "So, Mum was apparently evicted from Oak Hall. Indefinitely."

Amelia laughed through a mouthful. "What a great day."

He leaned back against the headboard. "Can I just hide up here with you for a while?"

She nodded toward his glass. "Only if you bring more wine."

He poured them both another, but before either could sip, a firm knock echoed through the house.

Arthur groaned. "You must be joking."

Downstairs, they heard Lady Edith's unmistakable voice floating through the hall. "Why, hello dear!"

Arthur frowned and rose, setting the glass aside. "Who now?"

Amelia listened. A beat later came a softer, trembling voice. "Hello, Lady Edith. Is Amelia here?"

"Wendy?" Amelia whispered.

Lady Edith ushered her in like an old friend. "Please, come in. Arthur! Amelia's friend is here."

"I'll get you a glass of wine!" Rosie called, already clattering toward the kitchen.

Arthur leaned over the railing. "Amelia's upstairs, Wendy. Go ahead."

"Thank you." Wendy's voice was fragile.

Moments later, she appeared in the doorway of Amelia's room, a glass trembling in her hand. She looked paler than usual, her eyes red at the edges.

"Wendy," Amelia said, surprised. "Hi!"

Wendy crossed the room and perched beside her on the bed. "How's your knee?"

"It's not great, but I'll survive. What's going on?"

Wendy twisted her hands in her lap. "I needed to talk to you."

Arthur stood uncertainly in the doorway until Wendy turned and said gently, "Arthur, could I have a private moment with Amelia?"

He nodded, understanding the tone. "Of course."

The door clicked shut behind him.

Amelia leaned forward. "What is it?"

Wendy's voice cracked. "You know how my uncle's been helping out at the pub?"

"Yes?"

"Well... a woman came to the pub today looking for Harry. She said she was... family."

Amelia blinked, trying to make sense of it. "Say that again?"

"My uncle told her she must be mistaken, and then she pulled out this photograph."

Wendy reached into her purse and unfolded a crumpled picture. Her hand shook as she passed it over. Amelia stared. It was Harry—smiling, young, alive—his arm around a woman Amelia didn't recognize, with a small boy perched on his knee. The child couldn't have been more than seven.

"Oh my," Amelia breathed.

"Then," Wendy whispered, "my uncle told her what happened. That Harry's gone. The woman just... broke down. She cried so hard she could barely breathe, then ran out of the pub. She left this behind."

They both stared at the photograph, the silence in the room thickening. The only sound was the faint ticking of Amelia's bedside clock.

"Have you ever seen her before?" Amelia finally asked.

"Never."

"Did you tell Charlie? Or your mum?"

Wendy shook her head. "Only my uncle knows. And now you. I don't know what to do."

She broke then—the sobs she'd held back for hours collapsing all at once. Amelia reached out, pulling her close, holding her as she wept. Amelia looked over Wendy's shoulder at the photograph again, the boy's face—Harry's eyes, unmistakably.

"Oh, Harry," she murmured under her breath. "What have you done?"

Downstairs, the house hummed with uneasy quiet. Lady Edith and Rosie had settled at the kitchen table, the remnants of dinner scattered between them.

"Do you suppose she'll mind?" Rosie asked, pouring herself another half-glass.

"Who, dear?"

"Amelia. You being here."

Lady Edith smiled, folding her napkin. "Of course not. I am, after all, her future Mother-in-law."

Arthur appeared in the doorway, weary and silent.

Rosie shot him a look. "Whatever's going on upstairs, it's serious."

He nodded, pouring himself more wine. "Everything seems to be *serious* lately."

Lady Edith studied her son. "You're pale. And distracted. Is it the engagement that's unsettling you, or something else?"

Arthur didn't answer.

Rosie filled the silence. "He's just stressed. Between Helena reappearing, Amelia's surgery, and me showing up with two suitcases, I'd say he's earned a glass or ten."

Lady Edith raised a brow. "Helena?"

Arthur froze mid-sip.

Rosie realized too late what she'd said. "Oh, damn it."

Lady Edith folded her hands slowly. "I beg your pardon—*Helena Darling?* She showed up again?"

Arthur set his glass down. "It's nothing, Mother."

"Oh, it's never *nothing* with that woman," Edith said softly. "I warned you years ago, she was trouble."

Arthur stood abruptly. "Not now."

He left the room. The air crackled in his absence.

Rosie swallowed the last of her wine and muttered, "Well. That went well."

Upstairs, Wendy finally pulled back, eyes swollen. "I just don't understand any of it. Harry is such a good man, and Father."

Amelia rubbed her back gently. "He was. But sometimes even the best people have secrets."

Wendy nodded, gripping the photograph again. "I must tell my mum. But I don't know how."

Amelia reached for her hand. "You'll know when the moment's right."

They sat there in silence a long while—two women bound by grief, by the strange cruelty of truth arriving too late. Downstairs, a door slammed. A voice—Lady Edith's—sharp and echoing through the marble halls:

"Arthur, don't you walk away from me!"

Wendy looked up, startled. Amelia exhaled, shaking her head. "Welcome to The Park House," she murmured. "Where the ghosts are all still living."

Wendy almost smiled through her tears.

Outside, thunder rolled across the Nottinghamshire hills, low and distant, promising a storm that would arrive before morning.

And in the drawing room below, Lady Edith poured herself another glass of wine, eyes glinting in the candlelight.

"Helena Darling," she whispered to herself. "Back again."

CHAPTER THIRTEEN

THE SMELL OF BACON DRIFTED THROUGH THE CORRIDORS OF The Park House like a memory. Amelia stirred awake to the soft crackle of fat in a pan and sunlight filtering through the curtains. Her body ached, her knee throbbing faintly beneath its bandage—but when she shifted and tested her leg, she realized the pain was finally duller than it had been for days.

Beside her, Wendy slept deeply, still in yesterday's clothes, her hand resting across the blanket. Amelia smiled faintly. They had stayed up late, whispering through the dark about Harry, about loss, about the strange ways people broke and still somehow kept moving forward.

Quietly, she slipped from bed. Her feet met the cool wooden floor and she steadied herself on the carved bedpost before walking into the bathroom. The mirror showed dark crescents under her eyes, a sign of how much the past week had taken out of her. Still, she brushed her hair, washed her face, and dressed with a soft resolve.

When she descended the staircase—one careful step at a time—the morning light was spilling in golden sheets across the marble entryway. The scent of bacon and something buttery led her toward the kitchen, where she stopped short at the sight of Lady Edith, sleeves rolled up, standing at the stove.

"Oh," Amelia said, half-smiling. "Good morning, Lady Edith."

"Edith, darling," she corrected gently, glancing over her shoulder. "Good morning. How are you feeling?"

"Much better today." Amelia took a seat at the long oak table, still amazed to see Edith at the helm of the kitchen like an ordinary woman.

"Sit, sit," Edith insisted. "Tea or coffee? I made both—I wasn't sure which you preferred."

"Coffee, please. That was thoughtful of you."

Edith smiled to herself, sliding the pot across the counter. "I have a quiche in the oven—assuming I don't forget about it—and bacon for everyone. I'm going to run to the shops later, pick up something nice for dinner."

Amelia accepted her coffee, watching her move with surprising grace. "Where's Arthur?"

Edith frowned lightly. "He wasn't upstairs with you?"

"No. Wendy's still asleep in there. I think she needed the rest."

"I'm sure she did. Poor girl." Edith lowered her voice, curiosity dancing in her tone. "She looked heartbroken when she arrived last night."

Amelia checked that the hallway was empty, then leaned forward. "Something happened."

Edith leaned in too, conspiratorially. "What sort of something?"

"A woman showed up at Harry's pub yesterday. Said she was a friend of his. She even had a photograph—her, Harry, and a boy. Seven, maybe eight years old."

Edith's eyes widened. "You can't be serious."

"I wish I weren't. She left the picture behind. Wendy's uncle confirmed it—it's him."

Before Edith could answer, a hard knock echoed from the front door, startling them both.

"Who on earth would be here at this hour?" Amelia muttered, setting down her cup.

"Shall I get it?" Edith offered.

"No, I've got it."

She was halfway down the hall when Arthur emerged from the study, hair tousled, shirt wrinkled. "I must've fallen asleep in there," he said, rubbing his eyes. "Who's knocking?"

"I'll find out."

"I'll come with you." He fell into step beside her, lowering his voice. "How's the knee?"

"Much better," she said truthfully. "It doesn't hurt as much to walk on today."

"That's good." Arthur unlatched the heavy front door—and immediately froze. On the doorstep stood Gran, sharp as a blade in dove-gray wool, and Barnaby, cheerful but wind-ruffled in his cream hat and coat.

"Gran," Arthur said slowly.

"Arthur." Gran's tone was clipped, her eyes flicking briefly— dismissively—toward Amelia.

Barnaby, by contrast, brightened. "Do I smell bacon?"

"Uh... yes," Amelia managed. "Lady Edith's cooking."

Barnaby chuckled. "Edith? Cooking? The world truly has turned upside down."

"Won't you come in?" Amelia offered politely, stepping aside.

Barnaby's grin widened as he entered. "This place looks won- derful! The Park House is alive again." His voice echoed down the hall as he disappeared toward the kitchen.

Gran followed, her cane tapping on the marble floor. "I've come to speak to my daughter," she announced without looking at anyone.

Arthur slipped an arm around Amelia. "Welcome to our home, Gran."

"I thought this house belonged to your mother," Gran said coolly.

"It does," Amelia replied before Arthur could answer. "I gave it back to her. She's kind enough to let us take care of it for her."

Arthur hid a grin. "She's in the kitchen. Just follow the smell."

From upstairs, Wendy's voice called out groggily, "Do I smell bacon?"

Rosie appeared at the top of the opposite staircase, her hair in chaos. "You do, but don't bother—Gran's here."

"Oh no." Wendy turned back toward her room.

"Good idea," Rosie muttered, retreating as well.

Amelia sighed. "Well, that's the end of a peaceful morning."

Wendy came down the steps anyway, coat in hand. "I need to head home. Mum and Charlie are waiting." She hugged Amelia tightly. "We'll talk later, alright?"

"Of course," Amelia said softly.

Wendy smiled faintly at Arthur. "Bye, Arthur." And she was gone.

Arthur exhaled. "What was that about?"

"I'll tell you later," Amelia said. "Let's go see what fresh disaster awaits."

They entered the kitchen quietly. The atmosphere was dense with tension—and the smell of bacon grease. Barnaby was seated at the table, humming cheerfully, devouring a plateful of bacon. Lady Edith stood by the stove, arms folded, watching her mother sip tea like a monarch inspecting her court. "Did you offer your congratulations to Arthur and Amelia?" Edith asked sharply.

"Congratulations indeed!" Barnaby declared, mouth half full. "We're delighted about the engagement. Overjoyed." He clapped his hands together, beaming. "Now, Amelia, would you be a dear and show me this solarium I've heard so much about? I hear it's a masterpiece."

"Oh," Amelia blinked. "Of course. I'd love to."

As they left, Arthur stayed behind, planting himself by the counter like a silent bodyguard. Gran's spoon clinked against her china cup. "Arthur, we were just discussing living arrangements.

It seems clear your mother should take up permanent residence here. You and Amelia could use the time to establish yourselves properly—in town, perhaps."

Edith's eyes flashed. "Mother, please. This hasn't been my home for years. It's theirs now—they've made it something special."

Arthur stepped forward. "Mother, I—"

Gran raised a hand. "Arthur, dear, you're sensible enough to see reason."

Arthur's jaw tightened. "Reason? You mean banishing your own daughter while you move back into Oak Hall?"

"Don't be melodramatic. She left of her own choice."

"That's not the point," Arthur said, voice hardening. "What is the point, Gran, is how cruel this all is. You talk about family, but you treat them like tenants."

Gran's lips pursed. "Careful, child."

"I'm not a child."

"Then act like a man," she shot back. "Are you certain about this American girl? She doesn't understand our world."

Arthur's eyes burned. "Our world? You mean this crumbling illusion of control you all cling to? Amelia's survived things none of us could bear for a week. She's stronger than all of us combined."

Gran sipped her tea, unfazed. "Be smart, Arthur. Your father left you a fortune, yes—but he left you expectations as well. Your choice in wife will determine the course of everything that follows."

Arthur's tone sharpened. "My father left everything to Kinsey. Kinsey chose Amelia. And so have I."

Edith's eyes gleamed with quiet pride.

Gran rose slowly, spine straight as a ruler. "Then you can make your own way, as your mother will now have to."

At that moment, Rosie appeared in the doorway, her expression defiant. "No, Gran. I'm staying with Mum." She crossed the kitchen and put an arm around Edith. "Wherever she goes, I go."

Gran's gaze hardened. "Very well. Then from this moment, you are both cut off."

"Cut off?" Edith gasped.

"If you don't need me," Gran said icily, "you don't need my money."

Barnaby entered again, halting in the doorway, his face conflicted.

"Barnaby?" Edith's voice trembled.

He sighed. "I'm sorry, my dear." He raised his hands helplessly and followed his wife out the door. Through the kitchen window they all watched as the car rolled down the long gravel drive, dust rising in its wake. The silence they left behind was almost holy.

Then—a sharp *beep!*

"Is something burning?" Amelia sniffed the air.

Smoke curled from the oven. Edith yelped, "My quiche!"

Arthur threw open the window while Edith pulled out a charred pan, coughing through the smoke. Rosie burst out laughing. "Well, at least we know breakfast's over."

Edith dropped the ruined dish on the counter and sank into a chair. "I can't even cook. I'm a Marchioness, a widow, a mother—and I can't cook a quiche without disaster."

Arthur knelt beside her. "It's not your fault."

Rosie leaned on the counter. "I'm twenty-two and have no idea what I'm doing either. Feel better?"

Edith gave a watery laugh. "A little."

Amelia's phone buzzed. She glanced at the screen. "Oh, it's my client. Sorry I have to take this." She hurried into the study, her voice brightening automatically. "Good morning, Eloise."

"Bonjour, Amelia," came the polished French accent. "My husband adored the bird idea for the master bathroom. He wants to meet at your office this afternoon. One o'clock."

Amelia froze. "This afternoon?"

"Yes. We'll finalize everything together. Oh, and *Elle Decor* wants to feature the house in their October issue."

Amelia's grip loosened. The phone slipped from her hand and clattered to the floor.

Arthur, hearing the noise, rushed in. "Are you alright?"

She bent to grab it—too quickly—and pain lanced through her knee. "Ow."

Arthur caught her elbow. "You shouldn't be moving like that."

She snatched the phone back just in time to hear Eloise's crisp voice: "We'll see you at one. Don't forget—*live birds*, plural."

"Plural?" Amelia echoed weakly. "I thought we agreed on one."

"Non, non. Birds. *Au revoir!*" The line went dead.

Amelia collapsed into the chair and stared up at the stained-glass rabbit. "I've got to go into town. I need to find a pet shop."

Arthur blinked. "A pet shop? Amelia, you just had surgery."

"Arthur, please, I can handle this. I've taken care of myself for years."

He exhaled slowly. "I know. But it's alright to let someone take care of you now."

She looked at him, softened by his sincerity. "You're right," she whispered. "But not today."

He smiled sadly. "Fine. I'm not going to argue with you. I've got class at eleven anyway."

Moments later, Rosie burst in, breathless. "Knock knock!"

Amelia laughed weakly. "Come in."

"I have a small favor," Rosie said. "Arthur told me you're working with *Eloise Kit*. The Eloise Kit. Do you think maybe I could help? Be your assistant or something? Just for the experience?"

Amelia thought of Peter, her actual assistant who'd moved back to London. "You know, I really could use one."

Rosie's eyes widened. "Are you serious?"

"Completely. But you'd have to start today."

"Five minutes!" Rosie squealed, bolting for the stairs. "Maybe ten!"

"Ten minutes!" Amelia shouted after her, smiling despite herself.

When she turned back, Lady Edith stood in the doorway, a hesitant grace about her.

"Do you have a moment, dear?"

"Of course."

Edith took the chair across from her. "I wanted to ask if it's alright for Rosie and me to stay here—just for a while. Until we find our footing."

"Lady Edith, this is your home. You don't have to ask me."

Edith smiled softly. "Still, I wanted to. I want us to have a good relationship, Amelia."

"I think we already do," Amelia said, smiling back.

Edith laughed quietly. "Now, perhaps."

Their laughter faded, and Amelia said, "Before you go—about Harry. What should I tell Wendy?"

Edith's eyes darkened with thought. "Sometimes, dear, ignorance spares pain. Perhaps she should leave the truth buried."

Amelia stood slowly. "But the truth always comes up, one way or another. Helena's proof enough of that."

Edith rose too, meeting her gaze. "Then you already know what to advise her."

Amelia nodded, touched by the unexpected wisdom. "Thank you, Edith. I will." She turned toward the door, pausing in the light that streamed through the window. "I'll see you at dinner?"

"I'll cook," Edith said brightly.

Amelia's lips curved, "Oh no, let's not test fate again."

CHAPTER FOURTEEN

THE BELL OVER THE PET SHOP DOOR JINGLED AS AMELIA pushed it open, holding it for Rosie, who followed reluctantly, her face twisted as if stepping into an unpleasant memory. "When you said I could help you, this is *not* what I had in mind," Rosie muttered, wrinkling her nose and eyeing the narrow aisles lined with cages, tanks, and the faint shimmer of feathers.

"You don't like pets?" Amelia asked, though she already knew the answer from Rosie's delicate recoil.

"No. I like *handbags*, not hamsters."

The shop smelled of sawdust and something faintly sour—like apples gone soft. Behind the counter, a young woman with hair streaked in pink, purple, and electric blue greeted them with a grin that could brighten a funeral. "Morning! What can I help you find?"

Before Amelia could answer, Rosie gasped, pointing to a glass case. "That's a spider! That's a *spider*, Amelia!"

Inside, a thick-legged tarantula crawled slowly across its tank, graceful in a nightmarish sort of way.

Amelia ignored Rosie's panic. "Actually, I have a question about birds."

"Who *wants* to have a giant spider in their house?" Rosie demanded, staring in disbelief.

"I do," said the clerk cheerfully. "His name's Leonard. He's a Sagittarius."

Rosie blinked. "You *live* with one of those? What if it escaped?"

"Oh, he's very friendly. I hold him all the time."

Rosie took a step back. "Right. I'll... stay over here."

The clerk leaned on the counter, still smiling. "So, what kind of bird are we talking about?"

Amelia hesitated. "It's for a client. She wants a bird—or maybe birds—to live in her... bathroom."

The woman tilted her head, as if deciding whether that was brilliant or insane. "That's... unusual. But I get it. I have a rabbit living in my kitchen. Rescued him last year. Name's Mr. Bongo."

Rosie blinked. "You're joking."

"He's litter-trained."

"Of course, he is," Rosie muttered.

"Well," the clerk continued, "a bathroom isn't ideal for most pets. Too damp, too cold. But if it's a big enough space, something like finches could do well. They're social, delicate—and they sing beautifully."

Amelia's mind sparked. "Finches," she repeated softly, turning the word over like a gemstone.

The clerk leaned closer, lowering her voice as if offering a secret. "You know, I've been building these custom aviaries from old furniture. My side gig. Look." She pulled out her phone and scrolled to a photo of an antique armoire transformed into a miniature indoor paradise—vines, gold lattice, the flutter of color behind wire.

Amelia's eyes lit up. "That's stunning."

"Isn't it?" The clerk's grin widened. "I could build one like that for you."

"I'm Amelia Levingston," she said, extending her hand. "And this is my—"

"Assistant. Rosie Bonneville," Rosie interrupted quickly, straightening her posture.

The clerk's eyes widened. "Wait. *Lady* Rosie Bonneville? I've seen you in magazines!"

Rosie blushed faintly. "Yes, well... not since being *cut off*," she muttered under her breath.

"I'm Chelsea," said the clerk. "Follow me. I'll show you, our finches."

The back of the shop came alive with soft music—the gentle trill of tiny birds fluttering in a large glass enclosure. Rosie leaned closer, enchanted despite herself. "They're so small. And look at those little stripes!"

"They're zebra finches," Chelsea explained. "They're calm, social, and happiest in pairs or flocks. You'll want at least four, but two is a good start."

Amelia smiled. "Perfect. I'll take two today."

Rosie groaned. "We're actually buying birds. This is happening."

"And," Amelia added, "I'm taking your number, Chelsea. I think I have the perfect project for you."

An hour later, they arrived back at *White Rabbit Interior Design.* Rosie pushed open the office door, balancing a glossy box with a picture of a gold cage on the front. Amelia followed carefully behind, cradling a small cardboard box with breathing holes.

"We have one hour before Eloise and her husband arrive," Amelia said. "If you can assemble the cage, we'll make it the reveal."

Rosie grimaced, setting down the box. "Wait. *Eloise's husband?* You mean *Teddy James?* The Teddy James, the rockstar?"

"Focus, Rosie."

"I'm focused."

Amelia placed the small box on her desk and whispered to it. "It's okay, little birds. You're about to have a beautiful home." She smiled softly, then opened her laptop, fingers flying across the keys.

She typed *mythical birds*—then *colorful birds*—then stopped when a photograph of a white peacock filled her screen, feathers fanned like moonlight caught in glass. Inspiration struck like lightning. A white peacock—elegant, divine—the centerpiece of a new stained-glass window.

She called Marcus, the artist who had helped her create the famous White Rabbit window that had made her career. When he heard her voice, he laughed. "You again. I've been waiting for your next mad idea."

"I have it," Amelia said, pacing as she described the concept.

By the time she hung up, her mind buzzed. This was it—the masterpiece that would cement her as more than just the "American girl with taste."

When Eloise and Teddy arrived, a ripple of excitement followed them down the street. Locals paused to snap photos as the couple—impossibly glamorous—swept through the door.

"Bonjour, Amelia," Eloise said, sunglasses perched on her hair. "You remember Teddy."

"Of course," Amelia said, shaking his hand. "Welcome. Please, sit."

Eloise turned to Rosie, who was standing at her best angle. "And you are?"

"Rosie Bonneville. Amelia's assistant."

"Ah, Bonneville," Eloise said, her eyes narrowing with recognition. "You have exquisite taste. That skirt is divine."

Rosie nearly glowed. "Thank you."

Teddy glanced at his watch. "We've only got an hour. Twins have a birthday thing."

"Understood," Amelia said, gesturing toward the corner. "Rosie?"

Rosie nodded and disappeared into the backroom. A faint chirping could be heard as she returned, carrying a covered cage. Eloise clasped her hands together, excitement sparking in her voice. "Mon Dieu. Is that what I think it is?"

Rosie placed the cage on the table, pulled off the coat, and two tiny finches blinked up at them.

Eloise gasped. "They are *adorable!* What are they called?"

"Zebra finches," Amelia said. "They'll sing while you soak in your copper tub."

"I love them!" Eloise bent closer, cooing at the birds. "Teddy, aren't they just perfect?"

He smiled faintly. "Whatever makes you happy, babe."

"Well," Amelia continued, "I wanted the space to feel like a sanctuary. You mentioned loving my stained-glass window—the one with the white rabbit—so I've commissioned the same artist again. We'll create a *white peacock* window that floods the room with color. The birds will live in a custom aviary—an antique cabinet transformed into art."

Teddy nodded, rhythmically tapping his sunglasses against his palm. "That's... genius."

Eloise looked spellbound. "A peacock of light, and little birds that sing. Amelia, this is why I adore you." Then, suddenly, she frowned at the cage. "But this one won't do."

Amelia smiled. "Of course not. It's temporary. The aviary will be magnificent—a jewel box of gold and glass."

Eloise turned to her husband. "Teddy, Elle Decor is coming to photograph the house for the October issue. We'll need everything done by August."

Amelia blinked. "That's eight weeks."

"Oui."

Her voice caught in her throat, but she smiled through it. "Then eight weeks it is."

Teddy clapped his hands. "Brilliant. Amelia, we're counting on you."

They all stood together, exchanged air kisses, and swept back toward the door greeting cameras flashing outside.

Amelia exhaled. "Oh, thank God."

Rosie grinned. "You were incredible."

Amelia laughed nervously. "I feel like I just survived a hurricane."

Rosie leaned over the birdcage. "What are we supposed to do with *them?*"

"Take them home with us, I suppose," Amelia said.

The finches chirped, as if in approval.

Rosie turned to her. "Amelia... can I ask something?"

"Of course."

"I don't know what I'm doing with my life," Rosie admitted. "You seem so sure of everything—like this is what you were born to do. I'd like to work with you. Properly. Be your assistant. Until I figure it out."

Amelia softened. "Then consider yourself hired."

Rosie's face lit up. "Truly?"

"Truly."

"Then we should celebrate. Cocktails?"

"We have to work Rosie."

Rosie groaned. "Fine. Lunch then."

"Lunch sounds great."

"Great. I'll pick something up while I'm out." Rosie grabbed her purse.

"Perfect. Be back in an hour."

Rosie hesitated. "You're serious, aren't you?"

Amelia smirked. "You're on the clock, Rosie."

Rosie saluted dramatically and left.

A few minutes later, Charlie arrived, looking drained but trying for a smile. "Did I just see Rosie sprinting down the street?"

"She's our new assistant," Amelia said, proudly.

He stared at her. "That's a terrible idea."

"She'll surprise you."

He leaned on his desk, listening to the faint chirping. "Why do I hear birds?"

Amelia gestured to the cage. "Meet our new project."

He laughed softly. "You never fail to surprise me, Amelia."

They worked in quiet rhythm for a few moments until Charlie spoke again. "Wendy told me she stayed with you last night. Thank you for that."

"Of course."

"The funeral's this Sunday," he said quietly. "Eleven at St. Mary's."

Amelia's heart sank. "So soon."

"There was a cancellation. We took it."

He rubbed his temples, staring at the floor. "No viewing. Just the service. He was cremated." Amelia nodded, choosing silence over questions she wasn't ready to ask. Charlie forced a smile. "Anyway, what's new with you?"

"Elle Decor's coming to shoot Eloise's house. We have eight weeks."

"Eight weeks?" He laughed. "Impossible."

"I have an unlimited budget."

"Then eight weeks will be *perfect.*" They both laughed, though exhaustion lingered behind their smiles. Charlie stared at the finches again. "They're singing. That's good luck, you know."

Amelia looked up from her sketches. "Is it?"

"Yeah. Birds singing indoors. It means hope."

She smiled faintly, watching the birds flutter in their cage. For once, she chose to believe it.

CHAPTER FIFTEEN

BY THE TIME AMELIA AND ROSIE RETURNED TO THE PARK House, the evening light had softened into a pale gold haze that settled across the estate. The drive up through the avenue of oaks always filled Amelia with a strange calm—but not today. Her shoulders ached, her head throbbed, and Rosie, clutching her heels in one hand, announced what Amelia already felt.

"I'm absolutely *exhausted*," Rosie groaned, kicking off her shoes at the door.

The moment the soles of their feet met the marble floor, they both stopped. A smell—dense, heavy, indescribable—clung to the air like fog.

Amelia wrinkled her nose. "What *is* that?"

Rosie's eyes widened in recognition. "Oh no. Mother's cooking again."

From the kitchen came the sound of pots clanging and a voice that carried cheerfully down the hallway. "Is that you, girls?" Lady Edith called.

Rosie turned to Amelia, whispering urgently, "Quickly. Call Arthur. Tell him to bring food. Tell him it's an emergency."

Before Amelia could move, Lady Edith appeared, radiant and

utterly unbothered by the olfactory chaos she had conjured. She wore an apron embroidered with tiny violets and held a wooden spoon like a conductor's baton. "I found the loveliest recipe in one of the cookbooks in the library," she announced proudly. "Cabbage soup—and I'm roasting lamb with mint jelly. Doesn't that sound divine?"

Amelia forced a smile. "That sounds... ambitious. You really shouldn't have gone to all that trouble."

"Nonsense. You've all been working so hard. I wanted to *contribute.*"

Before Amelia could respond, the front door opened, and Arthur stepped in. He stopped dead in the entryway, his nose twitching as if assaulted by an invisible wall. "What is that horrid smell? Did an animal die in here?"

Lady Edith's expression fell. "It smells?"

Arthur blinked, incredulous. "You don't smell that? It's like rotting seaweed in a sauna."

Offended, Lady Edith lifted her chin. "Perhaps I'll add more seasoning." She turned sharply on her heel and vanished, leaving a faint trail of something acrid in her wake.

"Why is mummy cooking now?" Rosie asked flatly. Arthur rubbed his temples in denial.

"She wants to 'contribute,'" Amelia whispered, making air quotes as Arthur groaned.

He kissed Amelia's forehead with a sigh. "I'll handle it."

Amelia watched him disappear down the corridor, brave and doomed. She followed a few cautious steps behind and peeked around the doorframe. The kitchen looked like a culinary battle-field. Pots steamed on every burner, cabbage leaves clung to the counter, and the oven door hung open while heat escaped into the room. "Hello again darling." Lady Edith said flatly, stirring something that hissed as if protesting. "How was your day?"

Arthur scanned the disaster before him, the bubbling pot, the smoke curling from the oven. "Mum, what on earth are you *doing?*"

"Cooking for my family," she replied with great dignity. "Although this blasted lamb just doesn't seem to cook fast enough."

Arthur crouched, closed the oven door, and said gently, "Because you keep opening it. You're letting the heat out."

Lady Edith paused, spoon midair, then nodded solemnly. "Ah. That does make sense."

From the doorway, Amelia surveyed the scene once more—the scorched smell, the cabbage water seeping onto the floor—and silently turned back down the hall. Her phone buzzed on the console table. Unknown number. She hesitated, then ignored it, setting the phone face down.

"Amelia!" Rosie's voice rang from upstairs.

Amelia looked up the staircase. "What?"

"Look at Eloise's Insta!" Rosie shouted, holding her own phone like it contained breaking news.

Amelia sighed, retrieved her phone, and glanced at the screen. A text from the unknown number flashed first: *It's me. Can we talk?* She frowned and typed back, *Wrong number,* before opening Instagram.

At the top of her feed was Eloise's post: a photograph of the finches from earlier, perched delicately on their swing. The caption read, *"A bird does not sing because it has an answer. It sings because it has a song."*—Chinese Proverb

Rosie leaned over the railing, grinning. "You're tagged. And look at your followers—they're going up by the second!"

Amelia stared, bemused. Indeed, the numbers ticked upward as if her screen had caught fire. Her career—or at least her name—was spreading. But before she could process it, another text appeared.

This time, the name was clear.

Helena. Let's talk.

Amelia's breath caught. Then she threw the phone down the hallway with startling force. The sound made both Rosie and Arthur jump. Rosie leaned over the banister. "Did you just *smash* your phone?"

Arthur, emerging from the kitchen, followed her gaze to the device lying on the floor. "Why on earth—" He bent to pick it up just as another message appeared, glowing on the cracked screen. Amelia snatched it from his hand and, without thinking, hurled it again—further this time, bouncing off the wainscoting.

Arthur blinked. "What is wrong with you?"

"I— I just... I need a minute," she stammered, cheeks flushed.

She scooped up the broken phone and darted into the small powder room at the end of the hall, locking the door behind her. Her heart thudded. She tried to swipe the cracked glass, but the message was frozen, fragmented across the screen. "Damn it," she whispered.

In the mirror, her reflection looked pale, frantic. She knew she'd have to tell Arthur eventually—about the texts, about Helena—but not tonight. Not with the house filled with smoke and cabbage. When she stepped back into the hall, the air hit her like a wall. The smell had grown stronger—a mix of burnt brassica and undercooked lamb—a culinary tragedy. Arthur was waiting for her, arms folded, studying her face with patient concern.

"It was..." she began, fumbling for a story, "Wendy. She wants to meet me at the pub. Alone."

Arthur tilted his head. "You're lying."

"I am *not*."

He stepped closer, blue eyes narrowing in gentle amusement. "I know you're lying."

Amelia froze, caught between guilt and absurdity. "You... do?"

He placed his hands lightly on her shoulders, leaning in until she could smell the faint trace of soap and smoke on his collar. "You're lying," he said softly, "because you're trying to escape my mother's cooking. And if you think for one second that you're leaving me behind, you're *dead* wrong."

Amelia pressed her lips together, trying not to laugh. "You're right. I can't keep secrets from you."

He kissed her forehead, pulling her into his arms. For a fleeting second, the warmth of it erased everything else—Helena, the texts, the noise. They had both told their share of half-truths, but somehow, they met in the middle, bound by affection and avoidance alike. "I'm coming with you," he said, and turned toward the kitchen. "Mum!" he called. "Amelia's meeting Wendy at the pub. I'll drive her."

Lady Edith emerged, wiping her hands on a towel. "Oh? Well, of course, dear. Rosie and I will just have a quiet dinner together."

Arthur kissed her cheek. "Try not to burn the house down."

Amelia had already retrieved her coat when Rosie appeared at the top of the stairs, arms crossed. "Wait—where are you two going without me?"

Arthur grinned. "Enjoy dinner, Rosie."

"What? That's not fair!" she protested as the front door closed behind them.

From the kitchen came Lady Edith's voice again, cheerful, and oblivious. "Rosie darling, could you help me find one of those thermometers for meat? What are they called again?"

"A meat thermometer," Rosie said flatly, resigning herself to fate.

"Ah yes! That's it. Fetch me one, please."

Rosie glanced toward the door where Arthur and Amelia had vanished into the evening, then sighed and disappeared into the kitchen, bracing herself for what awaited inside.

Outside, the last light was fading over the garden, the air carrying a chill and the faintest echo of laughter from the house. In the car, Amelia stared out the window, the cracked screen of her phone resting in her lap. Arthur said nothing for a long while.

Eventually, he reached over and took her hand. "Whatever it is," he said quietly, "we'll figure it out."

Amelia nodded, her reflection flickering faintly in the glass—tired, worried, and a little uncertain of what truth might come next.

But for the moment, she was grateful for the silence, for the warmth of his hand, and for the distance—however brief—from the smell of cabbage that still haunted the house behind them.

CHAPTER SIXTEEN

THE COUNTRYSIDE BLURRED BY IN STREAKS OF GREEN AND gold as Arthur steered the car away from the Park House. The low hum of the tires and the rhythmic flick of the turn signal filled the quiet between them. Amelia glanced sideways at him, watching the way his fingers brushed over the stubble on his chin—an old habit when he was nervous.

Something had changed in his energy. The warmth of their earlier laughter seemed to have cooled into a stillness that made her stomach twist. Her broken phone sat heavy in her purse, cracked screen and all, like evidence of something she couldn't yet confess.

Arthur broke the silence first. "So," he said slowly, "are you going to tell me why you destroyed your phone?"

She hesitated, tracing the edge of her coat sleeve. "I... I got some weird texts."

"Weird how?" His voice lowered a register, protective but edged with irritation.

Amelia swallowed hard. "I think... Helena tried to text me."

Arthur's hands tightened on the wheel. "What? How does she even have your number?"

"I have no idea," she said, genuinely baffled. "I swear."

He exhaled sharply, his jaw tightening. "And what? You weren't going to tell me?"

Amelia turned to look out the window. "Why did you turn right? The pub's left."

"We're not going to the pub." His voice was calm but clipped. "You weren't going to tell me that my ex is texting you?"

"Your *ex*," she repeated bitterly. "Now she's your *ex*. Two days ago, I didn't even know she existed, and now she's everywhere— your lectures, your phone, *mine* apparently. I don't know how she got my number, Arthur, or why!"

"Calm down." He reached for her hand, but she pulled it away.

"No, *you* calm down, mister!"

As soon as the word left her lips, Amelia wanted to laugh at herself. *Mister?* She had never said that in her life.

Arthur's lips twitched. "Mister?"

"Whatever. I'm mad at you."

"Mad at *me?*" He slowed the car and pulled off to the shoulder, putting it in park. "Mad at me? What did I do?"

"You kept this from me!" she said, pressing her hands to her face. "You let me walk around like an idiot, completely in the dark."

He took a deep breath, his voice quieter now. "Amelia, I can't apologize for this anymore."

"Well, it doesn't feel right," she murmured. "Everything feels... wrong lately."

Arthur studied her, his features softening. "I'd think getting engaged to the man you love isn't so wrong."

She lifted her eyes to him. "You proposed on the *bathroom floor*, Arthur. Even Kinsey would agree that isn't Austen-worthy."

"Austen-worthy?" He blinked, confused.

"It's something Kinsey and I agreed upon... just forget it," she muttered, turning toward the window again.

Arthur leaned back against the seat, hurt flickering briefly across his expression. "I proposed to you because I love you. But since you don't seem to think that counts…" He reached for her hand, gently tugging at her ring.

Amelia's breath caught. "What are you doing?"

"Give me the ring back," he said softly.

"What? No!" Her heart pounded painfully. "Arthur—"

"Amelia." His tone was gentle, almost tender. "Give it back."

Her throat tightened as she slipped the ring off her finger and placed it in his palm. The absence of it felt like a cold mark left behind. "So," she whispered, "you don't want to be engaged to me anymore?"

Arthur brushed a strand of hair from her face, his expression full of affection. "I love you more than anything in the world. I just realized the bathroom floor wasn't the place to profess it. Let me fix that."

Before she could speak, he leaned in and kissed her—slow, certain, steadying. When he pulled away, his forehead rested against hers. "No buts," he murmured. "If she tries to contact you again, I want to be the first to know. Do you understand me?"

Amelia nodded. "Yes."

"Good. Because there's absolutely no reason for her to contact you." He pressed another kiss to her temple before starting the car again.

As they rejoined the road, the tension seemed to dissolve between them. The fields rolled by, painted in the dimming light.

"Well," Amelia said after a moment, "when do I get my ring back?"

Arthur's lips curved. "Oh? You want it back already?"

"Yes, I do."

"Then you'll just have to wait until it's Austen-worthy," he teased.

She laughed despite herself. "That could take years."

He grinned. "Then we'll have a very long engagement."

Her stomach growled audibly, and they both burst into laughter. "In all seriousness," she said, "where are we going? I'm starving."

CHAPTER SEVENTEEN

DINNER WAS A BLUR OF WARMTH, CANDLELIGHT, AND TOO much wine. Amelia stared at her empty plate, feeling both full and exhausted. The restaurant had been quiet—white linen, soft jazz, the scent of rosemary and lamb. She couldn't help but laugh that after all the chaos, they'd ended up eating lamb anyway.

Arthur handed the waiter his card, smiling across the table at her. "Thank you for a lovely dinner," she said softly.

He nodded. "Of course. But what are we going to do about Mum?"

"You'll have to help her move her things out this week," she said, finishing her wine.

He groaned, pressing his hands over his face. "I do, don't I? What a mess."

"I still don't understand why your grandparents suddenly decided to move back to Oak Hall," Amelia said. "Your poor mother. That place was her home."

Arthur shrugged. "I haven't the faintest idea."

"One thing's for certain," Amelia added wryly, "your Gran does not like me."

Arthur looked up, amusement flickering in his eyes. "You mustn't let that bother you. She'll come around."

"I doubt it," Amelia said. "Women like your grandmother never come around. They wait for you to prove yourself worthy."

Arthur's reply was lost when Amelia noticed two women at a nearby table staring at him—younger, both leaning in, whispering behind their glasses of wine. Her stomach tightened. She wished her engagement ring was still on her finger. Arthur followed her gaze and caught one of them waving. "Ah," he said lightly, "one of them is my student. Marguerite, I think."

"They're *drooling* over you," Amelia said under her breath.

"Are they?" He raised an eyebrow. "Maybe I should trade you in."

"Arthur!" she said, half laughing, half scandalized.

He chuckled, stood, and offered his hand. "Come on. Let's go home."

As they walked past the table, Arthur leaned down and kissed Amelia's cheek in full view of the women. "Ladies," he said pleasantly, and they both flushed bright red. Amelia couldn't help smiling as they left.

When they returned to the Park House, the faint crackle of a gramophone echoed through the halls. Lady Edith and Rosie were curled up in the formal sitting room—Rosie sprawled across a velvet chair, her mother upright and elegant as always, glasses perched on her nose.

"How was the pub?" Lady Edith asked, setting her book aside.

"It was fine," Amelia lied smoothly. "How was dinner?"

Rosie glanced up from her book and made a dramatic gagging motion.

"Rosie," Lady Edith warned.

"I didn't *say* anything!"

Arthur smirked. "I'm sorry we missed it."

"It smells... smoky," Amelia said gently.

Rosie nodded. "Understatement."

"Rosie!" Edith warned.

"I didn't say anything!"

"Dinner was perfectly fine," Lady Edith said primly. "I'm simply getting used to your oven, Arthur."

Arthur bit back a laugh. "I'm going to shower. Are you coming, Amelia?"

"I'll be up in a minute."

He disappeared up the stairs, leaving Amelia with the women. She removed her shoes and sighed in relief as she propped her sore leg on a footstool. "What are you both reading?" she asked.

Rosie lifted her book without looking up. "*The Red Book.* Mum thinks it'll help me 'find myself.' It's actually quite good."

"I didn't know you were much of a reader," Amelia teased.

Rosie ignored her. "I am."

Amelia smiled faintly and turned to Lady Edith. "And you, Edith? What are you reading?"

Lady Edith held up an old, worn copy. "*The Garden of a Commuter's Wife.*" She paused, her gaze narrowing slightly. "Where's your engagement ring?"

Amelia froze, glancing down at her bare hand. "Oh. That's... a long story."

Both women exchanged a look over their books, then set them aside in perfect unison.

"Are you not engaged anymore?" Rosie demanded.

"No, no, we are."

"Then why aren't you wearing your ring?"

Amelia hesitated, caught between laughter and fatigue. "It's complicated."

Rosie gasped dramatically. "What did my stupid brother do now?"

"Do I need to have a word with my son?" Lady Edith asked, her tone all maternal authority.

Amelia raised both hands. "No, no, absolutely not. Everything's fine." She glanced at the grandfather clock and nearly laughed at her own desperation. "Goodness, look at the time! I'm off to bed."

"Trouble in paradise," Rosie murmured as Amelia retreated toward the stairs.

"Rosie," Lady Edith warned again, but there was no real conviction in it. Lady Edith closed her book and rubbed her eyes. "I'm going to bed as well, dear."

"Night, Mummy," Rosie said.

"Goodnight, darling."

The music played softly as Lady Edith left the room. Rosie sat back in her chair, flipping a page and muttering to herself. "Bathroom proposals. Burned cabbage. Missing rings. This family's a circus."

Upstairs, Amelia paused outside the bedroom door. She could hear Arthur humming softly in the shower, the sound of water steady and calm. For a moment she leaned against the wall, her bare hand pressed over her heart. Everything was fine, she told herself. Or it would be—once the ghosts stopped texting and the past finally learned to stay buried.

CHAPTER EIGHTEEN

THE SOFT TAPPING OF KEYS FILLED THE QUIET OF THE WHITE Rabbit Interior Design office. Amelia's coffee had long gone cold beside her, forgotten as she stared at the bright blueprints glowing on her computer screen. Her knee still ached, though she tried to ignore it, losing herself in lines, textures, and swatches. The hum of her focus was abruptly broken when the office door swung open.

Rosie burst in like a gust of perfume and noise, a white iPhone box in her hand. "That took *forever,* Amelia!" she groaned, tossing the box onto the desk before collapsing dramatically on the velvet couch, kicking off her pink Jimmy Choos.

Charlie raised his eyebrows over his laptop, phone still pressed to his ear. "No, I said *tomorrow at six,* not seven," he barked into it. "Yes, the list's been sent. You *saw* the list? Then why are we— never mind." He sighed, ending the call, and turned to Amelia with a weary look. "This is madness."

Amelia didn't look up. "It's going to be worth it, Charlie. This will be huge for us."

From the couch, Rosie groaned again and draped an arm over her eyes. "I'm taking my break."

"Rosie," Amelia said without looking away from her screen, "did you—?"

"Break," Rosie repeated, waving a hand lazily in the air.

Charlie smirked and leaned back in his chair, watching Amelia with a knowing glint that said, *You hired her.*

Amelia stood slowly, stretching the stiffness from her legs before crossing the room to the couch. "Hey, Rosie?"

"Yes?" Rosie answered without moving.

"We still have a lot to get through today. Maybe take *five* minutes, not fifty. And perhaps tomorrow, rethink the footwear." Amelia gestured to the bright pink heels lying like discarded candy wrappers on the floor.

"What's wrong with my Jimmy Choos?" Rosie asked, sitting up.

"Nothing," Amelia said patiently, "but when you're running errands and hopping between construction sites, you'll need something more practical. Maybe even—brace yourself—work boots."

Rosie gasped theatrically. "Work boots? Amelia, I'm not a miner."

"You're our assistant," Amelia said. "A very *stylish* one, granted, but still—our assistant."

Rosie crossed her arms. "I didn't want to hurt your feelings, since we're going to be family soon and all... but *you* could use some help with your style too."

Amelia blinked. "What about my style?"

Charlie was suddenly very busy packing up his things. "I'm going to grab lunch. My treat," he blurted, and bolted for the door. The bell above it jingled as if applauding his escape.

Amelia turned back to Rosie, hands on her hips. "Alright. Enlighten me."

Rosie stood, towering over her in effortless elegance. She wore fitted jeans, a silk blouse, and a blazer that probably cost as much as a month's rent. Even her messy ponytail looked intentional. "Amelia, you're gorgeous, but you hide it. You dress like you're trying *not* to be noticed. Burberry here and there, sure, but it's so... safe. So plain."

Amelia looked down at her soft floral dress, which she'd thought was sweet and professional. Rosie circled her like a hawk. "This dress, for example—if you added a belt here"—she reached around and tugged gently at Amelia's waist—"it would show off your figure. You have curves, you know. And your hair..."

"Not the hair," Amelia said sharply, her voice defensive before she could stop it.

Rosie paused, softening. "I know, I know. The cancer. We all know. But your hair's long and beautiful now. It could use a shape, maybe a bit of color—something golden, something alive. It's time, Amelia."

Amelia stared at her reflection in the small mirror across the office. Maybe Rosie wasn't wrong. Her hair was heavy, uneven. She looked... tired.

Still, she cleared her throat and returned to business. "We're getting off topic. We have a massive list today. I need you focused, not shopping."

Rosie smiled slyly. "Well, maybe I could *be* your stylist as part of my duties. Two birds, one stone."

Amelia hesitated. Rosie's eyes shone—really shone—and it was the first time she'd seen her so genuinely excited about anything since moving in. Against her better judgment, Amelia smiled. "Fine. I'll give you a small budget. If—and only if—we finish our work early, you can use what's left of the day for... styling."

Rosie squealed, throwing her arms around her. "You just wait! I'll transform you!"

The door opened. Amelia barely had time to turn before a familiar figure appeared—tall, poised, and unmistakably red-headed. Helena Darling.

Amelia froze. "What are you doing here?"

Helena's composure wavered for a split second, but she smoothed it over with a polite smile. "I'm sorry to intrude. I did try to text you."

Amelia's pulse spiked. Her new phone box sat unopened on her desk. Her old, cracked phone—still inside her purse—was silent. She could almost feel it buzzing phantom messages she couldn't bear to read.

Rosie stepped forward; arms crossed like a bodyguard. "Answer her."

Helena turned her attention to Rosie and offered a delicate nod. "Nice to see you too, Rosie. It's been a while."

Rosie didn't blink. "We have nothing to say to one another."

Helena's smile stayed fixed. "Listen, Amelia. I just wanted to apologize. I didn't mean to cause... any sort of mess between you and Arthur."

"What mess?" Amelia's voice sharpened. "There is no mess. I don't even know you."

Helena tilted her head, the corners of her mouth curling. "Well, when I told Arthur I was ready to get back together, I didn't realize he was already seeing someone."

Rosie's head whipped toward her. Amelia caught the glance—the look that said *she knew something.* "What are you talking about?" Amelia demanded. "What does she mean?"

Helena blinked innocently. "Oh. Arthur didn't tell you?"

"Tell me what?"

Helena sighed, as though she were the victim. "This is... embarrassing. I came to Arthur, explained that I'd made a mistake. I thought I'd fallen for someone else, but that man wasn't who I believed he was. Arthur has always been the steady one. The true one. I suppose I realized that too late. Surely you can understand a woman's heart changing."

Amelia's stomach dropped. Every word felt rehearsed—silky, venomous. She was searching for breath when the door burst open and Charlie walked in, holding a bag of sandwiches. "Lunch is here—oh, bloody hell."

Helena's eyes flicked to him. "Charlie."

Charlie froze. "Helena. What are you doing here?"

Amelia's gaze darted between them. "You know her?"

Charlie hesitated. "I worked for the Bonnevilles, remember? I knew everyone connected to the family."

Amelia's stomach twisted tighter. Before she could speak, Helena leaned forward. "I tried to text you to arrange coffee. A chance to talk privately."

Amelia's voice was ice. "You had no right to contact me. I never gave you my number. I don't know you, and I didn't even know you existed until this week. You've crossed a line."

Helena's eyes flickered to Amelia's bare hand. "I wanted to make peace, that's all. After all, Arthur and I work across the hall from each other now. But..." she gestured toward Amelia's unadorned finger, "perhaps things aren't as perfect as they seem."

Amelia's face flushed hot. "I don't have my ring on *right now* but let me be very clear—Arthur and I are engaged."

"Very well then." Helena smiled, slow and deliberate. "I'll be off. I have a class in an hour."

"Lose my number," Amelia said through clenched teeth.

Helena stopped in the doorway and turned, her gaze cool and predatory. "Is that a threat?"

Rosie stepped forward until she was shoulder to shoulder with Amelia. "Consider it whatever you like." Charlie crossed his arms behind them, silent but firm. The air between them thickened like storm clouds.

Helena's smile widened. "Listen, Amelia. Arthur and I share history. Deep roots. You're..." she gave a delicate shrug, "so American. There are things about his world you'll never quite understand."

Amelia's pulse hammered in her ears. She stood tall despite the pain in her knee. "Oh, I understand plenty," she said quietly. "And I see exactly what you're trying to do. So, consider *this* a warning—back off."

Helena laughed, soft and cruel. "I like you," she said, brushing past. Her oversized bag swung wide and caught Amelia sharply in the knee. Pain seared up her leg, and she gasped, clutching the desk for balance.

"Oh dear," Helena said sweetly. "You should probably have that looked at. Ta-ta."

The door clicked shut behind her.

Charlie dropped the sandwiches onto the counter and hurried to Amelia's side. "Are you alright?"

Amelia grimaced, straightening with effort. "I'm fine," she lied, though her knee throbbed fiercely. She grabbed her purse and the unopened iPhone box from the desk.

"Wait—where are you going?" Charlie asked.

"To find something I can turn into an aviary," she said, her tone clipped, controlled.

"Let me come," Rosie said quickly, reaching for her own bag.

"No." Amelia's voice left no room for argument. "I'll be back by four. You can drive me home then."

She strode to the door, every step a protest from her aching knee.

As the bell above the door jingled behind her, Charlie turned to Rosie, who stood with wide eyes and a box of untouched sandwiches.

"Well," Rosie whispered, "that was drama."

Charlie sank into his chair, running a hand through his hair. "You think that was bad? You've never seen Helena *angry*."

But Amelia wasn't there to hear it. She was already on the street, her reflection flashing in the glass of the shopfronts as she passed. Her hands trembled, but her expression was set.

Helena Darling had made her move. And Amelia Levingston wasn't about to let her win.

CHAPTER NINETEEN

MR. MCCLOUD'S BITS & BOBS ANNOUNCED AMELIA'S ARRIVAL with the small bell that hung over the door—a cheerful trill that always sounded like permission to breathe. The scent met her next: old paper and lemon oil, wool and dust, the faint whisper of lavender from a sachet retired to a high shelf. Time itself seemed to hang in the narrow aisles, portioned into neat decades on every wall.

"I'll be right with you," called Mr. McCloud from somewhere in the warren behind the counter.

Amelia closed the door against the street and stood for a moment, letting the hush of the shop settle around her heartbeat. Her knee—stitched, tender, and sullen about the damp air—protested as she shifted her weight. She didn't mind. Pain felt manageable here, softened by velvet and varnish and the polite ticking of a dozen clocks.

Mr. McCloud rounded a stack of hatboxes with his familiar jolly care, spectacles low on his nose and his smile already shaped. "Why, Miss Levingston," he said, as if she'd wandered in from a childhood, he'd kept safe for her on a high shelf. "Always happy to see you."

They had met properly the year The Park House had become hers. She had arrived timid and sunburned by grief, and he had placed the world back in her hands in the form of little things—brass doorknobs, a cut-crystal lamp, a stack of linen tea towels edged in blue. He had been the first person in Nottingham to call her dear without pity.

"Hello, Mr. McCloud." She moved toward him, limping more than she meant to.

"Oh, that's a limp," he fussed, kindness quick in his face. "What's happened?"

"Nothing dramatic," she said. "Small surgery. I'm fine."

"What can I help you find? Are you hunting treasure," he asked, "or simply hiding from the world?"

"A few things," Amelia admitted. "But mostly... the hiding."

"In that case, fancy a cuppa?" He lifted his brows like a magician about to produce a dove.

She sighed in genuine relief. "I would love one."

"Of course, you would. Anything for my favorite customer." He crossed to the door, flipped the paper sign to CLOSED with ceremony, and shot her a conspirator's grin. "Perfect time for a break, wouldn't you say?"

"Thank you," she said. "You're always so kind."

"Go on then—find yourself a throne," he said, scooping up his keys and disappearing through the muslin curtain toward the little back kitchen that managed to produce miracles.

Amelia drifted down the nearest aisle, fingers grazing carved chair-backs and a row of silver frames that reflected her in thin, wobbled slivers. She found a large velvet chair upholstered in a plum that had once been decadent and was now merely comfortable and sank into it.

The clocks spoke softly to one another—tick, tick, tick—each on its own small island of time. She closed her eyes and inhaled. She had always loved the smell of old books; to her they didn't smell like age but like concentration, like the air of a room where someone had once tried very hard to say something true.

When she opened her eyes again, a tall bookcase opposite drew her: a narrow ladder leaned against it as if someone had hurried down and left in a rush, promising to return. She rose and read spines the way other people scanned faces: **A Short History of the Tulip, Constance Spry's Garden, English Housewifery,** a thin volume about roses with a spray of gilt prickling down the spine. Mansfield Park peered down too—soft-leathered, the gold almost rubbed from the title. The sight thudded gently against her heart. Her mother had loved Austen; Kinsey had, too, though he liked to argue with Pride and Prejudice as if Elizabeth Bennet were seated across from him at breakfast.

The first-edition set he and Merry had left for her sat locked away now in a fireproof box, tucked into the study's darkest shelf, as if even air might be a thief. Sometimes she wondered whether those books were lonely. She toyed with the thought— of lending one to a small library or displaying them in a glass case where they might be adored. Then she pictured the day a careless hand tore a page and felt the thought snuff out like a candle.

The rose book slid easily from the shelf. Lady Edith, whose mornings lately were equal parts wilting and stubborn bloom, might like it. Amelia tucked it under her arm.

"Here we are," Mr. McCloud said, arriving with a tray. The cups were mismatched, the milk in a miniature pitcher shaped like a cow. He passed a cup to her and glanced at the book in her elbow. "Oh, excellent choice. Some things improve with pruning. Roses, tempers... households," he added dryly, then blushed at his own boldness.

Amelia smiled around her sip. The tea was strong enough to steady her. "Business been alright?" she asked.

"A touch slow this month," he admitted, lowering himself into a buttoned leather chair. "August holidays beginning earlier every year. People drive through on the way to elsewhere. Still. The faithful come." He winked at her.

"I'll take pictures and post them," she said. Habit had her patting her bag for her phone before she remembered. "Oh—right." She grimaced. "New phone. Still in the box."

"Never mind," he said, stirring. "We survived trade without the internet for a thousand years."

"It certainly helps, though," Amelia said, and he hummed agreement.

The shop breathed. Soft music unspooled from somewhere—something with a clarinet and a sunny melancholy—and the clocks, the clocks kept counting. Mr. McCloud asked, lightly, where she went when the present grew too loud; she confessed that lately she went nowhere at all.

"Bath," he said decisively.

"Bath the place," Amelia asked, "or take a bath?"

He waggled his spoon. "Both. But I mean the city. My wife's family keeps a house there—let out most of the year. When we wish it, we have it." The pleasure of the sentence lit his face. "Have you been?"

"Not yet." She realized, with a little embarrassment, that she'd stitched her life between Nottingham and London out of necessity and love and left the rest of England to postcards. "I've been remiss."

"What are you waiting for?" he asked gently. "The earth is not endless. One should see as much of it as one can manage. And the Roman baths rather put one in mind of empires and smallness at once, which is good for the soul."

She thought of Harry's hand slipping from life to sheet, of Betty's palm closing over his ring, of how quickly laughter arrived after a sob, the human heart incapable of any single weather for long. She thought of chemo—the sterile light, the beep-beep-beep—and how it had somehow led her to Kinsey's cane by the fireplace and his stained-glass rabbit with a bowler hat who looked like time itself interrupting. Life was unbearable and marvelous and always frighteningly present. She finished her tea. "I needed this," she said. "A shop full of sentences. And a perfect cup of tea."

"We all need to step sideways sometimes," Mr. McCloud said, and stood, patting his pockets for keys. "Now, what treasure did you promise yourself?"

"An armoire," Amelia said, lifting herself carefully. "A large one. I'm going to convert it into an aviary."

He stopped, then laughed so delightedly a china shepherdess nearly rattled. "An aviary?"

"For a client," she added. "Finches. She wants birds in her bath."

"As one does," he said, eyes twinkling. "Well then, let us fit your finches for a palace."

He led her through the aisles like a tour guide moving backward across history. He showed her three candidates: a Regency piece too narrow in the shoulders, a Victorian wardrobe whose mirrored doors had seen too many ghosts, and—oh.

The third was walnut, deep and calm. Two paneled doors rose like closed books; the cornice had a gentle broken-arch pediment that gave the impression of a small crown. The inside was empty but dignified, smelling of polish and old winters. It felt less like furniture than like a promise.

"That one," Amelia said at once, laying her palm against it. "It has a spine."

"Ha," Mr. McCloud said, pleased. "You hear them speak the way I do."

She imagined it transformed—solid ash perches inset like a lattice of air, brass-capped feeders tucked into the corners, a removable tray at the base, hidden casters so the whole could be wheeled closer to light. And at the back—a panel of stained glass in white and palest blue, a peacock's fanned tail turned to light so the morning would pour feathers across tile. She could already hear the small, precise music of the finches, the hush of a copper tub filling, a woman exhaling the day.

"We'll take this," she said.

"*We'll?*" Mr. McCloud teased.

"I mean I will," Amelia corrected, laughing. "And I'll need a large mirror to throw light back. Not too new. Something with a little foxing but not so much that Mrs. Eloise will think she looks ill."

He considered. "There's a French gilt piece in the back that flirts without trying," he said. "Come along."

The mirror he showed her was perfect—taller than she was, its frame a thicket of laurel leaves and tiny birds if you cared to notice them; the silvering had softened at the edges like dawn. "Yes," she said, and then she saw them: a vase of peacock feathers, not gaudy but midnight, and beneath them a few loose quills with eyes the green-blue of rumors. She gathered two.

"For the photos," she said. "And for the birds, a bit of camouflage. Makes them feel like there are always a few friends hiding."

"You speak bird," he observed.

"I try," she said. "They're clients with wings."

They were nearly back at the counter when something gleamed in the corner of her eye—ceramic blue peering between a stack of music boxes and a silver salver. She turned, and there he was: a tall blue vase painted with a white rabbit. The white of him was brilliant against the cobalt, and the look on his face—good heavens—the look said *There you are. I've been waiting.*

Amelia picked it up and felt the small, ridiculous happiness of recognition. Kinsey would have adored it. He would have made a speech. He would have set it somewhere mischievous and moved it when no one was watching.

"Mr. McCloud," she said, cradling the vase, "I'm taking this."

"I'll add it to your account, darling," he said without glancing at his ledger, as if the rabbit had chosen her and the shopkeeper's job was simply to say amen.

He wrote up the armoire and mirror and feathers with his careful pen and offered to have the larger pieces delivered in the morning. "Be kind to that knee," he added, eyeing the tension she tried to hide. "Stitches sulk if you make them do too much."

"Thank you again," Amelia promised.

"I always look forward to when you stop by," he said, shooing her gently. "now go before I sell you half the shop."

She left with the rose book under her arm, the rabbit vase wrapped in brown paper, and the day steadier beneath her feet. Outside, the light had gone honey-thick; traffic groaned and then gave up, letting the town breathe. She turned toward the office, rehearsing how she would tell Charlie about the armoire so he could calculate the reinforcement panel and how she would tell Rosie *no, we cannot put sequins on the aviary*, and how she would tell Arthur— a flicker of color caught her eye with movement at the end of the lane. Red hair catching a lick of sun. Helena, leaning against a lamppost as if she belonged to it. Watching her.

Amelia's body registered her before her mind had formed a sentence. Her stomach clenched. She tightened her grip on the rabbit's papered ears. Helena's mouth quirked—not quite a smile—and then she pushed herself from the post and slipped around the corner with the fluid, practiced ease of a woman who knew which eyes were on her and which to avoid.

The square resumed its ordinary clatter—the bus wheezing to a halt; a boy laughing too loudly at something in his headphones; a dog hauling its owner toward a butcher's window—but the world had shifted a half-inch to the left. Amelia stood still a long breath, listening to the after-silence that follows a slammed door.

This was going to be a problem.

She started walking again, faster now, and it was hurting her knee with every step. The rabbit thumped softly against her ribs. She did not look over her shoulder because she had taught herself, long ago, not to feed fear with attention. Instead, she named what could be managed: the armoire (handled), the mirror (handled), the feathers (handled), the stained glass (Marcus had said yes), the timeline (eight weeks and no slippage), the birds (Chelsea's number waiting), the delivery (morning), the knee (rest tonight), the heart (later, but yes, handled).

She reached the office and paused with her hand on the door, letting the bell's future chime steady her. Inside would be Rosie with a million opinions and perhaps a sensible one hidden among them, and Charlie pretending not to worry about finances the way a father pretends not to worry about his child touching the sea for the first time. Inside would be work, and work had always been the rope she could hold when other things tried to sweep her away. She pushed the door open. The bell rang its bright note into the room.

"Amelia?" Charlie called from the drafting table, relief already folding into his voice. "Tell me you found magic."

She held up the rose book, then the parcel with rabbit ears, and finally she said, "Better. I found a spine."

Rosie appeared from the back with a tape measure around her neck like a stole. "And I found you twenty-seven new followers since Eloise's post," she announced, then stopped, squinting at Amelia's face. "What happened?"

Amelia set the rabbit gently on the counter and smoothed the paper over his painted hat. She thought about telling them she had just seen Helena, then she changed her mind and said, "Good news, tomorrow morning," she said evenly. "Delivery. A walnut armoire, a French mirror, and a project that's going to land us in a magazine or kill us trying. Let's be brilliant."

Charlie exhaled, the ghost of a grin returning. "Brilliant I can do."

Rosie brightened. "And after we're brilliant," she said, tapping the tape measure against Amelia's shoulder, "we're getting you a belt."

Amelia laughed then, properly. The sound made the clocks in the shop seem to tick a little lighter. The white rabbit—ridiculous, dapper, inevitable—tilted his painted face toward the window as if quite pleased with the afternoon's arrangements.

Outside, the light thinned toward evening. Somewhere beyond the square a red head turned another corner and disappeared. Inside, the work assembled itself: sketches and schedules, purchases and prayers. And Amelia—limping, stubborn, absolutely present—set the rabbit on the shelf and set herself to the task of making beauty strong enough to hold the day.

131

CHAPTER TWENTY

THE EARLY MORNING LIGHT FILTERED THROUGH A VEIL OF damp mist, soft and gold, glancing across the glistening lawns of The Park House. After last night's storm, the estate looked like a watercolor left in the rain—muted, blurred, and heavy with silence. The gravel drive was waterlogged, the puddles deep and the stones slick beneath Amelia's boots. Each step gave a faint squelch as mud pressed up through the gaps, clinging to the soles.

She inhaled the cool air, earthy and sharp. It carried the scent of wet grass, clay, and woodsmoke—the signature perfume of Nottinghamshire after a storm. Despite the peaceful dawn, she couldn't shake the faint unease that had settled in her chest.

Behind her came the sound of a long, drawn-out yawn, followed by the soft click of the front door closing. "I heard someone outside last night," Rosie announced, her voice groggy but alert.

When Amelia turned, she nearly laughed. Rosie, as usual, looked utterly unbothered by the mud or the chill, dressed as though she were heading to a fashion editorial rather than trudging through muck. Her ensemble was a symphony of coordinated cream and blush—silk blouse, tailored jacket, flowing skirt—and the pièce de résistance: bright pink rubber boots that gleamed like patent leather jewels in the morning light.

"I'm serious," Rosie added, rubbing her arms. "I heard someone on the gravel drive."

Amelia froze for a moment. "Yes," she said slowly, "I heard it too. A car. Around three, I think."

Rosie's eyes widened. "Then I wasn't imagining it. Who on earth would be out here at that hour?"

"I haven't the faintest idea," Amelia replied, though her mind was already forming one: Helena.

Before she could say more, the door swung open again and Arthur emerged, adjusting his coat and squinting against the rising sun. "What are you two talking about?" he asked.

"We both thought we heard someone outside last night," Rosie answered, folding her arms like a prosecutor about to deliver her evidence.

Arthur's head snapped up. "What? Why didn't you wake me?"

Amelia's guilt prickled. "I didn't want to panic you," she said. "I thought maybe it was nothing. I was in the study and heard what sounded like a car on the drive—just once, then silence."

Rosie nodded. "I swear I saw lights through my window too."

Arthur's jaw tightened. He scanned the tree line, his gaze darting across the mist as though expecting movement. The storm had left everything washed and quiet, yet that quiet felt loaded, expectant.

Finally, he turned back to them. "Let's just get to the car," Amelia said, breaking the uneasy pause. "We'll be late meeting Eloise."

Arthur hesitated another beat before nodding. "Alright. I'll grab the keys." He disappeared back inside, leaving them standing in the wet morning air.

"Rosie," Amelia said quietly, "be honest with me. Is Helena dangerous?"

Rosie pursed her lips, thinking. "I always thought she was perfectly normal—charming, even. However, I don't know anymore."

Amelia hugged her arms around herself. "I can't imagine her actually hurting anyone, but still—someone was here, Rosie."

"Maybe it was just a wrong turn."

"Down a private, gated drive?"

"Well, the gate's been unlocked for ages."

"Perhaps," Amelia said softly, "it's time we changed that."

Rosie sat in the backseat, tapping furiously at her phone as Arthur steered them through the slick countryside roads. The rain had ended, but the clouds still hung low, bruised and heavy, threatening to spill again.

Arthur's grip on the steering wheel was too tight, his knuckles pale. Amelia could feel the tension vibrating through the car, subtle but relentless.

"Are you alright?" she asked.

"No," he admitted curtly. "Not really."

"Maybe it was just someone lost," she offered. "Took a wrong turn, realized it was private, and turned around."

Arthur gave a dry laugh that held no humor. "Oh, yes, Amelia. Someone accidentally drove a mile down a clearly marked private road at three in the morning just for fun."

Rosie lowered her phone, her brows furrowing. "Then who was it?"

Arthur didn't answer right away. His gaze flicked to the rearview mirror, scanning the road behind them. "I don't know. But I'm having cameras installed around the house."

Amelia blinked. "Cameras?"

"It's time," Arthur said. "And we'll change the locks while we're at it."

"No," Amelia protested. "Not the lock on the front door."

Arthur frowned. "Amelia—"

"That skeleton key is part of the house. It's magic. You can't replace it with something digital and soulless."

"This isn't about aesthetics. You've been posting photos of your projects, your home—your face—all over the internet. There are people out there who aren't your friends."

His words hit her harder than she expected. "What's that supposed to mean?"

Arthur glanced at her. "It means you have an audience. And not everyone watching is harmless."

"Oh, that's rich," she said sharply. "You're the one teaching half the female population of Nottingham University. You're a young, charming, eligible marquess—if anyone should be worried about stalkers, it's you."

He smirked faintly. "I'm not eligible."

"Well, they don't know that," she fired back.

He turned toward her, amused despite himself. "Who doesn't?"

"Your admirers," she said, gesturing vaguely. "Your students, that overly friendly receptionist at the clinic—don't tell me you haven't noticed."

"You can't be serious," Arthur said.

Rosie groaned. "Enough, both of you. Honestly, it's like watching an old married couple bicker about the weather."

Amelia's cheeks flushed. "We are engaged," she reminded her.

"Which makes it worse," Rosie replied dryly. "But—" she straightened in her seat, her tone shifting to something surprisingly authoritative—"you both have a point. Amelia, you're known now, not just here but abroad. You've been featured online, your work is public, your life is becoming public. And Arthur, you've got a title and a family history that journalists salivate over. You're both walking invitations for curiosity."

Arthur's eyes met Amelia's in the mirror. "So, what do you suggest?"

"Make it official," Rosie said simply. "An engagement announcement. Print it in the Nottingham Post, the Chronicle—hell, even Town & Country if you want. That way everyone knows you're spoken for. Including your little red-haired problem."

Amelia's mouth opened, but no words came. Her gaze drifted

down to her hand—bare, ringless, the skin pale where the band had once rested. She hadn't realized how naked it felt without it.

Arthur noticed. "I really don't think that's necessary," he said.

Rosie rolled her eyes. "Arthur, you're such a man of the last century. You don't seem to understand that this is what people expect. Appearances matter, especially now that you're marrying into—well—someone who isn't part of our... world."

Amelia gave a half laugh. "It's 2025, Rosie. We don't need to announce our engagement in the paper like it's 1813."

Rosie met her eyes in the rearview mirror. "Oh, but we do. Because while you might think you're living in a modern world, the society you're marrying into hasn't evolved as much as you think. Titles still matter. Appearances still matter. And the press—especially the glossy society kind—eats this stuff up."

Arthur sighed. "Rosie—"

"I'm serious," she interrupted. "You need to control the narrative before someone else does. Especially after what happened yesterday."

Amelia turned to her, uneasy. "What do you mean—what happened yesterday?"

Rosie looked between them. "You didn't tell him?"

"Tell me what?" Arthur asked sharply.

Rosie crossed one long leg over the other, perfectly composed. "There was a photographer outside the office yesterday. I thought at first, he was taking pictures of me, but it was Amelia he was watching."

"What Rosie? You didn't say anything about that to me?"

Arthur's grip tightened on the wheel. "What kind of photographer?"

"The kind who hides behind sunglasses and pretends he's texting," Rosie said. "Paparazzi, I think. Or maybe a tabloid freelancer."

"I didn't even know there was someone taking photos?" Amelia worried.

"I'm used to spotting them." Rosie said casually.

"Why would anyone—" Arthur began, but Amelia interrupted softly, "Maybe it's connected to Eloise. Or Teddy. They're well-known. Maybe he was just there for them."

"Or maybe not," Rosie said. "You've been tagged by Eloise on social media now, haven't you? That means you're in her orbit. You're news."

Arthur exhaled, long and slow. "Wonderful. So now we have a stalker, a paparazzo, and a mad ex-fiancée all circling our home."

Arthur's attention shifted between them, suspicion growing, but Amelia quickly diverted. "Look, let's just get through today. We'll deal with everything else later."

The car fell silent except for the hum of the tires on wet pavement and the faint tapping of Rosie's nails against her phone screen. Outside, the countryside blurred into gray-green streaks. The mist thickened as they neared town, swallowing the horizon, and for a fleeting moment, Amelia saw her own reflection in the car window—pale, tired, but determined.

Rosie was right about one thing. Appearances mattered. And if Helena Darling thought she could rattle her into running, she was sorely mistaken.

CHAPTER TWENTY-ONE

T HE DRIVE NORTH UNFURLED LIKE A RIBBON THROUGH WET pasture and hedged lanes, the morning light sharpening from pewter to silver as the clouds lifted. When the car turned past the stone piers and along the beech-lined approach, Amelia felt the usual quickening that Eloise's estate produced in her—a designer's alertness, like a tuning fork struck. Here, the Georgian proportions soothed the eye: a clean, symmetrical façade; honeyed brick banded by pale limestone; a portico set with fanlight and slim columns. Rock-star money had a way of arriving with flash; this place, at least externally, had been left to speak in the measured vowel sounds of its own era.

They parked beside a white van and a skip that had reached comic abundance—offcuts, shattered tile, the husk of an extractor hood, a carcass of cabinetry jutting like ribs. Charlie stood near it, sleeves pushed up, hair in untidy waves, conferring with a man in paint-spattered work trousers. He looked older than he had last week, and not only because of grief.

"Hey." He lifted a hand when he saw them.

Amelia shut her door and scanned the skip. "When is someone switching that out? It's beyond the point of charming."

"Thursday," Charlie said. "Earliest they can manage."

Arthur waved over Amelia, "Do you mind if I wait in the car. I have some phone calls to catch up on."

"Okay. This might take an hour or so."

"Perfect," she nodded. "Rosie walk with me, Charlie catch me up."

"I'm so excited to see her home! This is so great." Rosie giggled with glee.

"Focus Rosie." Amelia nodded. She tipped her head toward the house. "Is everything in the kitchen cleared? DeVol arrives this weekend for their delivery."

"This is Ned," Charlie said, nodding to the man beside him. "Plumber."

Amelia shook his hand. "Good to meet you. What happened to Bernie?"

Ned winced with gentle diplomacy. "Bit overcommitted, miss. I'm happy to step in."

"We're grateful." She smiled. "Welcome to the circus."

"I need to pop into town for a few parts," Ned added. "Back by eleven. Anyone need anything?"

Before Amelia could answer, a battle-cry whoop tore from the doorway. Two small boys—identical, all elbows and knees and shining hair—came hurling out and cannoned down the steps like greased marbles.

"Boys!" a voice called. "Don't scream." Eloise emerged with the nanny—a woman in crepe-soled shoes and battlefield calm. The designer wore a cardigan like armor and a mouth painted a flattering, ferocious red. Even harried, she was precise. Her gaze flicked to the skip, and her lips flattened.

"Amelia. Mon dieu. Have you seen this?" She pointed as if to a crime scene.

"They'll switch it Thursday," Amelia said, keeping her voice even. "We're on schedule."

"Tick-tock." Eloise tapped her watch.

Rosie, crouched as if greeting a pair of untamed foals, smiled at the twins. "Hello. I'm Rosie."

"You're pretty," one announced, exactly as if delivering the results of a study.

"Well, thank you." Rosie ducked her head with theatrical modesty. "Close my eyes; you hide. One... two..."

The boys scattered like swallows, the nanny half-laughing, half-groaning as she gave chase. Eloise's expression—irritation shaded with tenderness—softened fractionally. Interesting, Amelia thought; Rosie was, unexpectedly, very good with children.

"Shall we?" Amelia asked.

"Follow," Eloise said, and led the way inside.

The hall smelled faintly of beeswax and turpentine. Amelia had spent six months in and out of these rooms, coaxing the house toward a version of itself that felt both truer and more modern. There was the runner she had argued for—hand-knotted, low pile, just enough pattern to grin against the formal staircase. There is the console she had wrestled from a dealer in Newark, now miraculously proportionate under a new-gilded mirror. She always felt a flicker of gratitude at this stage of a project: a half-finished thing already showing its bones, the promise of it visible to those who knew where to look.

"How are we doing today?" Amelia asked as they passed into the back hall.

"Tired," Eloise said flatly. "I adore my sons; but sometimes I want to ship them to Switzerland. I told Teddy last night I would accept boarding school as an anniversary present."

"Where is he?"

"London. Recording for a week." The 'week' had the fatalism of sentence length. "Back next Wednesday."

They stepped into the kitchen. The room was a gut—clean, efficient ruin. Subfloor exposed. Wiring tidied into new runs. A painter on scaffolding drew a roller through a rectangle of deep, naval blue.

"First reaction," Eloise said, hands on hips. "This blue—is it too... police?"

"It will warm," Amelia said. "Remember the basalt mural

going in that corner is bronze-heavy. Once the copper pendants and hardware are in, the reflection will make the blue read a like shadow, not like a bruise. It's civilized, trust me."

Rosie entered behind them, cheeks bright from playing, hair a little windblown. "Your boys are sweet."

Eloise's eyes flicked from Rosie's face to the jacket she wore—charcoal with a razor-sharp shoulder, nipped at the waist. She reached, proprietary and unembarrassed, to pinch the fabric. "This is good. You styled the look?"

"I did," Rosie said, flushing with real delight.

"Could you go grab my notebook, Rosie?" Amelia asked. "I left it in the car."

"Of course." Rosie went, a flick of perfume in her wake.

Eloise watched her go, then tilted her head at Amelia. "What do we think of her?"

"Rosie?" Amelia bought herself a second. "She's Arthur's sister."

Eloise's gaze dropped, swift as a hawk's, to Amelia's bare left hand. She took it, turned it in her palm, and raised a brow. "Boyfriend? I thought fiancé. What happened?"

Amelia slid her hand free. "Nothing happened. Not really. I just... prefer not to wear jewelry on-site. It gets filthy."

"You're lying." Eloise said it gently, almost amused. "It's one of my gifts."

"A renegotiation of the proposal," Amelia said, aiming for light. "He wants to do it properly. Not on a bathroom floor."

Eloise's mouth curved. "C'est très étrange."

"What?"

"Very strange," Rosie supplied from the doorway, holding out the notebook. Her eyes darted between them as if she'd stumbled into a scene at intermission.

"How did he propose?" Eloise asked, eyes still on Amelia.

Rosie, torn between loyalty and the social theater of it, said—softly, betraying affection, not her brother—"On the bathroom floor."

Eloise's expression sharpened; she loved eccentricity in clothing but not, it seemed, in ritual. "Hmmm."

"Upstairs?" Amelia asked, both to redirect and because time pressed. "The bathroom's been stripped. I'll walk you through the window cut."

Eloise allowed herself to be steered. They crossed the hall where the new portrait of Johnny Cash watched from his gilded frame—Amelia's quiet coup, a sly nod to Teddy, a bit of American myth swaggering through English formality. The twins' voices—counting, squealing—rose and fell somewhere in the garden.

The master suite gaped like a theater set mid-change. Stud walls exposed. The old tub gone; its ghost traced in discolored tile. Morning light pooled through the existing casement; the tape outline Amelia had marked for the new opening climbed several feet beyond it—grand, yes, and right.

"The plumber finishes setting supply today," Amelia said, checking that Ned's plan matched reality. "Tomorrow the glazier removes the casement and cuts out to the header. We'll board it temporarily until Marcus delivers the panel."

Eloise folded her arms. "I detest surprises."

"Then you'll especially like this one," Amelia said, and felt the quick pinch of nerves. She could see the white peacock in her mind with an almost physical clarity; she could feel how the afternoon sun would ignite the tail, how morning would cool the glass to a milk-glow. The room would hold a living thing in its corner—the finches flickering in their tall antique aviary—sound softened by water and stone. There were commissions you did because they paid for lightbulbs, and commissions that stitched themselves into your name. This, she thought, would sew itself tight.

Rosie hovered behind Eloise. "Amelia has a way of doing what you didn't know you wanted," she said earnestly. "And then you wonder how you could have wanted anything else."

"Flatterer," Amelia said, but the comment steadied her.

"I'm measuring that corner for the aviary," she added, moving to the opposite wall. "I'll be out of your hair in five."

Eloise gestured to the hall. "Rosie, I want to show you something. You come with me."

Rosie glanced at Amelia, who nodded. "Go on. I'll catch you up."

They went, voices lowering as they disappeared down the stair. Left alone with her tape measure and her ghosts, Amelia ran numbers, sketched an outline, and wrote in her notebook: CHELSEA—armoire dimensions; sound baffling behind; tray for seed; hidden sweep-out drawer; perch hierarchy; safe plants. She tucked a loose curl behind her ear and stood very still, listening to the house breathe. Beyond the wall, a painter's radio murmured a song from her Los Angeles years; she felt, stung and unexpectedly tender, how far that life had drifted.

She set the notebook under her arm and followed after them.

The path to the garden building sloped between trimmed box and a drift of lavender that, even out of season, smelled faintly of summer and bees. The 'garage'—a polite word for something near the size of a small chapel—was dressed in ivy and fitted with a keypad. Eloise tapped the code, the door yawned, and the space hummed to light.

It made Amelia happy, privately, every time she came in here. The studio was the first room of the project she had completed; it had been her test case with Eloise, a way to prove—quickly, containedly—that she understood the client and the house. Now it lived: four industrial tables for machines, a wall tiled in rainbow spools, cutting islands, mannequins in various stages of undress. Racks of muslins and toiles; on the far wall, pinned sketches like a flight of birds.

"Bienvenue," Eloise said, the word softened by pride. She moved toward a drafting table where a spread of drawings lay. Rosie, thrown into delight like a child at the gates of a fairground, circled slowly, reaching—then checking herself—then reaching again.

"I love these," she breathed, fingers hovering above a pencil rendering of a coat: austere line, supple waist, a surprise of embroidery like frost along the hem.

"This was my reset," Eloise said. "When I sold the brand, I promised myself I would build a room where I could hear my own thoughts again. Amelia gave me exactly that. Look—she hid outlets inside the worktables; she put my iron on a swing-arm so I stop scalding my thigh. Genius."

Rosie laughed, a ripple of sound, and then Eloise, as if she'd reached the point without meaning to, said, "I can tell you like fashion?"

"I love it," Rosie said simply. "I've followed you for years. I still have two pieces from your Paris show—the draped dress in pewter and the cropped jacket with the satin collar."

"You were very young," Eloise said, amused.

"My grandmother... was very indulgent," Rosie said, matching amusement with her own dry truth.

"I sold the company when I had the boys." Eloise tapped a pencil against the edge of the table. "I was tired of being a CEO. But they're in school now, and I'm bored. I've been sketching. Quietly. Thinking about shape as defense and softness as rebellion. I'm launching again next year."

Rosie's eyes widened. "You are?"

"Would you like to see the line sheets?" Eloise asked as if offering tea.

"Yes," Rosie said, breathless, then steadied herself and added, "Please."

Eloise spread the papers—silhouettes labeled with a code only designers understood—while Rosie leaned in, ignoring the impulse to squeal. Eloise watched her watching, thoughtful. "You have poise, you have how you say... em... presence." Eloise said after a moment. "Taste. Children like you; you have an easy way with them. You carry clothes beautifully, and you already have a following. Representation matters. Would you consider working with me?"

Rosie's jaw dropped. For a heartbeat she was all Bonneville—bred-to-the-ballroom composure—then the girl under it burst through. "Are you serious?"

"I am always serious," Eloise said. "You would start here. Learn the rhythms. Eventually—if we fit—you'd travel. Shows. Press. Fittings. We'd build a role around what you do best."

"I was thinking of going back to uni," Rosie said, dazed, "for business."

"Then learn business from a business," Eloise said. "Ask Amelia—I am a benevolent tyrant. I teach by setting deadlines and handing you the table saw."

"I—" Rosie said, then laughed helplessly. "I'd be honored. I mean— I ought to ask my..." She caught herself. "I'll think about it. Quickly."

A scuff sounded at the door. "How's it going in here?" Amelia asked, stepping inside.

She paused, as she always did, to look. The studio pleased her; more than that, it stilled her. She saw the additional pegboard now crowded with tools, the pattern weights exactly where she'd imagined they would land, the tilt of the task lights, and felt the sweet click inside her—design doing what it was meant to do: ease a life.

Eloise turned, eyes bright in that particular way that meant she'd made a decision and was prepared to defend it before she was asked. "I've just offered Rosie a job," she said, and smiled.

CHAPTER TWENTY-TWO

T HE PARK HOUSE SMELLED LIKE BURNT TOAST AND DESPAIR. Steam hissed from a pot somewhere in the kitchen, and the faint sound of a wooden spoon scraping the bottom of a pan came through the open doorway. At the dining table, Amelia sat beside Arthur and Rosie, staring at the meal before them with a kind of cautious reverence.

Amelia stared down at a soup the color of beige wallpaper, a heap of limp carrots drowned in sticky honey glaze, mashed potatoes with the texture of pudding, and a slab of meat that might once have been corned beef—or at least a distant cousin.

Lady Edith swept into the dining room at last, dressed immaculately in a pale silk blouse and pearls, her hair perfectly set as if she were preparing to host an ambassador rather than serve a home-cooked disaster. She placed a silver dish piled high with toast—scorched and crackling—on the table with a very proud look on her face.

"Shall we pray?" she asked, folding her hands with grace.

They all bowed their heads. Amelia silently prayed that she wouldn't die of food poisoning. When Lady Edith finished, Rosie opened her eyes and smiled too brightly. "Looks wonderful, Mummy."

"Yes, thank you for cooking again," Amelia added diplomatically.

Lady Edith beamed. "You're very welcome. Arthur, dear—pour the wine, would you?"

Arthur reached for the bottle and did as told, filling everyone's glass a little higher than usual. Amelia took one grateful sip—rich, dry, and mercifully safe—and then reached for the mashed potatoes. The watery mixture slid from the spoon with a disheartening plop.

"Rosie has some exciting news to share," Amelia said, eager to shift the attention elsewhere.

"Oh, do you, darling?" Lady Edith's eyes gleamed with curiosity.

"Well, sort of. I haven't decided yet." Rosie turned red as the carrots.

"Oh, you must!" Amelia nudged.

Arthur smirked. "Don't hold us in suspense."

Rosie squared her shoulders. "Fine. Eloise Kitt offered me a job today."

Arthur nearly dropped his wine glass. "That's incredible Rosie?"

"Who is Eloise?" Lady Edith asked, slicing a burnt carrot with delicate determination.

Amelia leaned forward, suddenly energized. "She's one of my clients—an international fashion designer. Rosie helped me on the project and impressed her so much that Eloise offered her a position."

"How marvelous," Lady Edith said. "Though I thought you were going back to university."

"I was. But... what's the point?" Rosie twirled her fork dramatically. "Why study business when I can learn directly from someone who built an empire?"

Arthur, already chewing, froze mid-bite. A strangled sound escaped him. He coughed violently into his napkin. "Good Lord, Mother!" He drained his glass of wine in a single gulp.

Lady Edith's expression flickered from pride to alarm. "What is it?"

Arthur looked at the meat in horror. "What *did* you put in this?"

"Oh, it can't be that bad," Lady Edith said defensively. "Let's all try it together."

She took a forkful. The others reluctantly followed suit. On the count of three, they all took a bite—then immediately spat it into their napkins in unison.

"It's vile!" Rosie gasped, reaching for her wine.

Amelia chased the taste down with another swallow and muttered, "We need more wine."

Lady Edith set down her fork, utterly defeated. "That's it. We need a cook. I cannot go on like this."

There was a moment of silence—then Rosie giggled. Amelia tried to hide her laugh but failed. Arthur joined in, his deep chuckle echoing through the room until even Lady Edith surrendered, laughing so hard she dabbed tears from her eyes.

"Why don't we all go out?" Arthur suggested.

"I'll get the car!" Rosie jumped up.

"Shouldn't we clean up first?" Lady Edith asked, ever the hostess.

Arthur offered his arm. "We'll clean up later. Tonight, we celebrate your retirement from the kitchen."

Lady Edith smiled and took his hand. "Very well. But I'm choosing the restaurant."

They returned hours later, warm from laughter and wine, the night air cool and sweet after the noise of the city. The drive through the dark countryside was peaceful at first—until it wasn't.

As Arthur turned down the long gravel road to The Park House, the headlights cut across the front lawn—and something glistened red against the stone steps.

Amelia's stomach tightened. "Arthur... slow down."

He did. The car rolled forward, and the shape came into focus. A deer—its legs twisted, its body limp—lay sprawled before the front door. Its flank was matted with blood.

Rosie gasped. "Oh my God."

Arthur's hand shot out, stopping Amelia from unbuckling her seat belt. "Stay here."

He parked, opened the door, and stepped into the night. The air smelled of wet leaves and iron. His shoes crunched on the gravel as he approached the house, the headlights throwing long shadows across the drive.

Amelia watched him move closer to the deer. Her pulse quickened. There was something unnatural about the stillness, the deliberate way the animal had been left.

Arthur crouched beside it, studying the wound. A single bullet hole. Then he saw it—the blood-smeared trail leading up the front steps, ending at a sheet of paper pinned to the door. A note.

He stood there for a moment, reading. Then, without touching it, he backed away and returned to the car. His expression was pale, rigid.

"What is it?" Amelia asked, her voice unsteady.

Arthur reached into his pocket and pulled out his phone. "I'm calling the police."

Edith leaned forward. "What was that on the door?"

He didn't answer. His voice stayed low and deliberate as he spoke into the phone. "Yes, I'd like to report a trespassing incident. Possibly still active. We've just come home to find a recently killed deer at the entrance to our property. Yes... it appears to have been shot. There's also a threatening note attached to our front door."

Rosie's face went white. "What did it say?"

Arthur ignored her, giving their address to the dispatcher. Amelia could hear the faint voice on the other end—calm, procedural, distant. The words *stay inside the vehicle* floated through the static.

Arthur hung up. "They'll be here soon. No one gets out until the police arrive."

Rosie gripped her seat belt. "Arthur, what did it say?"

He hesitated, his knuckles whitening around the phone.

Amelia's voice broke the silence. "Arthur, please."

He exhaled slowly. "It said... *Stay away from Helena.*"

For a long moment, none of them spoke. The rain began to fall again—soft at first, then heavier, pelting the car roof in a steady rhythm.

Amelia felt the world tilt slightly. The inside of the car suddenly seemed smaller, the air tighter. She stared out through the fogging glass, watching the headlights blur against the rain.

Rosie whispered, "Oh my God. This is... this is mad."

Arthur rested his head against the steering wheel, jaw clenched. The muscles in his neck flexed as he tried to steady his breathing. "This ends now."

Amelia's mind raced. Helena—again. The name had begun to haunt the corners of her life like a ghost she couldn't exorcise. From the texts to the office, to now this. It felt deliberate. A message meant to pierce her peace.

Outside, the wipers groaned across the windshield. In the glare of the headlights, the deer looked like some kind of offering—its eyes dull, the once-white fur of its chest stained dark.

The police arrived within minutes, blue lights cutting through the trees. Two officers stepped out, their boots sinking into the wet gravel as they approached. Arthur got out first to meet them, speaking in quiet urgency.

Amelia, Edith, and Rosie stayed inside, watching through the rain. The older officer examined the deer, then the note, shaking his head grimly. The younger one took photographs.

Amelia could read their body language—the mix of disbelief and caution. This wasn't a random act.

When Arthur returned, his clothes were damp, his expression

harder than before. "They're taking the note for prints. They'll leave a unit outside tonight."

"Do they know who might've done this?" Rosie asked.

Arthur's jaw tightened. "Not yet."

Amelia wanted to ask what he hadn't said—*Do you think it was her?*—but the words caught in her throat.

Instead, she placed her hand gently on his arm. "Let's go inside."

He nodded. Together, they stepped out into the rain, the smell of wet earth thick around them. Rosie hesitated at the car, glancing at the deer before following behind.

Inside, The Park House felt colder than usual. The marble floor gleamed under the dim light. Amelia closed the door and locked it herself, her hands trembling.

Arthur lingered near the window, watching as the police car's lights flashed through the fog before fading down the drive.

Rosie wrapped her arms around herself. "Do you think this was meant for you... or for Amelia?"

Arthur didn't answer right away. "It doesn't matter who it was meant for. It's a threat to this house—and to all of us."

Amelia looked toward the front door, where faint muddy footprints now trailed across the tile. She felt the weight of the note in her mind, the crimson letters burned behind her eyelids.

Stay away from Helena.

It echoed like a curse.

CHAPTER TWENTY-THREE

THE SILENCE IN THE LIBRARY FELT ALIVE, PULSING WITH THE faint crackle of the fire and the occasional tick of the grandfather clock. It was nearly midnight, and exhaustion hung heavy over the room.

Lady Edith, Rosie, and Amelia sat together on the velvet sofa, their faces drawn and pale from the long, harrowing night. Every sound outside—every creak in the house—made them glance at the window. The police cars had only just driven off, their fading lights leaving behind a suffocating stillness.

The click of the front door startled them all. Rosie flinched, and Amelia's hand instinctively reached for the arm of the couch. Then Arthur appeared in the doorway.

Amelia exhaled, standing quickly. "Oh, thank God."

Arthur raised a hand, trying to settle them. "Please, everyone sit."

He crossed the room with steady but heavy steps and poured himself a glass of whiskey from the decanter on the sideboard. The amber liquid caught the firelight, glinting in the stillness before he sat opposite them. His expression was grim—controlled, but only just.

Rosie leaned forward anxiously. "What did they say?"

Arthur took a long sip before answering. "They didn't quite know what to make of it. They searched the grounds, checked the perimeter, looked for tracks. Nothing. Whoever it was, they were long gone."

Lady Edith's voice cut clean through the room. "Aside from a murdered deer and a note warning you to stay away from your ex."

Arthur froze, then sighed. "Aside from that, yes, Mother." He finished his glass and set it down hard enough that it echoed.

A long pause followed. The shadows danced against the book-shelves. Amelia twisted her hands together, unable to look away from him. "What do we do now?"

"I'm calling a security company tomorrow morning," Arthur said firmly. "We'll have cameras installed by the end of the week. I should have done it long ago."

He glanced toward the dark windows. "And we'll start locking the front gate again."

A collective groan filled the air. Rosie slumped back. "Arthur, that gate weighs as much as a small elephant."

"I know," he admitted. "But it's the only way to keep cars from driving in."

Amelia straightened, thinking aloud. "Maybe we can add an electric latch—something remote-controlled. You'd still have the old gate for show, but we could modernize it."

Arthur gave her a tired smile. "Yes. Bring us into the twenty-first century, Amelia. Please."

Rosie lifted her glass in mock salute. "To progress—and to not being murdered in our sleep."

Lady Edith didn't smile. She sat perfectly upright in her chair, her expression unreadable. "And what about Helena?"

The name settled into the air like a chill draft. Amelia's heart clenched. She hadn't wanted to hear it again—not tonight. Arthur stared into his empty glass for a long moment. "I'll speak to her first thing tomorrow."

Amelia's head snapped toward him. "What good will that do?"

"Because," he said evenly, "whoever did this knows her name. If this was meant as a warning, she could be in danger too."

"...Or you," Lady Edith said sharply. "You've been careless, Arthur. Too visible. If this person knows where you live, they might know where she works. What if it's a student? Someone watching you from campus?"

Arthur shook his head. "Unlikely."

"Or another teacher," she pressed.

"Mother, please," he muttered, rubbing his temples. "I doubt anyone at the university is shooting deer and leaving bloody notes."

Lady Edith crossed her arms. "And you're certain it's not Helena herself?"

The room went still.

Arthur's jaw tightened, but he didn't rise to it. "No. I'm not certain. But I need to be sure."

Amelia's voice was low, fragile. "You said whoever did this could be dangerous to her. But it feels like it was meant for me."

Arthur turned toward her, guilt flickering in his eyes. "It wasn't. Amelia—"

"Wasn't it?" she snapped. "A dead animal on *our* doorstep, Arthur. A note that says to stay away from your ex—your ex who showed up in *my office* to confront me. Do you really think that was random?"

Her voice broke. She hadn't meant for it to.

Rosie reached over and touched her arm. "Hey. It's alright."

Arthur set the empty glass aside and rubbed the back of his neck. "I'll handle this. I promise. I'll speak with her, find out if she's seen or heard anything strange."

Lady Edith frowned. "I don't think that's wise. Let the police handle it."

"They can't. Not yet. There's no proof of who did it."

"And if this person's still watching us?" Rosie asked. "What then?"

Chapter Twenty-Three

Arthur looked up at her. "Then we make sure they have nothing to watch."

He stood abruptly; the decision made in his body before his mind could catch up. "It's late. Everyone should get some rest."

Lady Edith gathered her shawl and rose gracefully. "Rest, he says," she muttered. "As if any of us will sleep tonight."

Amelia didn't move. She watched him as he crossed the room, pouring himself another half-glass of whiskey. The firelight flickered across his profile, throwing the sharp planes of his face into relief. There was something distant in his eyes—something she hadn't seen before.

"Arthur," she said quietly, "if this gets worse—"

"It won't."

"How can you be so sure?"

He glanced at her, a thin, forced smile on his lips. "Because I won't let it."

Hours later, the library was dark again. The house had fallen into uneasy silence.

Amelia sat alone in bed, staring at the faint line of moonlight slipping between the curtains. Her knee throbbed from the cold. Every time she closed her eyes, she saw the deer—its lifeless eyes, the glint of the nail through the note.

Beside her, Arthur slept heavily. But she could tell it was a forced sleep—the kind that came from whiskey and exhaustion, not peace. She rose quietly, careful not to wake him, and walked barefoot down the hall. The old floorboards creaked under her weight. She peeked into Rosie's room as she passed. Rosie was fast asleep, her phone still glowing faintly on the pillow beside her.

Amelia descended the stairs and paused at the base, listening. The house groaned softly—the wind against the windows, the faint ticking of the hall clock. She walked into the library. The fire had long since gone out, leaving the air cold and heavy with the scent of smoke and whiskey. She sat in Arthur's chair, tracing the rim of his glass where he'd left it.

Her mind refused to rest. Whoever had done this—whoever had left that message—wanted her afraid. And it was working. She thought about Helena's face in her office that day, the calm smile that didn't quite reach her eyes. The way she'd said, *"There are some things you'll never understand."*

Amelia closed her eyes and whispered, "What do you want from us?"

The wind rattled the windowpanes in answer.

By morning, the house was gray and quiet. Lady Edith emerged first, dressed impeccably as always, her posture unshakable despite the sleepless night. Rosie stumbled in behind her, hair tangled, clutching a cup of tea.

Arthur was already outside, standing in the cold mist with a mechanic from the village, speaking with urgency. Through the window, Amelia watched him. His breath fogged the air as he gestured, his expression resolute. Whatever guilt he felt last night had hardened into purpose.

She joined them on the gravel path, her boots sinking into the wet earth.

"Any luck?" she asked.

Arthur looked over, his face softening just slightly at the sight of her. "He's going to rig a chain system for now. A stopgap until the electrician comes to install a motor."

The mechanic nodded. "Should keep most people out unless they're determined."

Amelia forced a small smile. "And if they're determined?"

Arthur met her eyes. "Then they'll have to get through me."

She didn't argue, but her stomach twisted. She didn't want him to fight. She just wanted this to stop. When they turned back toward the house, Rosie was standing in the doorway with her coat half on, her face pale. "There's someone on the phone for you, Arthur. The police."

He jogged back up the steps and disappeared inside. Amelia followed more slowly. Lady Edith was in the hall, wringing her hands—an unusual display of nerves for the usually composed matriarch.

"What's happening?" she whispered.

"Not sure," Amelia said.

Arthur returned moments later; his expression unreadable. "They found tire tracks on the main road—fresh, about a hundred yards from the gate. Likely from last night."

"Do they know whose?" Rosie asked.

He shook his head. "No plates, no leads."

Lady Edith pressed a hand to her chest. "This is intolerable."

Arthur nodded. "Which is why I'm going to the university today. To speak to Helena directly."

Amelia stared at him. "Alone?"

"Yes."

"No." The word escaped her before she could stop it. "You can't go alone."

Arthur's gaze softened, but his tone was firm. "I have to. If I don't face this now, it will never end."

Amelia's throat felt tight. "And if you're wrong?"

He stepped closer and kissed her forehead. "Then I'll come home, and we'll find another way."

But as she watched him drive away an hour later, the mist swallowing the car, Amelia couldn't shake the feeling that something terrible was waiting on the other side of that day.

CHAPTER TWENTY-FOUR

THE MORNING LIGHT SLANTED ACROSS AMELIA'S DESK IN ribbons of pale gold, catching the corner of her phone and the half-finished mug of tea that had gone cold an hour ago. The office was still and silent except for the faint hum of the radiator. She sat with her elbows on the desk, staring at the long list of messages and call-backs that loomed over her like an accusation. Her mind drifted, the words blurring together into nothingness.

Her eyes flicked toward her left hand—bare. That small, empty space where her engagement ring should have been seemed louder than the silence itself. The door opened suddenly, and she jumped.

Rosie burst into the room like a gust of fresh air, her perfume bright and her smile brighter. "You are coming with me," she declared, setting a cup of tea and a small container of biscuits on the desk as if they were an offering.

"What?" Amelia blinked, startled. "Where are we going?"

Rosie was already halfway across the room. "I made an appointment for you this morning at my salon. They've squeezed you in—miraculously—and we're leaving right now."

Amelia glanced helplessly at the stack of notes, sketches, and unanswered emails that cluttered her desk. "Rosie, I can't. I have far too much work to do. Look at all these messages—"

"I'll handle them," Rosie interrupted with a grin that made it sound as though she'd just offered to slay a dragon. "But first, you're coming with me. No arguments."

Amelia hesitated, torn between the weight of her responsibilities and the rare, tempting idea of letting someone else take control for a moment. The thought of leaving everything—even for an hour—felt like a tiny rebellion against the chaos that had taken over her life.

"I don't know..."

Rosie clasped her hands together dramatically. "Please, Amelia. You need this. You deserve this. I promise it'll be worth it."

Amelia sighed, defeated by the younger woman's relentless optimism. "Fine," she murmured, standing to grab her purse.

"That's my girl." Rosie smirked, spinning the "open" sign on the door to "closed" with a flourish before locking it behind them.

Fifteen minutes later, Rosie parked her small silver car in front of an elegant boutique salon tucked between a bakery and a flower shop. The polished gold lettering across the window read *Maison de Beauté.*

As soon as Amelia stepped out, a wave of nostalgia hit her. The scent of freshly shampooed hair, the faint sweetness of hairspray, the distant whirr of dryers—it all transported her back to her early years in Los Angeles, when she'd worked the front desk at a salon much like this one. It had been a different lifetime—before Kinsey, before Arthur, before The Park House.

"Come on," Rosie said, looping her arm through Amelia's as they walked inside.

The salon was luminous and warm. A wall of mirrors reflected an assembly of women draped in black capes, each mid-transformation. The soft chatter mixed with the hum of blow dryers; the rhythm oddly comforting.

"Welcome back, your ladyship!" called the young receptionist behind the counter, her tone cheerfully reverent.

Rosie rolled her eyes. "How many times do I have to tell you? It's *just* Rosie." She gestured to Amelia. "This is who I called for—my soon-to-be gorgeous sister-in-law, Amelia Levingston."

Heads turned. A few women glanced up from their foils, curious, and Amelia offered an awkward smile. "Hello."

From across the room, a tall, striking man in a perfectly tailored black shirt appeared, his smile as warm as his voice. "This is Amelia?" he asked, his accent lilting faintly French.

Rosie beamed. "Amelia, this is my dear friend, Paul. He's a magician."

Amelia extended her hand. "Hi, Paul."

He took it, turning it slightly before pressing a polite kiss against her knuckles. "It is a pleasure to finally meet you, Amelia. Rosie has told me all about you. I follow your Instagram—your work is exquisite. You have a rare eye."

She flushed, a little flustered. "Thank you. That's very kind."

"Come, we'll make you even more exquisite."

Rosie's phone buzzed. "Oh! I've got to run—Paul will take good care of you."

"Wait—where are you going?" Amelia asked, half-panicked.

"To work, of course!" Rosie winked. "And no excuses—relax!"

Amelia watched her sweep out the door, radiant as ever, before turning back to Paul, who was gesturing toward a private room at the back.

The private suite was quiet, bathed in soft amber light and the faint scent of coconut. Amelia sat down in the large black salon chair and stared at her reflection. The woman in the mirror looked tired—her hair too long, her eyes shadowed with stress.

Paul caught her gaze in the mirror. "So," he said gently, "Rosie mentioned you're a little... attached to your hair."

Amelia hesitated, then nodded. "It's not that I'm attached. I just—haven't cut it since it grew back. I'm a cancer survivor."

Paul met her eyes through the reflection, something tender passing between them. "Then we have something in common," he said softly. "I'm a survivor too. Testicular cancer. Four years ago."

Surprised, Amelia turned to look at him fully. "Really?"

He nodded, his expression calm but meaningful. "Really. I'm fine now. But we both know—we're never quite the same afterward, are we?"

Amelia's throat tightened. "No," she whispered. "We're not."

He smiled knowingly. "Then maybe today, we let go of who you were before—and make space for who you've become."

She wanted to argue that she didn't have time for this. That she had deadlines, phone calls, a business to run. But before she could speak, Paul's assistant appeared with a flute of champagne and a reassuring smile.

"May I offer you a glass?"

Amelia hesitated—then laughed softly. "Oh, what the hell." She took the glass, the bubbles tickling her lip as she drank.

Paul gathered her hair gently in his hands, assessing its texture. "So, Amelia Levingston," he said, his voice melodic, "what are we doing today?"

She met his eyes in the mirror. "Make me look... sophisticated."

Paul grinned. "I know exactly what to do."

When the transformation was done, Amelia hardly recognized herself. Her hair was a shade darker, cut in layers that framed her face perfectly, falling in a smooth wave past her shoulders. The sleekness made her eyes appear greener, her cheekbones sharper. She felt—different. Stronger.

As she left the salon, the afternoon air was cool against her skin. For the first time in weeks, she felt light.

When she opened her office door she was greeted by Rosie with open arms. "You look wonderful Amelia. How do you feel?"

"I feel great." she smiled, "Thank you Rosie. I needed that."

Rosie ran to the side of the office and showed two bags. "New look for your... new look." She giggled. "Arthur is going to be so surprised."

By the time Rosie's car rolled up the long drive to The Park House, the sun had begun to set. The light glowed across the estate's pale stone façade, warm and honey colored. Lady Edith stood on the steps waiting, handbag in hand, looking as though she'd stepped out of a 1940s portrait.

"What's she waiting outside for?" Amelia asked.

Rosie grinned. "I'm taking her out to dinner. You and Arthur have the house all to yourselves."

Amelia raised an eyebrow. "You're serious?"

"Deadly."

Lady Edith approached Amelia's window and tapped it gently. When Amelia stepped out, Edith's eyes widened.

"Oh my," she breathed. "You look..."

Amelia's hand flew self-consciously to her hair. "Is it too much?"

"No," Edith said softly, and to Amelia's surprise, pulled her into a warm hug. "You look perfect." The hug lingered a moment longer than expected, and when Edith stepped back, there was something tender in her expression.

"Wish me luck," Amelia whispered.

"Good luck!" Rosie and Edith called in unison as they climbed into the car, laughter following them down the drive.

The house was quiet when Amelia stepped inside. She slipped off her heels by the door and shrugged off her coat, the faint echo of her own movements sounding impossibly loud in the stillness.

"Is that you?" Arthur's voice carried faintly from down the hall.

"I think so," she called back, smiling.

He appeared a moment later, holding two glasses of red wine, and froze. For a long heartbeat, neither of them spoke. His eyes traveled from her hair to her heels and back up again, a slow, reverent study. "Wha—" he started, then stopped, utterly lost for words.

Amelia bit her lip, her pulse fluttering. "Do you like it?"

He crossed the space between them, eyes soft with disbelief. "Like it?" he murmured, reaching out to brush a strand of hair from her face. "My God, Amelia Levingston... you are beautiful."

Her breath caught. The sincerity in his voice felt like a physical thing—warm, grounding, undeniable. He handed her a glass of wine, and their fingers brushed.

"Careful," she teased, "you'll spill—"

Too late. A splash of deep red stained the front of her new dress.

Arthur swore under his breath. "Oh no. Did I ruin it?"

Amelia looked down at the droplets of wine like rubies against the fabric and laughed. "It's fine. I can always get another one."

He set the glasses aside, eyes dark with affection. "I'm not taking another chance," he murmured, before kissing her.

The kiss deepened quickly, laughter giving way to something hungrier. They stumbled together against the wall, a centuries-old painting hanging askew before crashing to the floor with a muted thud.

They broke apart, breathless, staring down at it.

"We can always get another one," Amelia whispered.

Arthur laughed. "I'm not sure we can. That painting's about three hundred years old."

She grinned. "Then I suppose we're both in trouble."

He scooped her into his arms before she could protest, carrying her up the wide staircase as she half-laughed, half-squealed, "I can walk, you know!"

"I know," he said, his voice low and playful.

In their room, the air was thick with the faint scent of old wood and roses. He laid her gently on the bed, kissing her neck, his fingers trailing through her hair. "God, you smell incredible," he murmured.

"It's the shampoo," she whispered, smiling.

He laughed softly against her skin, and the world fell away. For a while there was nothing but them—the warmth, the closeness, the unspoken relief of finding each other again after days of tension and fear.

Then, a faint scent drifted through the air. Amelia frowned, pausing. "Do you smell something burning?"

Arthur froze, sniffed, then groaned. "That would be our dinner."

He leapt from the bed, pulling on his shirt as he ran. "You're turning into your mother!" she called after him, dissolving into laughter.

When he returned a few minutes later, he looked sheepish. "Well," he admitted, "I hope you aren't hungry."

She patted the pillow beside her, her smile slow and mischievous. "Actually," she said softly, "I'm famished."

Arthur's grin returned as he crossed the room to her.

And for the first time in a long while, the night belonged entirely to them.

CHAPTER TWENTY-FIVE

S T. MARY'S LOOKED DIFFERENT IN MORNING. JUST WEEKS EAR-
lier it had been dressed like a storybook—flowers spilling
from pew ends, candlelight glimmering over silk and lace, the
sanctuary a soft chorus of happiness. Now, the same nave held
a hush so deep it pressed against skin. The lilies were gone. In
their place: white chrysanthemums and laurel, solemn and orderly, framing a large photograph of Harry behind the lectern.
He was mid-laugh in the picture, head tipped back, as if he'd
been caught in one of the pub's better jokes.

Amelia stood with Arthur until the verger motioned them
into a pew. The wood was cool through her coat. People kept arriving—locals from every corner of Nottingham, faces she knew
from the high street and faces utterly new—filling the church
until latecomers were forced to stand along the stone walls. It
said something about a man when the turnout for his funeral
rivaled a town festival.

Harry had probably known more secrets than the priest did,
Amelia thought. Running a pub turned you into something between confessor and companion. People told barkeeps their truth.

On the aisle across from them, Charlie held himself stiffly, jaw clenched, fingers interlaced so tightly his knuckles blanched. Wendy kept one arm around him, cheek pressed to his shoulder. Beside them, Betty sat proudly upright in her wheelchair, her hands folded, her expression composed in a way that felt like defiance against grief. She had chosen not to speak during the service, she had told Amelia; the eulogy, if it mattered, would be how they carried on.

The priest's voice rose and fell, the words washing over her in a gentle tide. Amelia tried to focus and found herself drifting. Funerals had a way of dragging old shadows into the light. She remembered her mother's service. There had been no casket— her mother had donated her body to science, of course she had, practical to the end.

The gathering had been small, the church in Los Angeles nowhere near as beautiful as this one but dear to the tiny circle who came. Amelia spent the entire time crying into a wad of tissue while Aunt Tessa sat stiffly beside her, eyes forward, as if angered by grief itself.

She remembered nothing of her father's funeral; she had been too young. A gap in memory where a goodbye should have been.

A warm pressure wrapped around her hand. Arthur, eyes rimmed red, squeezed her fingers once. The gesture startled her—the reminder that he carried his own ghosts. She'd been thinking only of Wendy and Charlie and had not considered how a church, a hymn, a reading about loss might rake across the ache of his father and brother.

She tilted her head and rested it on his shoulder. He slid his arm around her and pulled her closer. For a breath or two the sanctuary and its collected sorrow fell away, and there was only the quiet exchange between them: I'm here. I know. Me too.

Above the nave, gilded angels peered down from their carved wooden cloud. Amelia followed their gaze to the photograph of Harry and felt, fleetingly, something like thankfulness settle inside her chest. For survival. For this improbable new family who had insisted on making space for her. For a love that felt like a mercy.

When the last hymn faded, Wendy made her way to the lectern. She had her father's dark eyes, steadier today than Amelia expected.

"You are all invited," she said, clearing her throat when it caught on the first word, "to the pub. We'd like to give my dad—" she paused, changed course, "—Harry—one last goodbye."

A low assent rustled through the congregation. Wendy met Amelia's eyes and Arthur's and gave a small nod.

As they stepped out beneath the cool grey sky, Arthur asked his mother and Rosie, "Are you coming?"

"I wouldn't miss it," Lady Edith said. She threaded her arm through Rosie's and led the way down the church steps.

By the time they reached the pub, the wake had turned noisy, the way wakes do when memory collides with whiskey. The front room was packed shoulder to shoulder, people spilling onto the pavement outside with pints and stories. Laughter rose and fell like birds startled from a hedge, startling even the people who made it. The urn—a modest, handsome thing—sat on the bar beside a framed photograph of Harry in his apron, one hand on a tap handle as if he were still mid-pour. Someone had arranged a ring of small tumblers around the urn, each filled with Scotch. One by one, patrons walked up, spoke a few words to the photograph or to the urn or to the bar itself, took a glass, and swallowed.

Arthur found a corner table for the four of them—Amelia and Lady Edith on one side, he and Betty on the other—while Rosie, with the unerring magnetism of a sparrow for crumbs, drifted toward a pair of handsome strangers who were laughing too loudly at nothing at all.

The pub smelled of malt and fry oil and a hundred colognes. Beneath it all hung grief, invisible and heavy, and yet Harry's place had a way of insisting on warmth.

"How are you holding up, dear?" Lady Edith asked Betty, leaning in so she wouldn't need to raise her voice.

Betty's hands stayed folded, the knotted knuckles spotlit by the table lamp. "I'm going to be all right," she said. "Charlie and Wendy have started moving in. I never liked that guest room but I do like the sound of them in the kitchen, fussing with the kettle."

"I'm sure they've been a great help," Edith said. "It's a comfort, having the house full."

"If there's anything you need," Amelia said, "anything at all—we mean it. I can pop by in the mornings before I head to the office. Or we can arrange the pantry so you can reach what you need from the chair—whatever would make it easier."

Betty turned her face toward Amelia and smiled, the kind of smile that made the skin around her eyes soften. "As it happens," she said, "there is something."

Arthur, who had been watching the line at the bar, turned back. "Anything," he said.

Betty lifted a hand and gestured, palm open, to the room around them. "This."

"The pub?" Amelia asked, careful.

"The pub," Betty confirmed. "Wendy's running it now, and—well, it's going to be hard for her as it is. The place is soaked in him. Every tile, every cabinet door. He had his ways, did our Harry. He could be stubborn, especially when she suggested changing the menu. It kept us going, I won't pretend otherwise." She looked toward the bar, where Wendy was bending to listen to an elderly regular whose blue eyes shone with tears. "But I want Wendy to have her own vision here. Not to spend the next twenty years inside her father's shadow."

Amelia felt a flush rise under her collar. "Are you asking me—us—to take on the pub?"

"If you've room," Betty said. "I know you've your famous client and the magazine sniffing round. But I thought—maybe with the life insurance—maybe we could do this properly. A rework. Still roots down deep, mind you. Nothing cold or fancy. Just... hers."

Arthur's hand found Amelia's knee under the table and gave it an encouraging squeeze. "I think it's a wonderful idea," he said quietly.

"Does Wendy know?" Lady Edith asked.

"She will," Betty said. "Tomorrow, when I've worked up how to say it without her feeling she's letting her dad down."

"She won't," Amelia said. She pictured the bar without its scuffed shelves, the space lighter, kinder; a menu that had her friend's handwriting all over it. "If you want it, we'll make room. Always, for you."

They raised their glasses. "To Harry," Amelia said.

"To Harry," echoed Betty and Lady Edith and Arthur, and then—because sound carries in rooms where people want to be together—the entire pub lifted pints and glasses and plastic tumblers and shouted it back: "To Harry!"

As if summoned by the wave of tribute, the door from the back snug opened and Wendy stepped out with two people Amelia didn't recognize—a woman in her thirties, draped in a simple navy salwar kameez that made her look impossibly elegant amid the denim and jumpers, and a boy of seven or eight, thin, watchful, dark hair clipped neatly above wide eyes.

Amelia felt the air around their table contract. Betty's gaze swung toward them, and something in her face—surprise, yes, and also a careful composure—made Amelia's stomach tighten. She pushed back her chair. "Oh—Betty—" she started, meaning to offer a warning, a pause, something, but the older woman was already wheeling herself forward through the crowd with a purpose that made people step aside instinctively.

The woman in navy saw her and hesitated, as if bracing for rejection. Then, not quite believing it, she smiled. Betty reached for her hand; the woman took it with both of hers and bent to hug her, and for a breath they stayed like that—two women in the eye of the room's noise, steadied by each other. "I'm so sorry we missed the service," the woman said when she straightened, voice soft and accented. "Our train—there was a delay."

"Nonsense," Betty said briskly, patting the woman's wrist with her thumb. "You're here now. That's what matters. Come. Sit with us."

Wendy's eyes flicked to Amelia, then down to the floor. She looked frightened and brave at once. She guided the boy by the shoulder toward the table, hovering a step behind him as if keeping him in her orbit could keep him safe.

Arthur leaned toward Amelia. "Who are they?" he whispered.

"Shh," Amelia said, barely moving her lips. In the corner of her vision, she saw Rosie straighten away from her pair of admirers, attention pulled like a compass needle.

Betty reached the table and turned her chair, so she faced the room. With one hand, she gathered the boy's fingers into her palm; with the other, she gestured to the woman. Her voice carried farther than Amelia would have thought possible, given its gentleness.

"Let me introduce you," Betty said, and the thread of conversation around them thinned, then stopped. "This is Manish."

Silence fell so swiftly the ice machine's low rumble sounded like thunder.

"Harry's son," Betty finished.

The word seemed to travel in widening concentric circles, like a pebble dropped in a still pond. Harry's son. A woman at the end of the bar dropped a stirrer. Someone somewhere muttered "what?" to no one in particular.

The boy looked at the floor. His hands went still in Betty's. Amelia's throat tightened. She recognized the posture intimately—the bone-deep awareness of being the reason a room changed temperature.

Wendy moved closer to the woman—Manish's mother, Amelia guessed—and placed her hand lightly between the woman's shoulder blades. A steadying touch. She looked across at Amelia, and in that look Amelia read a hundred unsaid things: I didn't know how to do this. I'm doing it anyway. Please.

Arthur rose first. "Hello, Manish," he said, voice pitched low, the way he spoke to skittish horses on the park grounds. "I'm Arthur."

Manish lifted his head, considered, then nodded. "Hello," he said. His voice was surprisingly clear.

"I'm Amelia," she said, and her chest eased when the boy's mouth tilted toward something almost like a smile.

Betty squeezed his fingers. "We'll have none of that whispering," she said to the room at large, with a firmness that reminded Amelia of the way she had once watched Betty shoo three burly men from a bar fight with a single look. "Harry loved with his whole silly heart. That's who he was. Love is messy. But look at this boy." She tipped her head toward Manish.

The quiet didn't break so much as lift. People started to move again—the barmaid resumed pulling pints; someone at the far end lifted a glass and said, too loudly, "To Harry," and a ragged chorus answered it, grateful for something to do with their hands.

Amelia looked at Wendy. Tears glistened without falling. Wendy managed a small nod, and Amelia felt something like pride pull through her, bright and fierce.

Arthur's hand found hers under the table. His thumb brushed along her knuckles once. Outside, a burst of laughter rose, not unkind.

In a pub that had belonged, for so long, to one man's particular gravity, a new map was drawing itself in real time: lines of responsibility, of tenderness, of future. Wendy would have decisions to make in the morning that might break her heart and heal it at once. Anita and her son would have to stand inside a thousand uninvited opinions. Betty would hold the center with an iron will and gentler words.

And Amelia—Amelia felt the old scaffolding of her life make room for one more beam. She could already see the changes in the pub that would carry Harry forward without pinning Wendy to his past. She could picture a corner where a child might do homework before the dinner rush; a chalkboard menu Wendy could rewrite each season; a back-room Anita might repaint the color of monsoon clouds if she liked.

"Manish," she said softly, "do you like chips?" His eyes flicked up. He nodded. "Well," she said, "I happen to know this place makes the very best ones."

He looked uncertain, then, more certainly, curious.

"Come on," Rosie said to Anita with the kind of cheerfulness that's actually courage, "let's order one of everything and decide together what stays on our menu."

Manish trembled into a smile, "All right."

As they moved toward the bar, the regulars shifted aside to let them through, and a lane opened in the crowd as if the pub itself wanted to make this easier. Amelia slid the empty tumblers away from the urn and replaced them with fresh ones. She caught the photograph of Harry in the edge of her vision—caught that open-mouthed laugh—and felt an unexpected calm.

"Goodbye, you silly, dear man," she thought. "We'll take it from here."

CHAPTER TWENTY-SIX

A HUSH SETTLED OVER THE PUB AGAIN—QUIETER THIS TIME, more tentative. Enough chairs had been pulled up that nearly every patron within earshot had drifted closer, drawn by the sudden gravity around Betsy and the small family standing beside her.

Betsy adjusted herself in her wheelchair, clearing her throat with a composure that only half hid the tremor in her voice. "This," she began evenly, "is Nivetha, and her son, Manish." Her eyes swept the room. "We've never spoken about this because, frankly, it was no one's business."

"Mum!" Wendy's voice broke with disbelief. "How could you not tell me?"

The air tightened again, the crowd hovering between curiosity and discomfort. Arthur leaned forward, resting his elbows on his knees, while Amelia's heart thudded in her chest.

Betsy held her hand up to calm her daughter. "Now, listen. There's nothing to be upset about. I can explain."

The room seemed to lean in as she continued, her tone softening, her eyes finding Wendy's. "After my accident, your father and I were struggling. I couldn't walk. I could barely manage to lift you Wendy, and he was running this pub—day and night. We needed help, desperately. That's when Harry hired Nivetha."

Amelia's gaze flicked toward the woman. Nivetha's eyes were warm and cautious, her dark hair neatly plaited, a single silver bangle glinting on her wrist as she comforted her son.

"She stayed with us for almost three years," Betsy went on. "She was young, far from home, and she became... family. She wasn't just an employee—she saved me. She gave me hope again. You were only a toddler then, Wendy. You adored her. Followed her everywhere. But her work visa expired, and there was nothing we could do. She had to go back to India. We were heartbroken."

A murmur spread through the crowd. Amelia caught Rosie wiping discreetly at her cheek. Betsy exhaled. "We kept in touch all these years. Letters, calls when we could manage. Then I learned she'd married—a good man, by all accounts—but he passed suddenly before their son was born."

Her eyes drifted to the boy beside her. "That's Manish."

He looked down at his shoes, one foot fidgeting nervously against the floorboards. Betsy reached out, squeezing his small shoulder gently. "Harry and I did what we could. Sent money when it was needed. Birthdays, Christmas, even when the post lost half of it. It was never charity. It was love."

For a long moment, the only sound was the soft clink of glasses behind the bar.

When Betsy's voice returned, it was quiet, reverent. "Nivetha visited once a year ago and finally managed to return for a short visit. She came to see us last week—stopped by the bar before she even unpacked—and that's when she heard the news of Harry."

Amelia felt the sting of tears. The thought of Nivetha, newly arrived after all those years, walking into the pub expecting laughter and finding loss instead—it was heartbreak wrapped in fate. "I am so sorry for your loss," Nivetha said gently. "We loved Harry so much."

Betsy smiled weakly. "I know, dear."

But Wendy stood frozen. Her voice shook. "I don't understand why you never told me. All these years?"

Betsy sighed. "Because it wasn't about secrets, love. It was private. Harry didn't want to make a spectacle of his kindness, and I didn't want to confuse you when you were little. But I'm glad you know now."

The words didn't soothe Wendy immediately. Her eyes darted to Nivetha, then to the boy, then back to her mother. "You just thought you'd wait twenty years to tell me I have—what—another family?"

"Wendy," Betsy said gently, "we never hid love from you. We just... protected it. That's all this ever was."

The tension in the air was palpable. Amelia could almost feel it crackling against her skin. Then Nivetha rose, smoothing her skirt, and stepped closer to Wendy. Her voice was calm, melodic, touched by the cadence of another country. "If it weren't for your parents, Wendy, my son and I would have had a very different life. We are not here for anything except to say thank you—to tell you in person how much their friendship meant. They were our family too."

For a heartbeat, Wendy said nothing. Then she blurted out the fear sitting in her chest. "And I suppose you aren't here to ask for money."

The words hung in the air like glass about to shatter.

"Wendy!" Betsy gasped.

But Nivetha, to her credit, only smiled sadly. "No, my dear. We don't need money. I have remarried, and we're doing well. Truly." Her gaze softened. "We came to honor a man who gave us kindness when we had nothing. To tell you that his generosity lives on in us."

Manish nodded, stepping forward timidly. "I wanted to meet you," he said, voice small but sure. "Mum told me stories about you. You're kind of like my big sister. I always wanted one."

The transformation on Wendy's face was slow, like dawn breaking. Her eyes welled; her lips trembled. Then she bent down, opening her arms. The boy went to her easily, pressing his face into her shoulder.

"Well then," Wendy said, her voice breaking into a soft laugh. "I suppose I'll have to be that for you."

Around the table, the tension dissolved into something gentler—relief, affection, the kind of shared exhale that people give when a storm passes. Rosie sniffed loudly and muttered, "Oh, bloody hell," dabbing at her eyes with a napkin. Even Arthur smiled, one arm draped along the back of Amelia's chair.

Amelia, watching it all unfold, felt something inside her unclench. She had been so certain—so ready—to believe the worst of Harry when the mystery of his past surfaced. The late-night phone calls, the strange silences, the rumors about other women. She'd built her own quiet narrative of betrayal in her head.

And now, with one conversation, it had unraveled.

Harry hadn't been a cheater or a liar. He'd been a man who carried the weight of compassion quietly, privately. The kind of person who did good for the sake of it, not for the recognition.

In the warmth of the pub, the noise slowly swelled again—people laughing, clinking glasses, calling for another round. Someone began retelling an old story about Harry convincing a sheep farmer to trade lamb for beer. The laughter rolled like a wave through the room.

Amelia sat back in her chair, watching Wendy still holding Manish, and thought of all the ways grief could surprise people. Sometimes it tore open what had been hidden, not to wound, but to heal.

She thought of her own mother—of the secrets that had passed away with her, of the questions that would never be answered. She envied Wendy a little, that her father's kindness had been revealed in the end.

Betsy, her eyes glossy with fatigue, turned her chair toward Amelia. "I think he would've liked this, don't you?"

Amelia nodded. "Very much. He'd be behind the bar right now, pretending to complain about the noise."

Chapter Twenty-Six

Betsy chuckled. "Yes. And he'd charge us all double for the whiskey."

Arthur raised his glass again. "To Harry," he said simply.

"To Harry!" the others echoed, voices overlapping until the whole room caught the refrain.

Rosie, flushed and laughing, joined the toast from the other end of the bar, waving a glass of gin.

By the time the night grew late, plates of food had been cleared and replaced by trays of crisps and small sandwiches that vanished almost instantly. The fire crackled low in the hearth, throwing amber light across faces—old friends, new acquaintances, even strangers who had come simply because Harry had once bought them a pint when they were down on their luck.

Amelia sat back, head buzzing pleasantly from wine, and let the sound of laughter wash over her. She couldn't remember the last time grief had felt this alive, this full of love.

At one point, she caught Arthur watching her. He smiled—a quiet, knowing smile—and she smiled back. Around them, life went on: Rosie teaching Manish a silly card trick; Nivetha laughing with Lady Edith over something lost in translation; Wendy finally relaxing beside her mother, the two women leaning their heads together.

Amelia took a sip of wine and thought, *This is what redemption looks like.*

Harry's legacy wasn't just in the bricks of the pub or the stories people told—it was in the way everyone here belonged to each other now.

When the evening began to wind down, Nivetha and Manish prepared to leave. The boy clutched a small paper bag of sweets that Rosie had insisted he take. Wendy knelt and hugged him tightly once more.

"You'll visit again, won't you?" she asked.

"Of course," Nivetha promised. "Next time we'll bring sunshine with us."

As they disappeared through the doorway into the cool night, Amelia felt a small pang—part sadness, part gratitude.

The crowd began thinning, groups heading out arm-in-arm. Betsy lingered near the fireplace, a faint smile on her lips, her chair framed by the flickering light. Amelia approached and crouched beside her. "He really was a good man," Amelia said softly.

Betsy looked at her, eyes shining. "Yes. And now everyone knows it."

By the time they stepped outside, the air had turned crisp. The pub's sign creaked gently in the wind. Arthur took Amelia's hand, their fingers intertwining automatically as they walked toward the car.

Behind them, laughter still spilled from the doorway, and the golden light of the pub pooled across the gravel like a promise that even in loss, love remained.

Amelia looked back one last time. Through the window, she could see Wendy wiping down the bar, Rosie still talking animatedly to whoever hadn't yet left.

A new chapter was already beginning.

And for the first time in weeks, Amelia felt peace.

CHAPTER TWENTY-SEVEN

T HE ROAD TO OAK HALL WOUND THROUGH THE ANCIENT TREES
like a grey ribbon. Rain from the morning still clung to the
hedgerows, and Amelia's headlights shimmered against their
slick leaves. She wore the dress Rosie had chosen for her—soft
dove-grey silk that matched the storm clouds above—and though
she had spent the drive steadying her breathing, there was a
quiet defiance in her posture.

She was not the same woman who had once trembled before
titles and portraits. Today, she would walk into Oak Hall as an
equal.

As she turned into the sweeping drive, she saw him—a man
waiting in the distance, hands folded behind his back, his stance
oddly still. When she slowed the car, he stepped forward through
the thin mist. His face was familiar, and it took her a moment
to place him.

He smiled faintly. "Good afternoon."

Amelia stepped out of the car, her heels crunching against
the gravel. "I recognize you," she said, studying him.

"Oh?" His tone was polite, almost rehearsed.

"You were at Nottingham University. I saw you in the corridor the other day."

He gave a small, embarrassed smile. "Ah, yes. That's right."

"Are you a student there?"

He rubbed the back of his neck, avoiding her eyes. "Not exactly. I was visiting a friend that day."

His answer came too quickly. Amelia's instinct pricked. "I see. Forgive me—I'm Amelia Levingston."

At that, his dark eyes finally met hers. The smile that followed was thin and strangely forced. "Henry Hyde," he said. "I'm new here at Oak Hall. Just started this week."

The name landed awkwardly. Amelia smiled faintly. "Nice to meet you, Mr. Hyde."

"Henry," he corrected softly.

He moved closer than necessary, reaching past her to shut the car door, his arm brushing her shoulder. "Sorry," he murmured.

"It's fine."

"May I take your keys?" His voice lowered slightly. "We're expecting a large delivery, and I'll need to move your vehicle."

Amelia hesitated, but his expression was polite, deferential. "Of course," she said, handing over her keys. "I should get inside before I'm late."

"Pleasure to finally meet you, Miss Levingston," he said.

Her brow lifted. "Finally?"

He blinked. "To meet you," he corrected quickly, then turned toward the barn.

As Amelia walked toward the front steps, the back of her neck prickled. Something about him—the way he said her name, as if testing it—lingered uneasily in her mind.

The heavy front doors opened before she reached them. Leopold, Lady Newcroft's butler, stood with his usual impeccable posture. "Miss Levingston," he greeted with a faint bow.

"Oh. Yes?"

"Her ladyship is waiting for you. Tea will be served in the garden."

Amelia glanced at the looming clouds. "Outside? It looks as though it might rain."

"Her ladyship insists."

"Of course she does," Amelia murmured under her breath.

She followed him through the corridors, her heels clicking against the marble floors. Something about the house felt changed. The once-abundant floral arrangements—always fresh and fragrant—were gone. The air smelled faintly of polish and something older, like closed rooms and cold stone.

The warmth that had once defined Oak Hall seemed to have evaporated, leaving only the weight of its history.

Leopold opened the terrace doors. The garden spread before them in manicured perfection, though even the roses seemed to droop under the threat of rain. Lady Newcroft sat at a table of white wrought iron, perfectly poised despite the chill, while Barnaby wandered a few yards away, humming softly to himself as he bent toward a bush of fading roses.

"Ah, there you are," Lady Newcroft called, her voice crisp as porcelain. "We may need to make this quick—looks like rain."

"I can set the table inside if you prefer, your ladyship," said Leopold.

"Nonsense. This won't take long."

Amelia stepped forward, her smile polite. "Thank you for inviting me to tea."

Barnaby turned at the sound of her voice, his expression lighting up. "Hello, Amelia," he said, walking toward her with a single rose in his hand. "Would you give this to Edith when you see her? It's her favorite."

"Of course," Amelia said, touched by his simple sincerity.

He nodded absently and drifted back toward the house, his gait slow, distracted, as though following thoughts only he could see. Amelia watched him go, her chest tightening with something like pity. There was a sweetness in him, a gentleness that didn't belong in such a calculating world.

"Please, sit," Lady Newcroft said sharply, breaking Amelia's reverie.

Amelia sat opposite her as Leopold poured the tea. "Milk?" he asked.

"Please," she replied, her tone even.

When he had gone, Lady Newcroft folded her hands, studying Amelia as though she were a curiosity on display. "I've heard we are soon to be family," she said at last. "It's important, then, that we understand one another."

Amelia smiled lightly. "I agree."

"Unless I'm mistaken. I see you're not wearing a ring."

"Oh—that's a long story."

"Is it a happy one?"

Amelia hesitated. "I suppose that depends on your perspective."

Lady Newcroft's gaze didn't waver. "Should we even be having this tea? I hear you're quite the commodity these days. A flourishing business, front-page appearances."

She lifted a folded copy of *The Daily Mail* and slid it across the table. Amelia glanced down. The photograph showed her and Eloise laughing together in Nottingham, shopping bags in hand, sunlight catching the side of her face. The headline beneath read: *'Designing Woman: Amelia Levingston and Nottingham's Star Designer, Eloise Bellemare, Spotted Together.'*

"I hadn't seen this one," Amelia said, trying not to smile.

"This one?" Lady Newcroft echoed.

"I mean—yes, business is going well. I'm proud of that."

"Don't get ahead of yourself, dear."

The words landed like a pinprick. Amelia pressed her lips together and took a slow sip of tea. Lady Newcroft's condescension reminded her painfully of Edith's when they'd first met—the suspicion, the cold curiosity. And yet, beneath it, she saw something else. Fear.

"As for my relationship with Arthur," Amelia said carefully, "I can assure you, I love your grandson very much."

"Where is your ring?"

"I'm not wearing it right now."

"Why?"

"Because... well, there's always the chance of damaging it when I work. I'm in restoration—it's safer not to."

"Hmm," Lady Newcroft said, unconvinced. "And why do you love my grandson, precisely? His title? His wealth?"

Amelia's breath caught, but she refused to look away. "I wasn't searching for Arthur. We found each other through Kinsey. I believe fate—"

"You mean my late grandson Henry," Lady Newcroft interrupted.

"I knew him as only as Kinsey," Amelia said quietly, steady.

"Ah. Yes." Her smile was thin. "So, why do you love Arthur?"

Amelia met her gaze. "Because he is my person. My home. My everything."

"The title has nothing to do with it?"

"I'm not interested in his title."

"That's convenient. Because once those vows are said, everything changes for you, doesn't it?"

"I'm not sure what you mean."

"You'll be the new Marchioness," Lady Newcroft said, her voice clipped. "That title carries obligations. Appearances. Expectations. You don't strike me as someone... acquainted with our world. In fact, you seem rather naïve to it."

Amelia's temper flared, but she kept her tone cool. "I don't think that's fair. I'm much smarter than you may think."

"Oh?" Lady Newcroft arched an eyebrow. "You read?"

"I do," Amelia replied evenly. "Voraciously. And since being entrusted with the restoration of The Park House— I've dedicated myself not only to its design but to learning every detail of the Bonneville history. Every brick, every portrait, every name. Out of respect."

Lady Newcroft tilted her head. "Oh, is that so?"

"Yes. It is."

"And what of our history?"

"Which do you mean? The Newcroft name, or your late husband's? Ask me anything."

A roll of thunder cracked across the clouds, deep and resonant. Lady Newcroft's expression flickered, just for a moment.

"I was asking," she said, her tone sharpening, "about the history of the Royal Family—the lineage to which you will now belong."

Raindrops began to fall, soft at first, then steadier, scattering across the white tablecloth.

"Ask me anything," Amelia said again. Her voice was calm, but her eyes gleamed with quiet fire.

Lady Newcroft leaned back, her lips pressing together. "It's starting to rain," she said. "We'll continue this another time."

Leopold reappeared with two umbrellas as if summoned by the tension itself. He held one over Lady Newcroft and handed the other to Amelia.

"Thank you, Leopold," Amelia said politely.

Lady Newcroft stood. "We will meet again soon, Miss Levingston."

"I look forward to it," Amelia replied, though she doubted she meant it.

She left the terrace, the cold rain pinpricking against her skin. The house loomed ahead, all shuttered windows and shadowed corners. As she passed the corridor where she had once delivered Kinsey's ashes, a chill ran down her spine.

She tried to shake the memory—the echo of Edith's grief, the weight of that urn—and walked faster. Outside, the rain thickened to a downpour. Her car waited precisely where she had left it. No sign of Henry Hyde. The drive was deserted.

She paused, scanning the grounds. "Henry?" she called, but her voice was swallowed by the rain.

Amelia hurried to the car, pulling the door open. It was

unlocked. Her keys sat neatly on the passenger seat. A prickle of unease crept up her neck. She climbed in quickly, shutting the door behind her, and took a deep breath before starting the engine.

The rain hammered harder, obscuring the view of the house as she turned down the drive. She reached the end of the long lane, where the gravel met the narrow main road. The storm was gathering speed, branches swaying wildly.

She pressed the brake pedal—

Nothing.

The car kept rolling.

She pressed harder. Still nothing. The pedal sank, useless, to the floor. Her breath caught. The world narrowed to the sound of rain and the thudding of her heart. "Come on," she whispered, pressing again—harder—but the car didn't slow. Ahead, the road curved sharply toward the stone boundary wall of the estate.

Amelia gripped the wheel, rain streaking down the windshield, the wipers screeching against the glass as she fought to control her breath.

The car gained speed.

Her mind flashed—Henry Hyde. The unlocked door. The too-polite smile.

She opened her mouth to scream—

And the world went white with the glare of oncoming headlights.

CHAPTER TWENTY-EIGHT

A FAINT, RHYTHMIC BEEPING ECHOED IN THE DARK. IT PULSED softly at first, then grew sharper, insistent—a sound that felt far away yet unbearably close.

"Amelia?" A voice reached through the haze. "Amelia, wake up?"

She tried to open her eyes, but her body resisted. Her eyelids felt heavy as stone. The beeping merged with another sound—ringing, high and piercing.

"Amelia, please."

Darkness folded around her, thick and impenetrable. Then another voice—a voice she knew as surely as her own heartbeat. "Amelia, it's time to wake up."

It was Kinsey.

Her eyes fluttered open, expecting him—but instead, there was light, blinding and sterile. Figures hovered above her. Their voices were muffled, like sound underwater.

"Oh good, she's waking up." A woman's face appeared, masked but kind. "Amelia, I'm Doctor Burd. You've been in a car accident, and we're here to help you."

Amelia tried to speak, but her mouth wouldn't form the words.

Panic surged in her chest. Her head was locked in a brace; she could barely move.

"You've got a broken arm," the doctor continued gently. "We're going to take care of you, alright? Try not to move. Can you speak?"

She couldn't. Terror swept through her body—followed by pain, sharp and total, blooming in waves until tears slid from her eyes. "Doctor, we're ready," someone said.

"You're going to take a nice nap now," Dr. Bird said softly. "Everything is going to be alright."

A mask pressed over Amelia's mouth. Cool oxygen flooded her lungs. The beeping slowed. The room dissolved into white—and then, there was grass beneath her hands.

She sat in a meadow bathed in soft light. The air smelled of clover and rain. Across from her, Kinsey sat smiling—the same soft eyes, the same bald head. He took her hand in his, warm and steady.

"I missed you," he said.

"I missed you too." Her voice trembled with disbelief. "How long has it been?"

"Forever," he said with a small grin, "is just a moment sometimes."

She laughed through her tears. "How did we get here? What is this place?"

"Gran's new hire," he said, his tone darkening. "He tampered with your car."

"Who?"

"The one at Oak Hall. He took your keys, Amelia. He cut your brakes."

She shook her head. "That's— that's impossible. Why would he—?"

"Why indeed?" Kinsey said softly. "But you know how stories work. We don't learn the truth until the end."

Her hand tightened around his. "I don't want to go back. I just want to stay here with you. I've missed you so much, I have to fill you in on everything."

He smiled faintly. "You can't stay, darling. It's not your time."

"Please Kinsey." She leaned against his shoulder, breathing in the scent of wildflowers.

"I'm always with you."

Tears slid down her face. "Your brother proposed to me."

Kinsey laughed, that warm, familiar sound that filled the space around them. "Did he now? Was it Austen-worthy?"

"No. He proposed in the bathroom."

Kinsey groaned. "I'll have a word with him."

"What, haunt him?"

"Perhaps I'll pull a Christmas Carol. Rattle some chains, scare him into buying flowers."

"Don't you dare." She nudged him playfully—and a sharp pain shot through her ribs.

"Ouch!"

"Easy, darling. You're in surgery," he said gently.

"I am?"

"Yes. And it's almost time to wake up."

She turned to him, desperate. "Can't I stay? Just a little longer?"

He smiled, brushing a strand of hair from her face. "You've got too much left to do. Take care of them, Amelia. Take care of my family."

"I will."

"Good girl."

He kissed the top of her head, and the world began to fade. The meadow blurred into light, and his voice drifted away.

The world returned in fragments—the scent of antiseptic, the hum of machines, the cold weight of a cast on her arm. Her eyelids fought to open again. A man with a clipboard looked up from the foot of her bed and quickly disappeared into the hall. Moments later, a doctor returned.

"Amelia, I'm Dr. Bird," the woman said warmly, checking the monitors.

"Hello," Amelia whispered.

"How are you feeling?"

"Mummified."

The doctor smiled. "That's one way to put it. You've got a broken arm, severe whiplash, and a concussion—but considering what happened, you're very lucky."

"What... happened?"

"Do you remember anything?"

"I was driving up the road... that's all."

"Well, there's an officer here to speak with you, but first, there's a very impatient man named Arthur who's been camped outside since you arrived."

Amelia exhaled, relieved. "I want to see him."

"How's your pain?"

"I don't feel much of anything."

"Good," the doctor said, adjusting her IV. "Let's keep it that way."

When the doctor left, the silence pressed down heavy. Amelia stared at the ceiling, her heart pounding. Why did this have to happen? The door burst open. Arthur rushed in, his face drawn and pale. "They wouldn't let me see you." He dropped to his knees beside the bed, taking her face in his hands and kissing her forehead. "You're alright. My God, you're alright."

Amelia's eyes filled. "I don't know what happened."

"It doesn't matter. You're safe now."

He sat beside her, gripping her hand as though afraid to let go.

"Do you know what happened?" she whispered.

Arthur hesitated. "They said you drove straight into the main road. A truck hit your side. The driver said you didn't stop—you just pulled out. He tried to brake but couldn't avoid you."

She blinked, confused. "That's impossible. I hit the brakes."

Before Arthur could answer, Dr. Bird reappeared with a man in uniform. "This is Officer Derry," she said. "He just needs a few moments with you, Miss Levingston."

Arthur stood quickly. "Is this really necessary now?"

"It's alright," Amelia said softly.

Arthur sat again, never releasing her hand.

"Miss Levingston," said the officer, his tone careful, "we believe we know why this happened. Your brake line was cut."

Arthur froze. "What?"

Amelia's blood ran cold. "The man," she whispered.

Arthur leaned closer. "What man?"

"The one at Oak Hall. He took my keys. He— he said he needed to move the car."

Dr. Bird glanced between them. "Amelia, can you slow down? Who are you talking about?"

Her head swam. "Henry. Henry Hyde."

Arthur looked at her, bewildered. "You're sure?"

"I saw him at the university before. And then at your grandmother's. He said he worked there. He took my keys."

Arthur stood, pulling out his phone. "Officer, can we speak outside?"

The officer nodded, and the two men stepped into the hallway, leaving Amelia alone with the rhythmic pulse of the monitors. Her fingers trembled. She could still feel the chill of the rain, the way the brake pedal had sunk beneath her foot. And Kinsey's voice echoed faintly in her mind—*Take care of my family, Amelia.*

She stared up at the ceiling, a tear sliding down her temple. "I will," she whispered.

CHAPTER TWENTY-NINE

TWO WEEKS AFTER THE ACCIDENT, AMELIA STOOD IN THE marble-tiled bathroom of Eloise Kitt's grand home, her left arm still wrapped in a pale plaster cast. The air smelled faintly of turpentine and polished brass. She watched as a team of glaziers lifted the stained-glass masterpiece she and Charlie had designed—the white peacock window—and slid it gently into its frame.

The late morning sun filtered through the glass, igniting the iridescent feathers in hues of sapphire, gold, and pale green. It was as though the room itself had exhaled light. Amelia pressed her good hand against her heart, her breath catching.

Beside her, Charlie stood motionless, his hand clamped over his mouth. Neither dared to speak until the frame was secured. When the final latch clicked into place, both released the breath they'd been holding.

"We did it," Charlie whispered, his voice trembling with pride.

"They did it," Amelia corrected softly, nodding toward the craftsmen. "But yes—we really did."

The window transformed the room, bathing the white marble in a kaleidoscope of soft color. For the first time since her crash,

Amelia felt a weight lift from her chest. The project—the one she'd dreamed about for months—had survived her absence, her pain, her fear.

Charlie clasped his hands together, grinning. "Painters arrive in an hour. I'll stay to oversee the work. When does the aviary get here?"

"Tomorrow," Amelia replied. "Eloise said she wants to help set the finches in herself before the reveal."

"Perfect."

She smiled. "I still can't believe we pulled this together—especially after everything."

Charlie glanced down at her arm, his expression softening. "Neither can I. You scared the hell out of us, Amelia."

"I scared myself," she admitted. "And the fact that they still haven't found him—"

He sighed heavily. "Whoever he was. Hired under a false name, fake references, no record. The police think he vanished the same night."

"There's something connecting him to Nottingham University," Amelia said, her voice low. "It's no coincidence. I saw him there before Oak Hall."

"But why come after you?" Charlie asked, shaking his head. "What did you ever do to anyone?"

Amelia didn't answer. The question hung between them, heavy and unanswerable.

"Amelia?" Eloise's voice carried down the corridor.

Amelia jumped slightly. "No peeking!" she called back.

"I can barely stand it!" Eloise teased.

"One more day! You can wait just one more day."

Eloise appeared in the doorway, radiant as ever in a cream silk blouse and oversized sunglasses. "You sound just like me when I was your age," she said, offering a small laugh before setting down a tray. "Tea. You both need it."

Rosie followed close behind, balancing a second tray with her usual charm. "Here you go, my darlings—fresh from the pot."

Charlie poked his head from the bathroom doorway, delighted. "Did someone say tea?" He accepted a cup from Rosie, the steam fogging his glasses. Amelia bent awkwardly to retrieve her cup, struggling with her sling until Rosie helped her.

"Thank you," Amelia murmured, her cheeks flushed.

"Have you told the twins about the birds yet?" Rosie asked.

Eloise shook her head, eyes gleaming. "Not a word. My husband gets home tomorrow, and I want us all to see it together. You'll be there for the unveiling, won't you?"

"Of course," Amelia said. "But promise me you won't peek. Let the paint dry, let the magic breathe first."

Eloise sighed dramatically, placing a hand to her chest. "Fine. I promise. But you'd better bring Arthur—and we're opening champagne when it's done."

Amelia smiled faintly. "He'd like that."

Eloise's tone softened. "How is he holding up?"

Amelia hesitated. "Stressed. Trying to keep everything together. He's still... processing."

"The man who did it," Rosie asked, "they still haven't found him?"

Amelia shook her head. "No trace. It's as if he vanished into thin air."

Eloise crossed her arms, her brow furrowed. "That's terrifying. You could have—" She stopped herself, her voice tightening. "You're here. That's all that matters."

Amelia exhaled slowly. "I'm grateful every morning that I am."

Charlie, who had been standing quietly in the doorway, turned away suddenly. His shoulders trembled as he wiped his eyes with the back of his hand.

Rosie whispered, "He's such a sensitive man."

"You have no idea," Amelia said, smiling faintly.

Eloise placed a reassuring hand on Amelia's shoulder. "You're strong. Stronger than you think."

Amelia didn't feel strong—not really—but she nodded anyway.

"Where's Arthur today?" Eloise asked.

"At work," Amelia replied. "He's finishing early, around two. He said he'll pick me up here."

"Good," Eloise said. "He needs to see how incredible this is."

Amelia smiled, though she still felt a flicker of unease beneath the surface.

Arthur's day at the university had been long and restless. The hum of students in the corridor, the scuff of shoes on tile, even the chalk squeak on the board—it all felt wrong somehow, as though the world hadn't quite realigned since the accident.

He closed the classroom door behind him and exhaled, rubbing the bridge of his nose. He was halfway down the hall when someone caught his arm.

"Arthur," a familiar voice said.

He turned, startled. "Helena."

She smiled—but it was nervous, forced. "I've noticed you haven't been around much lately. Is everything alright?"

Arthur pulled his arm free, his tone colder than he intended. "Everything's fine. Just dealing with some personal matters."

"You don't have to be so rude," she said sharply.

He stopped, guilt flickering across his face. "I'm sorry. I didn't mean to snap."

Helena tilted her head. "What's happened? Did you and Amelia—?"

"No," he interrupted quickly. "We didn't break up, and we're not going to."

Helena held up her hands in surrender. "Alright, I was only asking."

He hesitated, then sighed. "Amelia was in a terrible car accident. She nearly died."

Helena's expression softened instantly. "Oh my God. Is she—is she alright?"

"She's recovering," Arthur said. His voice cracked slightly. "Her brake line was cut."

Helena froze, color draining from her face. "Cut?"

"Yes. The police confirmed it. They think it was someone who'd been working for my grandmother—hired under a false name. Amelia said she recognized him from here, at the university."

Helena's hand went to her throat. "What did he look like?"

Arthur reached into his jacket and unlocked his phone. "We pulled a still from the security cameras at Oak Hall."

He turned the screen toward her.

Helena's reaction was instant—a small, strangled sound escaped her lips. "My God." Her hand flew to her mouth.

Arthur frowned. "What is it?"

"That's him," she whispered. "Arthur, that's my ex."

Arthur's blood ran cold.

Helena's eyes were wide with terror. "His real name isn't Henry Hyde. It's—" She looked up at him, her voice trembling. "It's not the first time he's done something like this."

CHAPTER THIRTY

THE POLICE STATION SMELLED FAINTLY OF DISINFECTANT AND rain. Outside, the storm that had followed Amelia's accident seemed to have found its echo in the grey drizzle streaking the station's windows. Arthur sat stiffly on a wooden bench beside Helena, the fluorescent lights above them humming faintly. She was dressed impeccably as always, though her eyes looked hollow—shadowed with fatigue, or guilt, or both.

He shifted uncomfortably; his fingers interlocked between his knees. "I still don't understand," he murmured. "Why would he want to harm Amelia?"

Before Helena could answer, a uniformed officer opened a door. "This way, your lordship."

Arthur winced. "Please," he said quietly. "Just Arthur."

The officer nodded, motioning them through to a cramped office lined with file cabinets and half-drunk mugs of tea. They sat opposite his desk while he flipped through a folder brimming with paperwork. The rhythmic tapping of his pen was the only sound.

"So," the officer began, glancing up, "we have the identity of our suspect."

Helena folded her hands carefully in her lap. "His name is

Randolph Hale," she said, her voice calm but tremulous. "He's my ex-boyfriend. When Arthur showed me the photograph, I recognized him instantly."

Arthur tensed. "Then you can explain why he'd do this. Why he'd cut the brakes on Amelia's car."

Helena hesitated, her gaze softening toward him. "Because I told him," she said slowly, "that I was still in love with you."

Arthur's head snapped toward her. The words landed like a slap. The officer's pen stopped moving. Helena's lower lip quivered, but her eyes didn't leave Arthur's. "When I said it, he hit me," she whispered. "He hit me so hard I nearly passed out."

The officer straightened in his chair. "He struck you?"

Arthur turned sharply to her. "He what?"

She nodded, eyes glistening. "At first, he was wonderful—charming, attentive. But he changed. Became controlling, paranoid. I tried to end things, but he wouldn't let me go. He was so possessive it scared me."

Arthur sat back, processing her words, his jaw tightening.

"I should explain," Helena continued softly. "Arthur had proposed to me once."

The officer raised his brows. "Arthur?"

Arthur sighed, pinching the bridge of his nose. "Yes. We were engaged... a long time ago."

Helena looked down. "And I betrayed him. I was seeing Randolph while engaged to Arthur. When Arthur proposed, I panicked. I realized what I was doing—that I was with a good man while throwing myself at something or I should say someone so dangerous. So, I went to end it with Randolph." Her voice trembled as she went on, "Arthur saw us together. Randolph kissed me, and Arthur thought... well, he thought the worst. And that was that." She turned toward Arthur, her eyes filling. "But I did love you. I still do."

Arthur's stomach twisted. He turned toward the officer. "What happens next?" he asked abruptly, eager to move past her confession.

Helena's hand brushed against his beneath the desk, desperate, trembling. He pulled away instantly.

"I tried to leave Randolph after that," she continued, ignoring the rejection. "He followed me everywhere. He'd turn up outside my flat, outside my lectures, even at the market. He'd send letters. When I blocked him, he found new numbers. Two months ago, I finally left for good. I changed my mobile, moved flats. I should have gone to the police then." Her voice broke. "I never thought he'd be capable of this."

The officer looked from one to the other, his expression unreadable. "Are you two currently having an affair?"

Arthur's eyes snapped to him. "No," he said sharply. "Absolutely not. I'm engaged to Amelia Levingston."

Helena gave a brittle little laugh. "Oh? I thought you'd broken that off."

Arthur turned toward her, incredulous. "What on earth would make you think that?"

"Well," she said, feigning innocence, "she hasn't been wearing her ring. Word travels quickly in Nottingham, Arthur."

He stared at her, momentarily speechless. "We are very much engaged."

Before Helena could answer, the officer raised a hand. "Let's stay on track, shall we? Miss Darling, do you have any way to contact Mr. Hale?"

"No," Helena said softly. "He always just appeared. I never knew how he found me."

"Anywhere he might frequent. Friends, family?"

"We used to spend most nights at Ye Old Jerusalem—that pub in the caves near Castle Gate. But lately, I think he's been traveling back and forth to Greece. His brother lives there."

The officer wrote briskly in his notes. "If that's true, he may have already fled the country."

Arthur's frustration bubbled over. "And if he hasn't? What if he's still here? What if he comes after her again?"

The officer sighed. "Then we'll find him, Mr. Bonneville. But right now, we need evidence—camera footage, witness statements, anything to prove intent."

Helena leaned forward, her voice low. "He doesn't need intent. I know how he thinks. He wants Arthur to suffer. He wants him to lose what he loves—the way he lost me."

Arthur froze, her words slicing through the room. He had never hated anyone before, not truly. But the thought of that man—Randolph Hale—touching Amelia's car, knowing Amelia was inside—it ignited something primal in him.

The officer set his pen down and folded his hands. "At least we have a name now. That's a start." He turned to Helena. "Do you wish to pursue a restraining order?"

"I think I should," Helena said softly. She turned to Arthur, her eyes wide and hopeful. "What do you think, Arthur?"

Before he could answer, she reached for his hand again.

"What's going on here?"

The voice sliced through the tension like a blade.

Arthur jerked his hand away and turned. Standing in the doorway, rain-damp hair clinging to her cheeks, was Amelia—pale, fragile, and trembling with disbelief. Rosie stood behind her, arms crossed, her expression fierce.

Arthur's heart stopped. "Amelia."

Helena straightened, smiling faintly—almost smugly.

Amelia didn't move. Her gaze flicked from Helena's hand to Arthur's, then to the officer watching silently behind his desk. "Are we interrupting something?" she asked quietly.

Rosie folded her arms tighter. "Yes, Arthur. Maybe you should explain what exactly *this* is."

Arthur's mind spun. He rose slowly, desperate to speak, but Amelia stepped back. Her eyes were glassy with unshed tears.

"Amelia, please—"

"Don't," she said softly. "Not right now."

Helena sat perfectly still, her hands clasped neatly in her lap, the faintest hint of a smirk ghosting her lips.

Outside, thunder rolled again, shaking the windowpanes.

And in the suffocating silence that followed, the fragile peace between them all—between truth and trust, past and present—shattered completely.

CHAPTER THIRTY-ONE

THE RIDE HOME WAS QUIET AT FIRST. THE WINDSHIELD WIPERS beat a steady rhythm against the drizzle, and neither Arthur nor Amelia seemed ready to speak. The silence between them stretched like a taut string, thin and sharp enough to cut.

When Arthur finally broke it, his voice was calm but strained. "I swear to you, Amelia, nothing happened," he said quickly, almost too quickly, as if rehearsing the words.

Amelia crossed her arms, her cast resting awkwardly in her lap. "It didn't look like nothing," she replied. "From where I was standing, it looked a lot like you were holding hands with your ex at the police station."

He exhaled heavily, his fingers tightening around the steering wheel. "That's what it looked like," he said. "But that's not what it was. She tried to take my hand—I didn't invite it."

"You didn't let go."

Arthur's jaw tensed. He glanced at her before looking back at the wet road ahead. "It doesn't matter."

Amelia turned toward the window; her reflection blurred in the glass. "I think it does matter," she said softly. "It's obvious, Arthur. She's still in love with you."

His tone softened, quieter now. "How did you know?"

Amelia gave a dry laugh, a little bitter. "Give me some credit. I'm not blind."

Arthur slowed the car as they turned into the long, winding drive of The Park House. The mist hung low over the trees, and the familiar silhouette of the estate appeared through the fog— their sanctuary, or at least it used to be. When he brought the car to a stop halfway up the drive, Amelia frowned.

"Why are you stopping?"

He turned toward her, eyes fierce with emotion, and reached across the console to cup her face gently in his hands. Before she could react, he kissed her—firm and desperate, as if trying to silence every doubt with that one act. At first, she resisted, her lips cold against his, but then her resolve melted. When he pulled back, his voice was low and steady. "I love you," he said. "Just you. Don't you know that?"

Amelia searched his face. There was no deceit in those blue eyes—only exhaustion, fear, and something rawer, truer. Love, yes, but also the terror of losing it. "I love you too," she whispered.

Arthur smiled faintly, brushing his thumb along her cheek. "Then trust me," he said. "Part of love—real love—is trust. You must trust me."

Amelia hesitated. Her eyes dropped to her hand, still bare, her fingers tracing the pale indentation where her engagement ring had once been. "Can I have the ring back?" she asked softly.

Arthur's grin was almost boyish. He started the car again, steering up the rest of the drive. "No."

Amelia blinked, startled. "What do you mean, no?"

"I mean no," he said lightly. "I'm planning something special, and you'll just have to trust me."

"Arthur!" She tried to sound annoyed, but a smile was already threatening to betray her. "That's not fair."

"Life rarely is," he teased.

"But I want to be engaged again. I want to wear it. I want people to know. I want you to know."

He glanced at her as they neared the house. "Amelia, you already said yes. That's all I need to know."

"It's not all I need to know," she countered softly. "I want to marry you, Arthur. I'd marry you now if we could. Drive us to the church and I'll say yes all over again."

His laughter filled the car, warm and deep. "We are going to be married, Amelia," he promised. "When the timing is right. You don't really want to walk down the aisle with your arm in a cast, do you?"

She looked at her bandaged arm and smirked. "Why not? It's white—it'll match the dress."

Arthur laughed out loud and placed a hand gently on her lap. "Patience, my love. You were right, you know."

"About what?"

"The proposal." His grin widened. "The bathroom floor wasn't exactly... what did you call it? 'Austen-worthy'?"

Amelia's cheeks turned pink. "That's what I said."

"Well," he said, his voice tender now, "I intend to do just that. Something Austen-worthy. Something beautiful. You deserve that."

Amelia looked out the window at the soft green hills of the estate, the garden blooming wildly in the mist. "Arthur, I don't care about grand gestures," she said. "I care about you. About us."

"I know," he replied gently. "But maybe I care about both."

They pulled up to the front steps, the gravel crunching beneath the tires. Amelia gazed at the ivy-covered façade of The Park House and felt that familiar ache—the house that had once been haunted by loss was now filled with love. Their love. It wasn't perfect, but it was real.

Arthur parked and turned off the engine. For a long moment, neither of them moved. The rain had slowed to a fine drizzle, and the world outside seemed to hold its breath.

Finally, Arthur said, "I'll make this right, Amelia. Everything. I'll protect you, no matter what it takes."

She nodded, her throat tight. "I know you will."

He reached for her hand again, and she let him. They sat there, hands entwined, in the quiet that followed the storm.

That evening, the fire in the library glowed soft and golden. Arthur poured two glasses of wine while Amelia sat curled on the sofa, her cast propped on a pillow. He joined her, draping an arm around her shoulders. For a moment, everything felt normal again—the warmth, the peace, the domestic hum of a home alive with quiet love.

But beneath that calm was something unspoken—a shadow neither wanted to name. Arthur stared into the flames. "I keep seeing her face," he murmured.

"Helena's?"

He nodded. "It's strange. Once upon a time, I loved her. Or thought I did. But now... she feels like another life. Another person's memory. I look at her, and I just feel sorry for her."

Amelia's voice was quiet but steady. "I don't think she wants your pity."

He sighed. "No. She wants something far worse."

Amelia leaned into him. "She wants you back."

He didn't answer.

Outside, a gust of wind rattled the windows. The flames flickered.

Arthur finally turned to her. "I don't want her back," he said firmly. "I just want you. I need you to believe that."

Amelia studied his face—the faint scar near his temple, the worry lines that hadn't been there a year ago. "I do," she whispered. "But she's not done, Arthur. I can feel it."

Arthur kissed her forehead. "Then we'll face her together."

Amelia smiled faintly. "Together."

For the rest of the night, they said nothing more about Helena. But neither of them truly slept.

THE DINING ROOM AT THE PARK HOUSE GLOWED IN CANDLE-light, the kind of warm, honeyed light that softened every edge. A gentle rain brushed against the tall windows, and the scent of roasted chicken lingered in the air.

Arthur carefully sliced Amelia's food for her, the blade scraping delicately against the porcelain plate.

"Thank you," she said, her voice touched with a shy laugh.

Lady Edith smiled across the table. "How's the arm feeling, dear?"

"Itchy," Amelia admitted with a grin. "I have a follow-up in a few days. They'll cut the cast off and do another x-ray. Then I guess they recast it. I'm counting the hours just to have it off for a few minutes so I can get a good scratch session."

Rosie reached for her wine and took a sip. "The cast suits you, though—gives you a tragic-heroine kind of elegance."

Arthur chuckled. "A rather clumsy one, perhaps."

Amelia mock-glared at him, then softened. "Tomorrow's the grand reveal," she said, turning to Lady Edith. "At Eloise's. We're bringing the birds first thing in the morning."

Lady Edith paused, fork in midair. "Birds?" she repeated.

"What on earth are you talking about? I thought you were building a bathroom."

"We did," Amelia said, trying not to laugh.

"Then why are there birds involved?" Lady Edith pressed.

Amelia's grin widened. "My client wanted them. So, I had a massive French armoire refurbished into an aviary. It's going to be breathtaking when it's done."

Lady Edith blinked, as though Amelia had just announced she was opening a zoo. "Birds. In a bathroom," she said flatly.

Rosie leaned in, her voice lilting with excitement. "Mummy, it's brilliant. You'll see. Even *Elle Décor* is coming to photograph it. Amelia's being featured alongside Eloise for the cover. It's a huge deal."

Arthur reached over and brushed Amelia's hand. "I'm so proud of you," he said quietly.

Amelia's heart swelled. "Thank you."

Lady Edith was still frowning, though her tone softened. "I suppose I'll have to see it to understand. Birds in a bathroom. Good heavens."

The mood was light, laughter threading through the air—until a sudden, loud knock echoed through the hall. The laughter died instantly.

They all exchanged glances. "Who could that be at this hour?" Rosie whispered.

Arthur took out his phone and checked the camera feed by the front door. "What on earth?" he muttered, pushing back his chair. He crossed the hall, opened the door, and froze.

Standing on the doorstep, her expression stiff and solemn, was Gran—Lady Newcroft herself—with Barnaby at her side. She held her hands behind her back, her chin raised high in that familiar way that always preceded a lecture.

Barnaby gave her a gentle pat on the shoulder. "Go on, dear," he murmured.

"I'm here to speak with Amelia," Gran said.

Arthur's voice was cautious. "Oh? And why is that?"

She brought her hands forward and revealed a lush bouquet of ivory roses and lavender sprigs, tied neatly with a silk ribbon. "Because I came to apologize," she said.

Arthur hesitated, then smiled faintly. "We're having dinner. You're welcome to join us."

"Smells delicious," Barnaby said cheerfully, stepping inside without invitation.

The dining room went silent as they entered. Rosie half-stood, astonished. "Gran! What are you doing here?"

Gran looked straight at Amelia, the bouquet trembling slightly in her hands. "Amelia, I came here to—"

Barnaby nudged her gently. "Go on."

"To... apologize," she said, each word heavy, as though it cost her dearly to speak to them aloud. "For what happened. For hiring that man. For... all of it."

Arthur glanced at Amelia, unsure what she would say.

Amelia rose slowly from her chair and approached Gran. The flowers smelled like rain and forgiveness. "They're lovely," she said softly, taking them from her. "Thank you. Would you care to join us?"

Gran blinked, visibly thrown. "That's it?" she asked incredulously. "That's all you want to say to me? I hired a man who wanted to kill you."

Amelia met her gaze with calm resolve. "You didn't know. It wasn't your fault."

"It *is* my fault," Gran insisted. "Had I done a proper background check, none of this would have happened."

Lady Edith set her fork down with a clatter. "If you hadn't thrown me out of the house, none of *that* would have happened."

Gran's eyes flashed. "It's not your house to begin with."

"That's enough you two," Barnaby interrupted, his tone firm but kind. "We're not doing this again."

Amelia stepped between them, still holding the bouquet. "What I want," she said gently, "is for all of us to live in peace. Truly. We're going to be family soon. Let's start acting like one."

Arthur reached for her hand. "She's right."

Gran studied them both. "So, you're engaged, then?" Her eyes narrowed at Amelia's bare hand. "Where's the ring?"

Arthur sighed. "Gran, listen to me. Amelia is *the one*. There's no one else for me."

Gran tilted her head. "What happened to Helena?"

The room fell completely silent. Even the fire seemed to still.

Rosie finally broke the tension with an exaggerated groan. "Oh, for heaven's sake! Helena is *history*. Why does everyone keep bringing her up?"

Barnaby raised his glass with a grin. "Here, here!"

Arthur exhaled and gave a small laugh of relief.

"Now," Barnaby continued, cheerfully oblivious to the tension, "let's all sit down as a family and catch up, shall we?"

Arthur pulled out a chair. "Would you like to sit, Gran?"

Gran hesitated, then looked at Amelia. "Only if it's alright with her."

Amelia smiled gently. "Of course. We'd love for you to join us."

Gran nodded once, lips pressed tight, and sat down.

"Are you hungry?" Amelia asked politely.

"Famished," Barnaby said before she could answer. "Gran fired our cook."

"What?" Lady Edith nearly choked on her wine. "Mother, you *must* stop firing people."

"Oh, I didn't just fire the cook," Gran admitted. "I dismissed the entire staff. After what happened with that man, we're having every employee vetted before they return to Oak Hall."

Rosie's jaw dropped. "You're kidding."

Barnaby threw his napkin dramatically over his lap. "Barely survived the interim, I tell you. Your mother's cooking could kill a man faster than that assassin she hired."

"Barnaby!" Gran barked, scandalized.

"It's true, darling," he replied, utterly unbothered.

Rosie and Amelia both burst into quiet giggles.

Gran narrowed her eyes at them. "You think that's funny?"

"I'm *quite* sure I don't know what I ate last night," Barnaby said, entirely straight-faced. "But I certainly can tell you what it *smelled* like."

"Barnaby!" Gran snapped again.

"Burnt rubber," he said solemnly, raising his wine glass. "I swear to you all—it was burnt rubber."

That did it. The table erupted in laughter. Even Gran tried to hold her composure but failed miserably, breaking into an undignified fit of giggles that made her eyes water. Lady Newcroft laughed so hard she had to dab her tears with her napkin. "You're incorrigible," she said, still gasping.

Barnaby grinned proudly. "And you married me anyway."

"Regrettably," Gran teased, but her tone was lighter than it had been in years.

Amelia sat back, her heart swelling as she looked around the table. The flicker of candlelight played across every smiling face—Lady Edith laughing beside her daughter, Rosie wiping her eyes, Arthur grinning so hard he could hardly breathe, and Gran—the formidable Lady Newcroft—laughing freely beside her husband.

This, Amelia thought, *is family.*

Not perfect. Not simple. But real.

Arthur caught her looking at him and smiled softly, reaching under the table to squeeze her good hand. "You alright?" he whispered.

She nodded; her voice barely audible. "Better than alright."

He kissed her cheek, and for that brief, golden moment, everything felt whole again.

After dinner, the rain began again—soft, steady, and peaceful. The candles burned low, and laughter lingered in the air long after the plates had been cleared.

Later, when the others had gone to bed, Amelia stood by the

window holding her bouquet, the faint scent of lavender filling the quiet. She looked out at the dark, wet garden and saw her reflection staring back—calm, content, almost unrecognizable from the frightened woman she had been weeks before.

Arthur came up behind her, wrapping his arms around her waist. "They love you," he whispered against her ear.

She smiled faintly. "Even Gran?"

"Even Gran," he murmured. "Especially Gran."

She turned in his arms and kissed him softly. "Tomorrow's a big day."

"It is," he said, brushing a lock of hair from her face. "You're about to show the world what you can do."

Amelia leaned her head against his chest. "I already have," she whispered. "I found you."

Arthur held her closer, the rain tapping gently against the glass, the warmth of the fire fading into the quiet hum of their shared breath.

For the first time in a long time, peace felt possible—fragile, fleeting, but finally real.

CHAPTER THIRTY-THREE

MORNING SUNLIGHT SPILLED THROUGH THE GLASS ROOF OF Eloise's conservatory, cascading in ribbons across marble and mosaic. The scent of lemon oil and jasmine filled the air as Amelia oversaw the final touches of the project that had consumed her life for months.

The bathroom—or as the *Elle Décor* photographer called it, *"The Aviary of Light"*—gleamed like a painting come to life. The peacock-stained glass window, now radiant in the morning sun, shimmered with jewel-toned brilliance. Pale blues and emerald greens rippled across the walls like water.

At the heart of the room stood the refurbished French armoire, transformed into a grand aviary. Inside, a pair of golden finches fluttered and sang softly. Their song mingled with the hum of voices and the faint click of camera shutters as journalists and stylists filled the space.

Rosie was buzzing about, directing florists and making sure every vase was perfect. "Darling, no, no—that hydrangea is clashing with the marble!" she said, spinning the arrangement half an inch. "Better."

Amelia smiled despite her nerves. Her arm still throbbed

lightly beneath its brace, but the ache felt distant today—muted beneath adrenaline and pride. She stood back, watching her team polish, adjust, and capture.

Arthur leaned against the doorway, watching her with quiet admiration. He was dressed in a soft gray suit, his tie loosened just enough to make him look effortlessly dashing. Their eyes met and he mouthed, *you did it.*

She smiled back, her heart light.

Eloise entered with her twin boys trailing behind, both gasping as they saw the finished room. "Mummy! The birds!" cried one, pressing his nose to the glass.

Eloise's eyes shone with emotion. "Amelia," she said softly, "you've created something extraordinary. It's more beautiful than I could have imagined."

"Thank you," Amelia replied. "I wanted it to feel alive. To feel like peace itself."

"Mission accomplished."

The *Elle Décor* editor, a woman in sharp cream linen, stepped forward. "We've photographed a thousand interiors, but I've never seen anything quite like this. You've brought art and life together. Tell me, where did you find your inspiration?"

Amelia hesitated. The question was simple, but the answer wasn't. She looked at the glass peacock shimmering above them—its feathers glowing in light—and felt a rush of memory. Hospitals. Healing. Starting over. "It came from rebirth," she said finally. "From starting again, even after you think you can't. The peacock is a symbol of renewal, beauty from pain. I think... that's what we all want, in some way."

The editor smiled, touched. "That's going to make a beautiful quote."

Arthur stood quietly behind the camera crew; his expression full of pride. Rosie, meanwhile, was fighting tears with dramatic flair. "Well, now I'm going to cry and ruin my mascara," she sniffed.

Lady Edith and Barnaby arrived later, both impeccably

dressed for the occasion. Lady Edith looked around in astonishment. "My word," she breathed. "You really *did* put birds in a bathroom."

Barnaby grinned, lifting a glass of champagne. "And somehow, it works! Who'd have thought?"

Laughter rippled around the room. Amelia felt lighter than she had in months. The day stretched beautifully. The cameras clicked; the journalists scribbled. Amelia gave interviews beside Arthur, the two of them glowing with quiet joy.

By late afternoon, the guests had gone, the photographers packed up, and the room fell still again. The birds chirped softly under the fading light. Rosie poured herself a final glass of champagne and flopped into an armchair. "Amelia, I think you've officially arrived," she sighed. "Interior design royalty."

"Don't say that," Amelia laughed. "It's just one project."

"One project that's about to go viral," Rosie said, already scrolling through her phone.

Arthur chuckled and kissed Amelia's temple. "You deserve every bit of your success."

"I couldn't have done it without all of you," she said, her voice soft.

They lingered a while longer, basking in the glow of the day. As the sun dipped, they said their goodbyes. Rosie stayed behind to chat with Eloise, while Arthur helped Amelia into her coat. Outside, the air had turned crisp, carrying the scent of rain. "You look tired," Arthur said, brushing a strand of hair from her face.

"I'm good tired," she smiled. "Happy tired."

"Let's go home."

He opened the car door for her, and she sank into the seat with a sigh. The drive back to The Park House was quiet, the countryside fading into twilight. Amelia rested her head against the glass, watching the road curve through fields that glistened with dew.

Arthur reached over and squeezed her hand. "I'm so very proud of you," he said again, softly. "You've come so far."

She smiled faintly. "I still can't believe it's real."

When they arrived home, the house was dark except for the soft glow of the hallway lamp. Lady Edith and Barnaby had gone to bed. Rosie texted that she'd stay overnight at Eloise's.

Arthur hung up his jacket and poured them both a small glass of wine. "To you, Amelia Levingston—artist, survivor, miracle-maker."

She clinked her glass against his. "And to you, Arthur Bonneville—the man who believed in me when no one else did."

They drank, and for a few quiet moments, the world felt still. Then Amelia noticed something on the table. A small box. It hadn't been there before. Wrapped neatly in pale blue paper and tied with a white ribbon, it sat beside the bouquet Gran had brought earlier in the week. "Arthur," she said softly, setting her glass down. "Did you put this here?"

He looked over, puzzled. "No. Why?"

"There's a package."

He frowned and walked over. There was no card. No return address. The wrapping was immaculate—deliberate.

"Maybe a gift from the magazine?" he suggested.

Amelia hesitated. Something about it felt off. "It's not their style," she said.

Arthur examined it closer. "No name," he murmured.

Her heart began to thud in her chest. "Open it."

Arthur tore the ribbon gently and peeled away the paper. Inside was a small velvet box—the kind used for jewelry. For a moment, Amelia thought it might be her ring—the engagement ring she'd been longing to wear again. But when Arthur flipped it open, the air seemed to drain from the room.

Inside was a single **piece of her brake line.**

Arthur froze. "What the hell..."

Amelia stared, her breath catching. The wire was unmistakable.

Her pulse hammered in her ears. Tucked inside the box was a folded note. Arthur unfolded it carefully. One line, written in tight, slanted handwriting:

Next time, I'll drive.

The room felt suddenly smaller, the quiet deafening.

Arthur's expression hardened as he closed the box and took Amelia's trembling hand. "We're calling the police."

She nodded, too shaken to speak. As he reached for his phone, Amelia looked once more at the brake- line and back to her arm. Amelia knew—it wasn't over.

CHAPTER THIRTY-FOUR

Dawn broke slow and pewter over the parkland, the sky the color of an old coin. The Park House woke to motion—murmurs in the hall, the soft thud of careful feet, the burred voices of policemen lowered out of courtesy. Coffee steamed on a side table, mostly ignored.

Arthur stood with Officer Derry in the study, the velvet box open on the desk between them like a dare: coiled wire, the single line of tight, slanted script—*Next time. I'll drive.*

"Gloves, please," Derry reminded a young constable as he indicated the box. "Bag the wire and note separately. I want the note protected for prints and pressure analysis."

Amelia hovered near the hearth, her left arm in its brace, the ache dulled by the colder ache beneath her ribs.

Lady Edith appeared with a robe cinched over her nightdress, hair swept into a disciplined knot that failed to disguise the long night. "Tea," she said simply, pressing a cup into Amelia's good hand and another into Arthur's. When she looked at the velvet box, her mouth thinned. "He likes theatrics."

"Randolph," Arthur said. It wasn't a question.

Derry nodded. "We cannot say *with certainty* until the lab finishes, but the presentation is... targeted. "He wants to be seen."

"He's been seen enough," Arthur answered, too sharply. He caught himself, drew a breath. "What happens now?"

"Alarms, more cameras—already scheduled, I know," Derry said. "We'll add nightly patrols along the lane for the week and notify the county team to widen perimeter checks. If anything else appears—gift, letter, a scrap of ribbon—you call us first. Do not open, do not touch."

Amelia stared into her tea, its tiny constellations of steam. "He wants to scare us."

Something in the room softened—Lady Edith's hand settled at the base of Amelia's neck, a mother's wordless benediction. Arthur's jaw eased; the line between fury and fear blurred into something fiercer. Derry closed his notebook. "There's one more thing. Miss Darling—Helena—filed for the restraining order. She also delivered a detailed timeline of Randolph's habits. It's... helpful."

Amelia's eyes flicked to Arthur's, and for the briefest moment the air rippled with the old, raw awkwardness of that triangle. He met her look directly. "She did the right thing," he said.

"She did," Amelia agreed, and the truth of it, spoken aloud, seemed to drain a pocket of tension from the house.

They walked Derry and his team out to the door. The new gate—stubborn and black, newly locked each night—gleamed wet with dew. Beyond it, the long drive lay empty, but the hedgerows seemed to listen.

"Stay reachable," Derry said, offering Amelia a card and Arthur a look that was almost a vow. "We'll be in touch after the lab reports."

The door closed. Silence held for a beat and then Rosie's voice descended from the landing with the airy drama of a stage cue. "Is it safe to come down or shall I continue barricading myself with throw pillows?"

"Come down," Arthur called, the ghost of a smile surfacing.

Rosie came barefoot, cardigan thrown over satin pajamas, hair braided like a Rupunzel. She clocked the velvet box, the thinness of Amelia's mouth, the guarded brightness of Arthur's eyes, and veered to wrap Amelia in a hug that was soft and noisily perfumed.

"Disgraceful," Rosie said into her shoulder.

"He won't win." Amelia murmered.

"No," Rosie agreed. "We won't let him."

Arthur moved into the practical. "Cameras are being installed this afternoon. I'm picking up a keypad lock for the mudroom. The gate stays closed unless someone is expected."

"And a rather marvelous guard dog," Rosie added, brightening. "We need a wolfhound. Or two. Three would be chic."

"We're not getting three wolfhounds," Arthur said, deadpan.

Lady Edith considered. "One," she allowed, surprising them all. "We shall name him... George."

"*We?*" Arthur asked, but it was smiling now, the house released from the vise.

By midmorning, the project's glow had resumed its gentle radiance, warming the chill Randolph had tried to cast. *Elle Décor's* online teaser had gone live at dawn: a carousel of photographs from Eloise's bathroom—light flung across marble, the jeweled peacock, the armoire-aviary shimmering like a fairy tale. The caption quoted Amelia:

"The peacock is rebirth—beauty from pain."

Rosie ran a triumphant commentary from the breakfast table, where she had colonized the end with two mobiles, one laptop, and a cappuccino. "You're up eight thousand followers since six a.m. The comments are a shrine.

Amelia sat opposite with her planner open, pencil hovering over a growing list. The words *pub refresh for Wendy* held a tidy underline, a promise she'd made to Betsy and herself alike. A sketch bloomed in the margin—arched wood, a new bar curve, booths softened with velvet, a small stage for acoustic nights. *Harry's, remade for Wendy.*

Arthur came in from the mudroom carrying a box of glossy-black camera hubs. "Sayers is outside to wire the exterior first. He'll ring for me if he needs to come through your office."

"Put one on the solarium," Amelia said automatically. "And the library windows that face the lane. The back garden gate, too."

He paused, taking her in. "I will."

She found his hand with her good one and squeezed. "I'm fine."

"You're brave," he corrected, and kissed her palm.

Lady Edith traversed the hall in a navy skirt and field jacket, the brisk air of a woman with a list of her own. "I'm off to visit Betsy and to drop off scones because that is what one does when one cannot cook."

"You *can* cook mummy," Rosie said loyally.

"I can *order,*" Lady Edith replied, gathering her gloves. "Which, I assure you, is a superior skill in times of crisis." She kissed Amelia's hair, squeezed Arthur's arm, and swept out the door.

The house quieted into industry. The cameras went up with tidy efficiency: discreet eyes at the eaves, a neat monitor in the study. Arthur and the installer vanished and reappeared, the thrum of new tech joining the old tick of hall clocks. In the library, Amelia set out finish samples for the pub and pieced together the bones of a timeline—demolition in stages so the bar could remain open, a paint cure scheduled around live music nights. She texted Charlie: *Meet me tomorrow at the pub at 9? Walkthrough with Wendy and Betsy. Bring tape and your optimism.*

Always, he wrote back. *Proud of you for yesterday. Call if you wobble.*

She smiled at the term—Kinsey's word, then Arthur's, now Charlie's—and felt a steadiness settle. She could feel Randolph prowling the edges of their life, but he did not own the center of it. She did not have to live there with him.

Her mobile pinged. A message from Eloise: *The finches are singing. The twins have named them Fig and Fable. We adore you. Drinks soon?*

Soon, Amelia wrote back. *Thank you for trusting me.*

Another ping. Helena. She'd sent only three words: *I'm truly sorry.*

Amelia stared, feeling no heat, only a clear, cool boundary. She typed: *For the police file: if you receive anything odd—box, letter, ribbon—call them. And please, don't contact me again.* She hovered a second and hit send. The phone stayed quiet.

"Done?" Arthur asked softly from the doorway, as if he'd heard the hinge of that decision.

She looked up. "Done," she said.

Rosie entered the room, "Eloise asked again, about the job. The touring, the shows. She wants an answer by Friday."

"How do you feel about it?" Amelia asked.

Rosie turned the question in her hands like a coin. "Hungry," she said at last. "For something that's mine." She looked at Arthur. "But not at the cost of disappearing."

"Then say yes with limits," Arthur answered. "Make it work for you. That's business."

"You're right." Rosie nodded. "I'm going to say yes—*with limits.*"

She ran off excitedly off to make the phone call. Amelia and Arthur grinned at each other. "You want to go somewhere with me for a breather?" Arthur asked.

There they were together. Standing in front of the Major Oak in Sherwood forest. Arthur's favorite place in the world. Amelia leaned into him and they both sighed. "I needed this." Arthur shared.

"I need this too." Amelia sighed. "Too much drama."

"I'm barely hanging on right now. I just need them to catch

him, or maybe we should all just leave for a while. Just until it's safe again."

"You can't do that to your students," Amelia said.

He turned to face her. "I need to be there to protect you."

"You can't always be there and you will just have to accept that." Amelia leaned her head into his and kissed him sweetly.

Amelia noticed how tired he looked, faded, and his facial hair was growing longer and his shoulders slouched heavily. She leaned in and gave him a one armed hug. He held her back. They stood like that for minutes together. As if this hug was the cure for everything. He whispered, "I just want to run away with you."

"If that's what you want Arthur, I'll go anywhere with you. Let's just jump on a plane and disappear."

He let go and shook his head, "Amelia, I love you. Our time is coming."

"I can't wait." She grinned.

He took her good hand and they walked back. Unspoken thoughts traded between the both of them as they traveled their path together back to their car.

One thing was clear, they were ready for a new chapter to their lives, and were going to be together forever.

CHAPTER THIRTY-FIVE

MORNING ARRIVED WITH A POLITE KNOCK INSTEAD OF A BANG. The Park House breathed out the night in ribbons of pale light across the Persian runner, as if exhaling relief. A kettle hissed. Somewhere down the corridor a radio murmured the shipping forecast in a voice so calm it felt like prayer.

Amelia woke to the smell of toast that was, mercifully, not burnt, and found Arthur already dressed, hair damp, sleeves rolled, a domestic Roman general marshaling teacups and marmalade. Her left arm—still in its slimmer, lighter, prison of plaster—itched along the elbow crease. She flexed her fingers and winced, then smiled to show she could.

"Good morning, beautiful," Arthur said, placing a cup where her good hand would find it.

"Good morning," she answered.

Rosie drifted in wearing a cream sweater and an alarming amount of lip gloss for eight in the morning. She carried a stack of post and a tablet pressed to her chest like a shield. "Status report," she announced, sliding into a chair. "Gate—locked. Guards—swapped at four. Cameras—still blinking little red eyes at the yew walk. And this—" she tapped the tablet "—is going to make you both scream."

Arthur paused mid-butter. "We prefer coffee before screaming."

"Fine. Sip. Now look." She turned the screen toward them.

It was the *Elle Décor* homepage. " 'Nottingham's' New Secret" read the headline, a little breathless, the way magazines always were when they discovered something already beloved by everyone involved. Beneath it: Eloise in her new robe, Teddy with his casual, absurd star-smile, and a gleam of copper that made the bathroom look like it had been dipped in sunrise. The white peacock window bloomed behind them, luminous. For a heartbeat Amelia forgot about knives, and gates, and feathers tucked inside wardrobes. Her chest lifted.

"They ran it early I guess this months cover there was some sort of scandal between their star and a politician so they pushed this way up," Rosie said, practically vibrating with triumph. "The print issue ships tomorrow, but the teaser's live now."

Arthur leaned over Amelia's shoulder. "Congratulations Amelia. Look what you've made."

Amelia felt herself going a little watery. Lady Edith appeared in the doorway in a silk scarf and pearl studs, the portrait of a woman who had once relied on staff and now relied on herself— and had survived it. "I hear celebratory sounds," she said. "Please tell me there are celebratory carbs to match."

"There are," Arthur promised, lifting the toast rack like a trophy.

They ate and admired. On screen, the finches were a whisper of motion within their gilded armoire, rosy beaks like punctuation. The copy was kind—florid in places, yes, but it understood the central trick: make magic feel inevitable. Amelia scrolled, her good hand steady on the trackpad. A behind-the-scenes carousel sat at the bottom—stylist tags, gratitude captions, little hearts multiplying in real time. Rosie stopped chewing. "Wait."

"What?" Amelia asked, still smiling.

"Go back one."

Amelia swiped. The frame rewound to a shot of the copper tub being buffed. A stylist had posted it to her Stories, and the magazine had re-shared it: a cheerful, careless square no one would study except the people inside it.

Rosie pointed—not at the tub, not at the stylist, but at the window. "There."

Reflected in the lower corner of a pane—small, distorted by lead lines, but undeniable—stood a figure in a dark hoodie, head tipped down, phone in hand. There had been only four of them in the bathroom that day—Amelia, Charlie, the photographer, and his assistant. None of them wore a hoodie. The house seemed to contract, as if it too had spotted the smudge.

Arthur set his toast down with exaggerated care. "It could be someone in the hall," he offered. "A builder passing."

Amelia knew better. The door had been shut because they were handling the birds; she had insisted on it. A coldness tracked up her spine, not sharp like fear but low and resolute, the way water finds the quickest path downhill.

She took a screenshot. "I'll send it to Officer Derry."

Rosie recovered first, shouldered up next to Amelia and zoomed the image until the pixels broke. "If he wanted to be seen, he'd have stepped into frame," she muttered. "This is worse. He wanted to be almost seen."

Arthur's jaw tightened, the muscle ticking like a metronome. He reached for Amelia's hand, found it, held it. "We do not let him own this," he said quietly. "It's your work. Your triumph."

Lady Edith was very still, taking them all in. "I'll go into town," she said briskly. "Betsy asked me to look at tiles, and I promised her I would. Rosie, will you come?"

"Of course, Mummy."

"Good," Edith continued, already slipping into her coat. "And we'll pick up twenty copies of the magazine on the way."

"Twenty?" Arthur blinked.

"In this family," Lady Edith said, "we frame joy."

At Amelia's office, the bell over the door pinged shyly as Amelia nudged it with her hip. Charlie was already there, elbows deep in a box of brass hardware that smelled like warm pennies.

"Did you see?" he called, voice bouncing. "Look—look—" He held up his phone as if the internet might have crashed without him. "They used the shot with the window dead center. I could cry."

"You did almost cry yesterday over the grouting," Amelia reminded him, smiling.

He grinned back, then sobered when he saw her face. "What happened."

"Nothing, and also something." She told him, quick and lean, about the reflection. While she spoke, he fitted a latch into his palm and closed his fingers around it like a prayer.

"Officer Derry?" he asked.

"I sent it. He's looping in the digital team at the paper. They can pull metadata, timestamps, location tags..." She shrugged. "He said it's thin, but it's something."

Charlie nodded once. "We keep going," he said, as if reciting a creed. "That's what we do. Oh, and Betsy want's to reschedule the pub visit for a couple more days."

"Okay great," Amelia said.

That morning was busy, Amelia answered twenty seven emails, booked the tiler Betsy had liked, and drafted a gentle, brave proposal for the pub—Harry's beams kept bare, Betsy's chair in its same corner, Wendy's new menu framed with a botanical print that looked suspiciously like one of Barnaby's roses. She drank a coffee that went cold and then another that stayed hot long enough to help. When she flagged, she opened the Elle piece again and let the peacock blaze her awake.

Around noon, her phone buzzed. *Unknown number.* She stared at it until it stopped.

A minute later it buzzed again. *Rosie:* **Answer. It's the photographer.**

Amelia exhaled and called back.

"Amelia," the photographer said without preamble, sounding both exhilarated and wrung out. "Congratulations. The comments are bonkers."

"Thank you," she said. "And also…"

"I know," he said, tone changing. "The reflection. I've scrubbed through all the raw. There's a four-minute period where a shadow crosses the glass and then—poof—gone. We were resetting the light and I was arguing with Teddy about whether finches count as talent. Door was shut. I swear to you. No one came in."

Her heart did something complicated—fear and fury and a flicker of dark admiration for the audacity of it. "Send Officer Derry everything," she said.

"Already did."

"Thank you," she told him, and meant it.

When she hung up, she let herself put her head on the desk. The wood smelled like orange oil and she pressed her forehead there, steadied herself, then lifted again. Keep going. The bell pinged. Wendy walked in, hair pulled back, cheeks pink from the wind. She carried a paper bag that breathed warm. "I brought sausage rolls," she said, and smiled in a way that told Amelia the smile had been chosen on purpose. "Betsy is so excited about the pub. She keeps calling it 'our project' and then pretending she doesn't."

Amelia laughed and then—because the house had taught her the economy of tenderness—stood and hugged her friend. Wendy's shoulders were still their new shape, braced against the world, but they softened under Amelia's arm. "How are you?" Amelia asked.

"Better today," Wendy said. "Grief's a trickster. Yesterday a crate of oranges made me cry because Harry hated oranges. Today the bar top made me cry because he loved polishing it. So." She lifted the bag. "Rolls."

They sat, and ate, and made a list on the back of a delivery invoice: paint chips, framed photographs, a corner shelf for

Manish's comic when he visited. Wendy watched Amelia's pen move, the quick, confident hand of a woman who'd built a life out of making other lives more beautiful.

"I saw the feature," Wendy said softly. "It's... good for the soul, isn't it? Seeing something made well."

"It is," Amelia said. Then, because Wendy was one of the few she allowed into the darker rooms of her mind, she added, "There was a... thing. In the reflection."

Wendy didn't flinch. "Do I need to come sleep over," she asked, half-joking, "and brandish a rolling pin at the windows?"

Amelia smiled. "We have guards who are less wobbly with pastry."

"Still." Wendy rested her hand over Amelia's a moment. "He doesn't get to steal the good bits."

"No," Amelia agreed. "He doesn't."

At the university, Helena sat very straight at her desk, the blinds half-closed against a sky the color of pewter. She had filed the restraining order. She had given her statement. She had told the truth in a room that smelled like dry paper and old men, and she had watched Arthur turn his ring in nervous circles, though there was no ring there to turn. She had told herself she was done lying to herself. It was not a heroic feeling. It was a clean one.

Her phone pinged with an email from the department: *Faculty meeting moved to Friday.* Beneath it a second ping, from a private address with no name. She stared at it for a long time, a low animal part of her already knowing, then clicked.

You always did love a storybook ending, the email read. No signature. No attachment. Just a link. Against her better judgment she pressed it.

The link led to the *Elle Décor* piece.

Helena stared at her reflection in the laptop screen. She

looked pale and very tired and exactly like a woman who had made a series of bad bargains and wanted to stop. She closed the lid.

"What a long day" Amelia exhaled.

Amelia curled under a blanket on the sofa while Rosie read comments aloud with theatrical relish. The finches were "poems with wings." The peacock window was "like bathing inside a dream." There were too many heart emojis, but that was modern affection and Amelia accepted it.

Just as everyone started to relax a loud knock was at the door. "Now who could that be?"

Arthur showed himself and spoke, There is a patrol guard at the gate. They must have let whoever it is in.

"Check the cameras," Lady Edith reminded him.

Arthur made his way to the door while checking the camera's with his phone. From worry to happiness he opened the door.

"Who is it?" Amelia called out.

Moments later the door closed and Arthur appeared with a giant bouquet of flowers. It was outrageously large and adored with peacock feathers. "Oh my goodness," Amelia said.

Arthur set it down and handed the card to her. Inside it said, *"Congratulations on all your success. Let's chat about your next project, Our London residence and Teddy's studio.- Eloise"*

"So, what does it say?" Rosie asked.

"Let's just say, I think Charlie and are going to need to start hiring more people because we are expanding to London."

CHAPTER THIRTY-SIX

THE STUDIO WAS HUMMING AGAIN. AFTER WEEKS OF HOSPItals, inquiries, and restless nights, it finally felt alive—alive in that comfortable, ordinary way that made Amelia's heart ache with relief. Morning light poured through the tall windows, casting golden patterns over the tables where sketches, fabric swatches, and teacups balanced in delicate chaos.

Charlie stood at the drafting table, one pencil tucked behind his ear and another twirling between his fingers, the picture of quiet concentration. Rosie was perched on the edge of the worktable, scrolling through client emails on her phone while absently humming along to an old Fleetwood Mac song playing through the Bluetooth speaker.

For the first time in a long time, Amelia felt like herself again.

She sipped her tea, resting her still-healing arm carefully against her side. "I swear, I've missed this sound," she said softly, smiling.

Rosie looked up. "What sound?"

"This," Amelia gestured around—the scribbling of pencils, the faint rustle of tracing paper, the music, the life. "It's the sound of things coming together."

Charlie grinned without looking up. "And the smell of varnish, glue, and impending deadlines."

"Exactly," Amelia said with a small laugh.

It was a comfort she hadn't realized she needed. The ordinary rhythm of creation, the companionship, and the quiet satisfaction of work—it was all a kind of healing. For a little while, it allowed her to forget about police interviews, security gates, and sleepless nights haunted by questions with no answers.

The bell above the front door jingled. A deliveryman stepped inside, holding a wide glass vase filled with the most exquisite arrangement Amelia had ever seen—white roses, gardenias, and pale pink peonies, their fragrance spilling into the air like a sigh.

"For Amelia Levingston," he announced, smiling as he set them down.

Amelia blinked. "For me?"

Rosie's eyes widened. "More flowers? From who?"

The deliveryman produced a cream-colored envelope tied with a satin ribbon and handed it to her. "No card on the outside, ma'am. But he said you'd know."

Charlie leaned over the flowers, inhaling. "Oh, he's good. These are definitely not the supermarket kind."

Amelia untied the ribbon and opened the note carefully. The handwriting was unmistakable—strong, elegant, and distinctly Arthur's.

"Meet me at my favorite tree at one."
—A.

Her breath caught.

Rosie's hand flew to her mouth. "Oh my God."

Charlie dropped his pencil. "That's it. That's *the* note."

Amelia stared down at it, her heart thudding. There was no address, no time—just that one simple line. But she didn't need more. She knew exactly where he meant.

Sherwood Forest.

The Major Oak.

It was their place. Where they had walked hand in hand on one of their first weekends together, before the chaos and tragedy and family entanglements, before the weight of titles and expectations. It was there, beneath that ancient canopy, that Arthur had looked at her with a kind of quiet awe and said, *"This is the first place I've felt at peace since my brother died."*

The trees had indeed remembered them.

Rosie spun around, beaming. "Amelia! He's going to propose!"

Amelia blinked out of her reverie. "What?"

Charlie nodded fervently, joining in the excitement. "Of course, he is! Flowers, secret note, their *place*—it's classic Arthur."

Rosie fanned herself with a fabric swatch. "Oh, this is going to be perfect. Sherwood Forest? The Major Oak? Can you even imagine?"

Amelia tried to laugh, but her voice came out shaky. "You two are ridiculous."

Charlie pointed his pencil at her. "Admit it. You think so too."

She looked down at the note again. There was no denying how her heart fluttered. "Maybe," she said softly.

Rosie clasped her hands dramatically. "We have to plan what you're going to wear."

"Rosie—"

"No arguments. This is your engagement day!"

Amelia smiled, shaking her head, but inside she felt that bubbling, nervous excitement—the kind she hadn't felt since the day Arthur first kissed her in the rain. It was terrifying and wonderful all at once.

Charlie started pacing, muttering like a stage director. "We need something romantic but comfortable. You can't exactly hike through the woods in heels."

"Charlie," Amelia laughed, "I'm not hiking up a mountain, I'm walking through Sherwood."

"Still," he said, waving a hand. "Soft hair, minimal jewelry, that cream blouse you wore to the Nottingham showcase—it was very *English-rose-meets-fairytale.*"

Rosie clapped. "Perfect! And bring a wrap. It's chilly in the evenings."

They were both unstoppable now, like two happy conspirators. Amelia gave in to their enthusiasm, feeling the tension of the past weeks lift just a little.

By ten, the studio had erupted into something halfway between a workday and a celebration. Charlie was whistling as he worked, Rosie had put on an upbeat playlist, and Amelia caught herself glancing at the clock more than once.

Every tick felt like an echo of her heartbeat.

When the afternoon light began to fade, Rosie stepped beside her, touching her arm gently. "You're glowing, you know that?"

"Am I?"

"You are. You've been through so much, Amelia, and somehow... you're still shining."

Amelia swallowed a lump in her throat. "It's because I'm finally seeing the other side of it all. The good part."

Rosie nodded, her voice softening. "You deserve the good part."

Charlie peeked up from behind his drafting table. "And he deserves you, which is saying something."

She laughed, wiping a tear from the corner of her eye. "Oh stop, you'll ruin my makeup."

Rosie grabbed her bag. "Alright, that's it. You're leaving early. Go home, get ready, and don't come back until you have a ring on that finger."

Amelia pretended to protest, but she was already reaching for her coat. "You two are incorrigible."

"That's our charm," Charlie said.

Rosie pointed toward the door dramatically. "Go get your happily ever after, darling."

Amelia hugged them both before stepping outside into the late afternoon sun. The sky was streaked with pink and gold, and a light breeze stirred the edge of her coat as she walked toward her car.

For a moment she simply stood there, breathing it in—the world, the scent of flowers still clinging to her, and the promise of what waited among the ancient trees.

The drive to Sherwood was calm, familiar. The winding road through the forest seemed to welcome her back, each turn bringing with it a hundred memories—of laughter, of stolen kisses, of Kinsey's voice in her heart reminding her to be brave.

When she reached Sherwood forest, she parked and stepped out slowly, the scent of damp leaves filling the air. The late sun filtered through the massive branches like stained glass, soft and golden. The forest felt alive, watching, listening. Arthur's vehicle wasn't in the parking lot but she was to eager to wait. She nervously got out of the car and begin walking the long trail toward the Major Oak, her heels crunching on the gravel. Her breath came in shallow, nervous bursts.

She smiled faintly and stopped to brush her hand over the rough bark of nearby tree. The wind stirred, carrying a soft whisper through the canopy. Somewhere far off, a bird called out, and the forest seemed to hold its breath.

Amelia turned toward the sound of approaching footsteps on the path. Her heart lifted.

CHAPTER THIRTY-SEVEN

THE RAIN HAD BEGUN TO FALL SOFTLY AGAINST THE STUDIO windows when the bell above the front door jingled. Rosie barely looked up from her desk, her glasses sliding down her nose as she reviewed a design draft. Charlie was hunched over a stack of invoices, muttering about supplier delays. The atmosphere was quiet, routine—until a voice startled them both.

"Hello?"

Rosie blinked up. "Arthur?"

Arthur Bonneville stood just inside the doorway, tall and polished as ever but with an unsettled look in his eyes. His hair was damp from the drizzle outside, his navy coat flecked with droplets.

"Good afternoon," he said, forcing a small smile. "I came to take Amelia to lunch, but her car's not outside. Is she in the back?"

Rosie straightened, confused. "Her car's not—wait." She exchanged a puzzled glance with Charlie. "Arthur, she left here well over an hour ago."

He frowned. "Left? Where did she go?"

Charlie set his papers down. "To meet you."

Arthur stared at them, unblinking. "To meet me?"

"Yes!" Rosie said, laughing a little. "Don't act surprised—she was absolutely glowing when she left. You sent her flowers this morning, remember?"

"Flowers?" His voice sharpened slightly.

Charlie gestured to the empty vase on the counter. "Big bouquet. Roses, gardenias, the works. Beautiful, really. They came with a note.

Rosie smiled, oblivious to the creeping unease that had started to shadow Arthur's face. "It was so romantic, Arthur. Honestly, we all thought you were going to—"

Arthur read the note and the color left his face. He stepped back as if struck. "No," he whispered. "No, I didn't send this."

For a heartbeat, no one spoke. The only sound was the rain against the windows.

Charlie frowned. "Wait, what do you mean you didn't send it?"

Arthur looked between them, disbelief twisting into dread. "I never sent flowers. I didn't write any note. I haven't spoken to her since last night." Rosie's chair scraped loudly against the floor as she stood. "Who delivered them?" Arthur demanded.

"Just a courier," Charlie stammered. "Young, dark hair. Said the flowers were from you. Amelia opened the note, smiled, and said she knew where to go."

Arthur pressed a trembling hand to his forehead. "Dear God."

Rosie's voice cracked. "Arthur, what's going on?"

He didn't answer. He was already piecing it together in his mind—the false employee at Oak Hall, the man calling himself Henry Hyde, the one Amelia said she recognized from the university. A man who had taken her keys, vanished without a trace.

It all came rushing together in a sickening flash.

"It's him," Arthur said quietly. "The man who cut her brakes. He's setting her up."

Rosie's hand flew to her mouth. "Oh my God."

Charlie bolted for his phone. "We'll call her—"

He dialed Amelia's number, put it on speaker. The line rang once. Twice. A third time. Then her voicemail picked up.

Rosie tried next, her hands shaking. No answer.

Arthur was already moving. He snatched his car keys from his coat pocket, voice sharp and focused now. "She's gone to Sherwood Forest. To the Major Oak. That's where she'll be."

"Arthur," Rosie said, panic in her voice, "if this man's there—"

"I'm calling the police." He dialed with trembling fingers, his voice low but steady when the dispatcher answered. "This is Arthur Bonneville. My fiancée has been lured out of Nottingham under false pretenses. I believe she's in danger. Sherwood Forest—near the Major Oak. Yes, I'll meet officers at the entrance."

He ended the call, turned toward the door—but Rosie and Charlie were already grabbing their coats.

"You're not going alone," Rosie said firmly.

"You shouldn't come," Arthur warned.

Charlie threw on his jacket. "Don't argue with us, Arthur. She's family."

Arthur hesitated for a fraction of a second, then nodded. "Fine. But stay behind me once we're there."

They locked the studio and ran through the rain together, puddles splashing underfoot as they reached Arthur's car.

The tires screeched as he pulled away from the curb, windshield wipers slicing across the glass in frantic rhythm. Rosie sat in the backseat clutching her phone, redialing Amelia over and over. Charlie leaned forward from the passenger seat; eyes fixed on the road ahead.

Arthur's jaw was set like stone, his knuckles white around the steering wheel. "He's been watching her. Waiting."

"Arthur," Charlie said carefully, "you don't know that."

The rain fell harder, streaking the windows in gray sheets. The car sped through winding roads and open countryside, the forest drawing closer with every passing mile.

Rosie whispered from the back, "She's not answering, Arthur."

"Keep trying."

They passed the old sign for Sherwood, and the road narrowed beneath the thick canopy of trees. The air grew darker, heavier.

The sound of the rain changed as it hit the leaves overhead—a thousand quiet heartbeats in the dark.

When they reached the small gravel clearing near the trailhead, Arthur slammed the car into park. His eyes swept the lot—and then he saw it.

Amelia's car.

It was pulled over to the side, the driver's door closed, headlights off and Amelia was nowhere in sight.

Rosie gasped. "Oh no. No, no, no."

"That's Helena's Car." Arthur noticed it parked in the back corner.

"Why would she be here." Charlie said.

"Why?" He thought a moment and then realized in fear... "He's going for both of them."

Arthur stepped out into the rain, shouting her name. His voice echoed through the forest, fading into the distance. "AMELIA!" No reply. Only the rustle of leaves and the low groan of wind through the ancient branches. He turned back to Charlie and Rosie, his face pale but determined. "Stay here and wait for the police. The will be here any minute."

Charlie shook his head. "Not a chance. We're coming."

Arthur didn't waste time arguing. He started down the muddy path, his heart pounding so hard he could feel it in his throat. The forest swallowed them quickly—the light dimming, the sound of rain muffled by the thick canopy.

"Arthur, slow down!" Rosie called.

"She's here somewhere," he said, his voice breaking. "She's here."

Another distant sound—faint, metallic—echoed through the trees.

Charlie froze. "Did you hear that?"

Arthur did. It was the sound of something shifting, something unnatural in the rhythm of the forest.

Then—silence again.

Arthur's phone rang. He grabbed it instantly. "Yes?"

"This is Officer Derry. We're in route to your location now, sir. Please stay where you are."

"She's somewhere near the Major Oak," Arthur said breathlessly. "I'm not leaving her."

"Stay on the line," the officer commanded, but Arthur was already moving again.

The rain thickened, running down his face like tears. The deeper they went, the heavier the air felt—as though the forest itself was holding its breath. They reached the clearing where the great oak stood, massive and ancient, its twisted branches stretched out like arms. The earth beneath it was slick and dark.

Arthur slowed, scanning the shadows. "Amelia?"

No answer.

He took another step forward. His boot hit something soft in the mud—a scarf. Amelia's.

His stomach dropped. He crouched, lifting it with shaking hands.

Then, faintly, from somewhere beyond the tree line, came a sound that froze them all in place. A woman's voice. Calling for help.

Arthur's eyes widened. "That's her."

He started running.

CHAPTER THIRTY-EIGHT

THE AIR IN SHERWOOD FOREST HUNG HEAVY WITH MIST. RAIN trickled through the canopy and gathered in soft rivulets along the winding path. Amelia tightened her coat around her shoulders, stepping carefully over the muddy roots that lined the trail.

Despite the gray clouds gathering overhead, she felt a rush of excitement. Arthur's note had been brief, but she'd understood its meaning immediately. They would meet at The Major Oak. The idea that he'd chosen that spot to surprise her filled her heart with warmth. She could almost see him there now, waiting beneath the enormous branches, smiling that quiet, knowing smile of his.

She followed the path deeper into the woods, the rain coming faster now. The few hikers she passed were already heading back toward the car park, pulling up their hoods and laughing as they escaped the downpour. Her shoes were damp, her hair starting to curl from the moisture, but she didn't care. She'd been through worse. A little rain wasn't going to stop her from meeting the man she loved.

As the forest grew quieter, she finally caught sight of the

clearing up ahead—and the towering, ancient silhouette of the Major Oak. Its enormous limbs reached outward like something out of a dream.

And nearby it, a figure stood.

Her heart leapt.

"Arthur!" she called, her voice carrying across the clearing.

The figure didn't move.

Amelia laughed softly, mistaking his stillness for theatrics. "You're not going to make me walk all this way in the rain just to—"

She stopped.

Something was wrong.

As she drew closer, the figure's posture shifted, the shadows pulling back just enough for her to see his face. It wasn't Arthur.

It was *him.*

Her breath caught in her throat.

He smiled faintly—that same unsettling smile she remembered from the driveway at Oak Hall. His dark hair was plastered against his forehead from the rain. In his right hand gleamed the unmistakable edge of a knife.

Amelia's feet froze to the ground. "What... what are you doing here?"

"Waiting for you," he said calmly, his voice low and even. "You got my note."

Her pulse thudded in her ears. "You sent that?"

"Of course, I did. You didn't think Arthur was that romantic, did you?"

Her stomach turned. "Why are you doing this?"

"Because" he said, stepping closer, "Arthur Bonneville has taken everything from me. My future. My love. My name. And now he'll know what it feels like to lose *her.*"

"Please," she whispered. "You don't have to do this."

Before he could answer, a new voice echoed from behind them. "Stop!"

Both turned sharply. A figure emerged from the trees—Helena, soaked through from the rain, her coat clinging to her frame. She looked terrified.

"Randolph!" she shouted, her voice trembling. "Leave her out of this! She's done nothing to you."

He turned toward her, his eyes cold. "You came."

"I got the message," she said shakily. "You said you wanted to talk. I thought..." Her voice broke. "I thought you wanted to fix things."

He laughed under his breath—a cruel, humorless sound. "Fix things? You left me, Helena for him. You humiliated me. And now you're protecting *her?*"

He pointed the large knife toward Amelia, who stumbled backward, nearly slipping in the mud. Helena stepped forward instinctively, placing herself between them. "Randolph, listen to me," she said, her hands raised. "You don't want to do this. This isn't you."

"Oh, it's exactly me," he hissed. "Because of *him*—I lost everything. You, my job, my reputation. He gets to have his grand house, his perfect fiancée, his noble title. And I get nothing."

"You're sick," Helena said.

He pressed the knife into Amelia's back, forcing her upright. "Walk."

Amelia gasped as the blade nicked her coat.

"Randolph, please!" Helena begged. "Take me instead!"

"Move," he ordered. "Both of you."

They climbed the small rise behind the oak, the mud slick beneath their shoes. Amelia tried to steady her breathing. Her heart hammered so loudly she could barely hear the rain.Helena followed, her voice breaking. "Randolph, you don't have to do this. She's innocent."

"Innocent?" He let out a hollow laugh. "So was I, once. Until your *Arthur* ruined my life."

Amelia could barely speak. "He doesn't even know you."

"Oh, but he will," Randolph said quietly. "He'll remember me every day—when he visits your grave."

Tears stung Amelia's eyes as she stumbled forward. Helena moved closer, her voice steadying. "If you hurt her, you'll never get away with it. Arthur will find you. The police will…"

"Let them try."

He shoved Amelia toward a fallen tree trunk. "Sit."

Helena lunged forward, grabbing his arm. "Stop!"

He turned and hit her hard across the face. She fell back into the mud, her hand clutching her cheek.

"Helena!" Amelia cried.

"Quiet!"

His knife glinted again as he raised it slightly. "You'll sit there and wait with me. He'll come. And when he does, he'll see what happens when a man takes what isn't his."

"Arthur, wait!" Rosie yelled, but he didn't stop.

Up ahead, a couple appeared—a man and woman running back toward the parking lot, laughing nervously under their shared umbrella.

Arthur stopped them, breathless. "Did you see a woman? Brown hair, wearing a tan coat, heading toward the Major Oak?"

The woman nodded quickly. "Yes—she passed us a while ago.

Arthur's blood ran cold. "Where?"

"Up by The Major Oak."

Without another word, he ran. The rain came harder now, thunder rolling overhead. He reached the clearing—empty. No Amelia. No sign of movement except the whipping branches of the old oak, groaning beneath the wind. "AMELIA!" he shouted, voice cracking.

Nothing.

He turned in circles, scanning the trees, his heart pounding so loudly he could barely breathe.

He grabbed his phone with trembling hands and called the police again. "This is Arthur Bonneville. She's here somewhere—Sherwood Forest, near the Major Oak. You need to send everyone you have. I think he's taken her."

"Stay where you are, sir," the dispatcher said. "Officers are in route."

Arthur stared into the trees, the wind howling around him. Somewhere in the distance, faintly, he thought he heard a woman scream.

He started running again.

CHAPTER THIRTY-NINE

THE RAIN HAD TURNED TO A STEADY DOWNPOUR BY THE TIME Randolph forced them through the thick of the forest. Amelia's boots slipped on the slick ground; her good arm braced against tree trunks as he shoved her forward. Helena stumbled beside her, her sobs blending with the sound of water beating against the leaves.

"Keep moving," he barked. The knife gleamed in his hand, catching the flashes of lightning that lit the woods in stuttering bursts.

They broke through a clearing where the earth had been disturbed. A freshly dug hole sat in the center—a shallow grave, raw and ugly against the sodden ground. Mud clung to its edges. A shovel leaned against a tree nearby, its wooden handle slick with rain.

Amelia's stomach turned. The reality of what he intended struck her cold.

"Randolph," Helena whispered, trembling. "What is this?"

"What does it look like?" His voice cracked. He sounded unhinged, his breathing uneven. "It's where it all ends."

Helena let out a sharp scream that tore through the rain. Her voice echoed, fading into the distance.

"Stop it!" he shouted, gripping the knife tighter. "No one can hear you out here."

Amelia's mind raced. Her heart hammered as she analyzed every detail—the distance to the shovel, the slope of the ground, how close she could get before he'd notice. She needed to stall him, to find a way to make him hesitate. "You don't want to do this," she said softly.

He turned toward her, rainwater streaking down his face. "Don't tell me what I want."

"Then tell me," She urged, "Why are we here? What do you want, Randolph?"

He stared at her for a long moment, his chest rising and falling. Then, unexpectedly, tears began to well in his eyes. His grip on the knife faltered for a second.

"I loved her," he said hoarsely. "You don't understand. I loved her so much. I would've given her the world, but she chose him over me."

Helena's voice shook. "Randolph, please—"

He snapped, his grief twisting into fury. "You'll never love me, will you?"

Helena froze, her lips trembling. "I did care for you, but this—this isn't love."

He laughed, an awful, broken sound. "No. You're right. It's not love anymore. It's freedom." He looked at the grave. "Once this is done, I can start over. You both will be gone, and I'll finally have peace."

Amelia's blood ran cold. "Randolph, please think about what you're saying—"

"I have thought about it!" he shouted, the knife shaking in his hand. "I've thought about it every night since you left, Helena. Every time I close my eyes, I see him—Arthur Bonneville— the perfect man who took everything from me. So, I'll take everything from him. First you," he said, turning to Helena, "and then her," he gestured at Amelia, "and then after he's suffered long enough, him."

Amelia's throat went dry. She thought of Arthur, of the way he'd looked at her that morning when he told her to trust him. She realized then—she couldn't die here. She couldn't let this man destroy the life they had fought so hard for. If she was going to die tonight, she would do it saving someone else.

When Randolph turned his knife toward Helena, Amelia made her move. "Helena, RUN!" she screamed as loud as she could. She lunged forward, slamming into him with every ounce of strength she had left. The impact threw him off balance, and his hand jerked—the knife flew from his grasp and disappeared into the mud.

"Get out of here Helena!" Amelia screamed, shoving him again. Her arm shot through her body in pain.

Randolph roared, spinning around and striking her as hard as possible in the chest. The blow sent her flying backward. She hit the ground with a sickening thud—and realized too late that she had fallen straight into the open grave.

The air was knocked from her lungs. She gasped, coughing violently, struggling to breathe. Rain poured down over the edge of the pit, turning the dirt beneath her into thick, heavy mud.

Above her, Helena scrambled for the knife, but Randolph reached it first. "NO!" Helena screamed.

He raised the blade, his face contorted with rage. "You ruined everything!" But before he could bring it down, a sharp, metallic crack echoed through the clearing.

Randolph's body went rigid—then collapsed sideways into the mud. Behind him stood Charlie, breathless, gripping the shovel with both hands. Rain streamed down his face, mixing with tears and mud.

For a moment, no one moved.

Amelia lay gasping in the grave, the world spinning above her. She felt footsteps thud against the soft earth—someone was climbing down toward her.

"Amelia," came a voice, low and steady. "It's okay. I've got you." Charlie crouched beside her, his face pale but calm. "You're safe now."

"Arthur..." she whispered weakly.

"He's here," Charlie said, helping her sit up. "He's coming."

At the edge of the clearing, Rosie appeared, drenched and shaking. She dropped to her knees beside Randolph's unconscious body and kicked the knife away from his reach. Moments later, the forest exploded with blue and red lights—the wail of sirens cutting through the storm.

"Police!" a voice shouted.

Several officers rushed into the clearing; guns drawn. Within seconds, Randolph was restrained, his arms forced behind his back. He barely stirred as they hauled him upright, his face slack with defeat.

Arthur arrived just as they were pulling him away. Mud clung to his coat, his hair plastered to his forehead, eyes wide with panic until they found her. "Amelia!" He ran to the grave and dropped to his knees, reaching down for her.

She looked up at him through the rain, her chest heaving. He grasped her good arm, and with Charlie's help, pulled her out of the hole. Her legs gave way, and Arthur caught her against him, holding her so tightly she could hardly breathe—but she didn't care. He buried his face in her hair, his voice breaking. "I thought I'd lost you."

"I'm okay," she whispered. "I'm okay."

Rosie came over, covered in mud, her makeup streaked down her cheeks but smiling through her tears. "You scared the hell out of us."

Charlie leaned against the shovel, his chest heaving. "Never thought I'd knock someone out with a garden tool."

Despite everything, Amelia laughed—a shaky, tearful sound that turned into a sob.

Arthur pulled her closer, resting his forehead against hers. "It's over now," he whispered. "It's finally over."

The rain poured harder, soaking them all—Arthur, Amelia, Rosie, Charlie, Helena. Every one of them was drenched, muddy, exhausted, but alive. And as the police led Randolph away and the flashing lights illuminated the clearing, Amelia clung to Arthur with trembling arms, whispering, "I thought I'd never see you again."

He kissed her forehead softly. "You'll never lose me," he said. "Not ever."

For the first time in what felt like forever, she believed him.

CHAPTER FORTY

THE WORLD HAD GONE MAD IN THE DAYS THAT FOLLOWED. What had once been a quiet Nottingham story—a love affair, a family estate, a life rebuilt—had now become national news. Every paper wanted the same story: the glamorous interior designer nearly murdered by her fiancé's grandmother's employee; the noble lineage, the tragedy, the love affair. It was the kind of story that journalists salivated over.

Headlines flooded the stands:

"Designer's Nightmare: Attempted Murder in the Woods."

"Aristocratic Scandal: Bonneville Heiress Targeted in Forest Attack."

"Love and Survival: The Park House Affair Continues."

Every photograph, every detail—all of it had been dissected and fed to the public.

Amelia tried her best to stay away from it, but every morning a new article would appear on her doorstep. Even the radio spoke of her in a tone somewhere between pity and fascination. Strangers had begun leaving flowers at the gate of The Park House.

She didn't want any of it. All she wanted was quiet. Arthur

had done his best to shield her. After the police took Randolph away and the rain-soaked chaos had settled, he'd hardly let her out of his sight. He'd watched over her as if every moment she might slip away again.

Wendy and Charlie came by each day, bringing warmth and laughter to the somber halls of The Park House. But even their humor couldn't completely cut through the tension that lingered. The house—normally a place of peace—now felt heavy with the weight of what had nearly been lost.

Amelia woke often in the night, breathless, her dreams replaying flashes of rain, mud, and the sharp glint of a knife. Arthur would always be there, pulling her close, whispering, "You're safe now, love. You're safe."

And yet, safety felt fragile.

Each time she looked out at the fog-covered lawns, she half-expected to see a figure standing near the hedges—a shadow, a memory, something her mind refused to release.

The press grew relentless. Drones appeared near the grounds. Strangers camped by the gate, hoping to photograph the woman whose name now filled the gossip columns.

It was Rosie who finally said what they were all thinking one evening over dinner.

"This can't go on," she muttered, slamming the newspaper shut. "You two need to get away. Somewhere no one can find you."

Arthur agreed. "I've already been thinking the same thing."

Amelia looked up from her tea, exhausted. "Arthur, I can't just run away. What about the business? Eloise's projects? Charlie—"

"Rosie and I can handle everything," Charlie interrupted, crossing his arms. "You've done enough, Amelia. You nearly died. Let us take it from here for a bit."

Rosie nodded. "He's right. You need to heal—mind and body."

Arthur reached across the table and took Amelia's hand. "Please, love. Let me take you away for a while. Just us. No reporters. No cameras. No nightmares."

Amelia hesitated—the thought of leaving her routine felt

almost impossible. But when she looked into his eyes, she saw the same exhaustion mirrored there. He had carried her pain on his shoulders and was now quietly breaking under its weight.

"Alright," she whispered. "Just a few days."

Arthur's lips curved into the first genuine smile she had seen in weeks. "Good."

The following morning, Amelia awoke to the faint sound of rain tapping against the windows. She turned over in bed—Arthur's side was empty.

"Arthur?" she called softly.

No response.

She sat up, the scent of coffee drifting faintly through the open door. On her nightstand lay an envelope with her name written in his neat handwriting.

Meet me downstairs.

Amelia slipped on her robe and made her way through the quiet halls. When she reached the entryway, she stopped.

Two suitcases stood by the door. Arthur stood beside them, smiling.

"Good morning, darling," he said.

Her heart fluttered. "What's this?"

He poured her a cup of coffee and handed it to her. "You've been through hell. You need air, peace, and a little beauty again. So,"—he lifted one of the bags—"I'm taking you away."

Amelia blinked in surprise. "Away? Where?"

Arthur only smiled. "It's a surprise."

She laughed, shaking her head. "Arthur Bonneville, what are you up to?"

"Trust me," he said simply, leaning down to kiss her forehead.

By midmorning, they were in the car, the countryside rolling past them in streaks of green and gold. The rain had faded to mist, the sun occasionally breaking through the clouds.

Amelia leaned back in her seat, watching the road unfurl before them. "It feels strange to just... leave."

"That's the point," Arthur said. "Sometimes the only way to reclaim peace is to step away from everything that tried to take it."

She smiled faintly, his words settling into her heart. "Do you ever think about what might have happened, if Charlie and Rosie hadn't found us?"

He reached over, his fingers brushing hers. "I don't let myself go there. Because we'll never have to know."

She turned her gaze to the passing fields. "He said he was going to kill you next."

Arthur's grip on the wheel tightened, though his voice remained calm. "And he failed. Because love isn't something you can destroy with a knife."

Amelia glanced at him, the profile of his face steady and strong, and thought—*this man saved me.* Not just that night, but every day since she met him. He had taken the broken pieces of her life and shown her how to live again.

They passed a familiar road sign.

"Nottingham Station?" Amelia read aloud. "We're taking the train?"

Arthur smiled, eyes glinting. "We are."

Her heart lifted for the first time in what felt like forever. "You're serious?"

"Completely."

"Where to?"

"You'll see," he repeated with infuriating confidence.

CHAPTER FORTY-ONE

"WHERE ARE WE GOING?" AMELIA ASKED AS ARTHUR GUIDed her through the Nottingham train station, their suitcases rolling along behind them.

"You'll see," he replied with that secretive smile she'd come to love—the kind that promised mischief and magic all at once.

He handed her a ticket as they approached the platform. She glanced down at it and gasped. *"Bath?"*

Arthur grinned. "I thought you might like that."

A familiar flutter danced in her chest. Bath—the city of literature, of Georgian terraces and timeless grace. It was as if he'd plucked the destination from her imagination itself.

The train hissed to life, and once aboard, they settled into a private compartment. Amelia sank into the seat by the window as the countryside began to roll past—green fields stitched together with stone walls, villages that looked painted by some old master, and clouds drifting lazily through a pale-blue sky.

Arthur poured them both a glass of wine from the bottle he'd smuggled in his bag. "To peace and quiet," he toasted.

"And to getting away from everything," Amelia added. They clinked glasses.

The train rattled on. For the first time in weeks, they both felt free—no journalists, no questions, no past ghosts waiting in the corners.

Arthur leaned back, watching her as she read. "You know," he said, "you make reading look scandalously beautiful."

Amelia laughed softly, lowering the book. "Scandalously?"

"Positively indecent," he teased.

"Flattery will get you everywhere."

He kissed her then—a slow, lingering kiss that seemed to stretch out time itself. The rhythm of the train, the steady hum beneath their feet, made it feel as if the world had stopped to let them exist just like this—weightless, safe, and utterly in love.

By the time they reached Bath, the sun had begun to dip low, washing the city in a soft honeyed glow. The cab driver navigated the narrow streets, past crescents of Georgian buildings and flower boxes spilling with color. The air carried the faint scent of rain and roses.

When the driver stopped, Amelia peered through the window and frowned.

They stood before a quiet townhouse of pale stone—charming but understated. No grand hotel. No polished marble entrance. Just an elegant door, ivy climbing the brick beside it, and a discreet brass number on the lintel.

"Where are we?" she asked, stepping out. "I thought we were going to a hotel."

Arthur paid the driver, who smiled knowingly and drove off, leaving them standing alone on the cobbled street.

"I booked a very special place for us," Arthur said, lifting the bags.

"Arthur, why didn't you book a hotel?" she pressed, her tone caught between curiosity and amusement.

He turned to her with that infuriatingly calm grin. "You'll see."

They climbed the short steps and entered the townhouse. It was quiet, the kind of quiet that felt alive. The front hall opened into a warm, beautifully kept sitting room with a tall window that let in the soft light of early evening. A faint scent of old books and beeswax polish lingered in the air.

Amelia's eyes moved from the antique writing desk to the delicate fireplace and the framed sketches on the wall. "It's very nice," she said slowly. "But… this doesn't seem like your style."

Arthur set the suitcases by the stairs and turned to her, eyes glinting with excitement. "That's because it isn't about my style."

"Then what is it?"

"This," he said, gesturing around them, "is where *Jane Austen* lived when she was in Bath."

Amelia froze. "What?"

Arthur's smile softened. "It's true. This house was hers—between 1801 and 1805, she lived here with her family. I found it while searching for somewhere quiet. When I saw the listing, I knew it was perfect."

Her eyes widened in wonder. "Arthur, you can't be serious."

"Quite serious," he said.

She turned in a slow circle, taking in every detail with reverence—the symmetry of the room, the creak of the floorboards, the scent of history. "Jane Austen *lived here*," she whispered, goosebumps rising on her skin. "She wrote here."

Arthur watched her, a quiet pride in his eyes. "I thought you'd like it."

"Like it?" she breathed. "I adore it."

He chuckled. "Good. Go on, explore. I brought a bottle of champagne—I'll pour us a glass."

Before she moved, she turned and kissed him—sudden and impulsive, the kind of kiss that spoke a thousand unspoken things. "I love you," she murmured against his lips.

He smiled. "I love you too."

Amelia wandered through the house in a trance. Upstairs, she found a small study with a writing desk positioned perfectly by the window. The light fell across the wood in a golden beam, and she could almost see Jane herself there—quill in hand, writing her heroines into existence.

She touched the edge of the desk reverently. *This is where she dreamed,* she thought.

Downstairs, Arthur worked quietly, setting out glasses and a small bouquet of flowers he had smuggled into his bag—pale cream roses. When Amelia descended the staircase again, she stopped halfway, watching him.

He had changed slightly since they first met—softer, yet more grounded. He carried a weight of experience now, and yet, he still looked at her the way he always had: as though she was the first and last person in the world.

"Thank you for this," she said as she reached the bottom step. "It's the most thoughtful thing anyone has ever done for me."

Arthur smiled, holding out her glass. "To Jane," he said.

"To love," she countered, touching her glass to his.

They took a sip. Amelia leaned against the mantel, her eyes wandering to the window. The rain had started again, a fine mist brushing against the glass. The whole world seemed softer in that light—quiet, suspended, and utterly peaceful.

She turned back to him. "An old friend of mine once said, 'Let's have a drink for today and one for tomorrow.'"

Arthur tilted his head. "A wise friend."

She smiled. "You think you can do better?"

"I think," he said, setting his glass down, "I can."

Before she could respond, he took her hand, kissed her knuckles, and lowered himself to one knee. The sound of rain filled the silence that followed. Amelia froze, her heart pounding as he pulled a small velvet box from his pocket.

"Amelia Levingston," he began softly, his voice rich and steady, "you are the great love of my life. You've changed the way I see the world—you've brought warmth into every corner of it. I knew from the moment I met you that you were extraordinary, and every day since has only proven it true."

Her eyes filled with tears, her hand trembling in his.

"I've waited to find the right moment, the right place," he continued. "And I thought—what better place than where one of the greatest writers of love stories ever lived? So, my darling Amelia, will you do me the honor of becoming my wife?"

A small, choked laugh escaped her. "Arthur..." She pressed her hand to her mouth, tears spilling freely now. "Yes. Yes, I will."

He smiled—that boyish, breathtaking smile—and slipped the ring onto her finger. It caught the light and sparkled as though it had always belonged there.

Amelia threw her arms around him, and he rose, holding her close. The champagne, the firelight, the soft hum of rain—everything blurred into one perfect, breathless moment.

They kissed, slow and certain, as though sealing the rest of their lives together.

When they finally pulled apart, Amelia laughed through her tears. "You realize, of course, this is Austen-worthy."

Arthur brushed a tear from her cheek. "I'd say so. Though I think she'd prefer if I'd waited for a ball."

"Hmm," Amelia said playfully, "I'll settle for Bath."

He smiled and pulled her close again. "You have no idea how long I've wanted to do that properly."

"I think I do," she teased.

He lifted his glass and offered it to her once more. "To us—and to forever."

Amelia clinked her glass against his. "To forever."

They drank, laughing, the room alive with warmth and history and love.

Later that night, as they lay together beneath the soft linen sheets, Amelia rested her head against his chest. Outside, the rain whispered against the windows, and the city slept around them.

She looked down at the ring—at the promise it carried—and smiled.

"Arthur?" she whispered.

"Yes, love?"

"This is the happiest I've ever been."

He tightened his arm around her. "Good. Because this is only the beginning."

And somewhere beyond the window, Bath glowed beneath the rain—a city built on stories of love, now holding one more.

CHAPTER FORTY-TWO

T HAT FALL DAY FELT LIKE A DREAM—SOFT AND GOLDEN, A season caught between warmth and the promise of winter. The air carried the faint scent of rain, mingled with woodsmoke and the sweetness of turning leaves. The Park House, their beloved sanctuary, shimmered in the afternoon light, dressed in garlands of ivory roses, twining ivy, and autumn blooms the color of fire and honey.

Every detail of the day reflected the life Amelia and Arthur had built together—a life born of chaos and rebuilt in love. The long windows glowed, the polished wood floors gleamed, and music floated faintly through the halls.

Outside, rows of chairs had been arranged beneath the ancient oak trees, their branches still jeweled with the last amber leaves. Lanterns hung between them, swaying gently in the breeze, their glass catching the sunlight like fragments of dreams. The guests were arriving—Rosie and Charlie laughing together, Lady Edith in elegant champagne silk, Barnaby holding a bouquet much too large and yet somehow perfect.

It was the wedding Amelia never dared to imagine she would have.

Inside, Amelia stood before her mirror, her reflection haloed in soft light. Her gown was simple but timeless—silk that shimmered faintly when she moved, its hem brushing the floor like a whisper. Her hair was loosely pinned, one curl slipping to frame her face. She lifted her hand and touched her ring—the one Arthur had given her in Bath—the one she would never again take off.

Behind her, Rosie adjusted the veil and smiled in the mirror. "You look like you stepped out of a dream."

Amelia smiled softly. "It feels like one."

Rosie fussed with the lace a little more. "I still can't believe we're here. After everything... you both deserve this day."

Charlie appeared in the doorway, leaning casually against the frame in his suit, his tie already loosened. "If I cry, I'm blaming both of you."

Rosie rolled her eyes affectionately. "You'll cry anyway."

He grinned, walking over to Amelia. "You look perfect, boss."

"Thank you, Charlie." Amelia's voice wavered just slightly, full of affection.

Outside, the sound of strings began—soft violins tuning, then the first notes of the prelude.

Lady Edith entered the room. Her expression softened when she saw Amelia. "My dear, you are radiant."

"Thank you, Lady Edith."

The older woman took Amelia's hands, her eyes glistening. "I once thought I had lost my son to grief. But then you came along, and you brought light back into this family. You brought him back to life."

Amelia's throat tightened. "You all brought me back to life too."

Lady Edith smiled through her tears. "Let's not ruin our mascara, shall we?"

Rosie laughed. "Too late."

A soft knock came at the door—Barnaby's voice floated through. "Ladies, the groom's about to faint from anticipation. Shall we begin before he topples into the rose bushes?"

They all laughed.

Arthur stood beneath a tree at the center of the garden. He had never looked more handsome—tailored navy suit, crisp white shirt, no tie, his hair a little tousled by the wind. In his pocket was a handkerchief embroidered with his late brother's initials—Kinsey's—a quiet reminder that love never truly leaves.

He turned toward the path leading from the house, his breath catching when he saw her step into view.

Amelia.

The world seemed to still.

She moved gracefully down the aisle, the autumn light painting her in gold. Every step she took echoed with memory—the first time she walked through the doors of The Park House; the first time Arthur kissed her; the nights they had fought and forgiven, the laughter that filled their home. Every moment had led to this one.

As she reached him, Arthur's eyes glistened.

"You're the most beautiful thing I've ever seen," he whispered.

"And you're mine," she whispered back.

Lady Edith dabbed at her eyes as Barnaby squeezed her hand. Rosie stood proudly beside Charlie, both glowing with joy. Even Gran—seated a few rows back—was smiling, her face soft with a rare and quiet peace.

The priest began to speak, his voice low and melodic. The ceremony flowed like poetry—words of love, faith, and renewal. When the time came for the vows, Arthur took Amelia's trembling hands in his and spoke from his heart.

"I have loved you from the moment you walked into my life—stubborn, brilliant, and brave. You've taught me that love isn't about finding perfection but building it together. You've rebuilt me, Amelia, and I vow to spend the rest of my life protecting, cherishing, and growing old with you."

Amelia's tears glimmered like dew. "Arthur Bonneville," she

began softly, "you've been my anchor, my courage, and my heart. You've shown me that love isn't a fairytale—it's work, it's patience, it's choosing each other every day, even when the world is unkind. I choose you, in every life, in every story, forever."

The vicar smiled; voice full of warmth. "By the power vested in me, I pronounce you husband and wife."

Arthur grinned and pulled her close. The kiss that followed wasn't delicate—it was alive, fierce, full of every moment that had brought them here. The guests erupted into applause as the music swelled.

Barnaby whistled loudly. "That's how it's done!"

Rosie threw her arms around Charlie. "Finally!"

Lady Edith wiped her tears, laughing through them. "It's about time."

Gran clapped gently, her eyes wet, and whispered to Barnaby, "She's perfect for him."

As twilight settled over the estate, the celebration continued. The outdoors had been transformed into a wonderland of candlelight and flowers. Long tables gleamed in candlelight and the scent of garden roses mingled with fresh bread and champagne.

Music filled the air—a small orchestra playing gentle jazz as couples danced. Charlie spun Wendy across the floor; Lady Edith laughed as Barnaby insisted on leading her in a waltz; even Gran tapped her fingers against her champagne flute, her pride showing through her usual sharpness.

Arthur and Amelia danced slowly in the center of it all, the world fading around them.

"This feels unreal," Amelia whispered.

"It's real," Arthur murmured against her ear. "Every second of it."

"You've given me everything I ever dreamed of."

He smiled. "You built all of this. All of these people are here, because of you. I'm so proud of you."

She rested her head on his shoulder, eyes closing. The warmth of his heartbeat, the sound of laughter, the golden flicker of candlelight—it all felt eternal.

As they turned, Amelia caught sight of the stained-glass window she had designed for The Park House—the one that started it all. Light from the candles caught the colored glass. She thought she saw, just for a heartbeat, the faint outline of a figure standing in the reflection—Kinsey, smiling, watching them.

Arthur saw her gaze shift and followed it. He squeezed her hand gently. "He'd be proud, you know."

She smiled through her tears. "I think he's here."

Arthur pressed a kiss to her forehead. "He never left."

Later that evening, as the guests began to drift home, Amelia slipped away to the terrace for a moment of quiet. The night air was cool and crisp, carrying the scent of rain. She looked out across the gardens—the lanterns glowing softly, the distant laughter still echoing through the halls.

Arthur joined her, draping his jacket over her shoulders. "Cold?"

"Just taking it all in."

He followed her gaze over the sprawling lawn, the home that had seen every shade of their story—love, loss, fear, and now, peace.

"It's beautiful, isn't it?" she whispered.

"It's perfect," he said. "Because you're in it."

She turned to him, tears filling her eyes. "This place saved me."

He brushed a curl from her face. "No, Amelia. You saved it."

For a long moment, they stood in silence, watching as the last of the lanterns flickered in the breeze. Somewhere inside, Rosie began to play the piano—a gentle tune that drifted through the night.

Arthur took Amelia's hand, lifting it to his lips. "Shall we have our forever now?"

Amelia smiled, eyes glimmering. "Yes. Let's have our forever."

He kissed her again beneath the starlit sky, the Park House standing proudly behind them—the house that had once been a mystery, now a home filled with love.

And as the night deepened and the music played on, the world outside faded away, leaving only them—Amelia and Arthur—in their timeless, perfect, ever-after.

CHAPTER FORTY-THREE

One year later.

THE COBBLED STREETS OF BATH GLISTENED WITH EARLY morning light. The air was crisp, tinged with the scent of rain and distant flowers. The grand white façade of the Jane Austen Centre stood proudly against the sky, draped in bunting and garlands of pale roses. It was a day for celebration, a day for remembrance, and, most of all, a day for love.

Amelia stood outside the entrance, smoothing her cream-colored coat and glancing down at her watch for what must have been the tenth time in as many minutes. Her heart raced—not with nerves about the event itself, but because one important guest had not yet arrived.

Inside, she could hear the faint murmur of voices, laughter, and the distant pop of champagne corks. Through the glass doors, she caught sight of Rosie chatting animatedly with Eloise, while Lady Edith inspected one of the floral arrangements with her usual perfectionist eye.

Arthur appeared behind her, his voice warm and teasing. "He'll come; you know."

Amelia turned, relief washing over her as she saw him. He looked effortlessly handsome as ever, his dark blue suit perfectly tailored. But it was what he carried in his arms that made her heart soften.

Their two-month-old son stirred gently against his father's chest, wrapped in a soft white blanket. Arthur shifted the baby carefully. "I think he's wondering why we're not inside yet."

Amelia smiled, brushing her fingers lightly over the baby's tiny hand. "He gets that from you. Always impatient."

Arthur chuckled. "He's hungry for life, like his mother."

The baby whimpered softly, and Amelia reached out to take him. "Oh, it's alright, Kinsey," she whispered. "Shhh... it's okay, my love."

The moment she said the name, she felt a quiet ache and a deep joy all at once. Their son's name—Kinsey Bonneville—was both a tribute and a promise.

Arthur watched her lovingly. "He would have been proud, you know."

"I hope so," she said softly. "I still feel him sometimes... especially today."

Arthur opened his mouth to respond when a familiar, exuberant voice cut through the quiet.

"Amelia, darling!"

Amelia froze, then turned around just in time to see a flash of bright color sweep through the crowd. There he was—Merry—dramatic as ever, in a flowing silk kimono of swirling blues and greens, his silver hair tied back with a velvet ribbon, his grin wide enough to rival the sunrise.

"Merry!" Amelia cried, laughing as he flung his arms open and hurried toward her.

He reached her in seconds, enveloping her in the warmest, most theatrical embrace. "My love! My muse! My miracle!"

Amelia laughed into his shoulder. "Oh, Merry, I can't believe you came!"

"Of course I came!" He pulled back, clutching her hands dramatically. "I would not have missed this for all the tea in Bath! Oh, look at you! Marriage agrees with you—your skin is practically glowing, like some sort of English goddess!"

Arthur grinned. "Still as modest as ever, I see."

Merry gasped as his gaze fell on the small bundle in Amelia's arms. "Oh... my... heavens." He pressed his hand to his heart. "Is this him? Is this the little prince?"

"Meet Kinsey," Amelia said softly, beaming with pride.

Merry's eyes shimmered with emotion. "Kinsey." He whispered the name like a prayer. "Oh, Amelia, give me that child right now. I'm holding him."

"Make sure to hold his neck." Arthur said.

Amelia laughed as Merry scooped up the baby with the utmost reverence, his kimono sleeve fluttering as he gently rocked him. "Hello, darling boy," he crooned, "You look just like your father, but with your mother's light. How perfectly unfair!"

Arthur chuckled. "You see what I live with every day, Merry."

"Tragic, absolutely tragic," Merry replied with mock solemnity, cradling Kinsey closer. "I shall have to visit often to provide this child with proper artistic influence."

"You mean chaos," Rosie teased from the doorway, waving them inside. "Come on, the program's about to start!"

Inside, the Jane Austen Centre was transformed for the occasion. Glass cases gleamed under soft lighting, each displaying letters, early editions, and delicate illustrations from Austen's works. But at the heart of the exhibit stood something new: a velvet-lined display containing a pristine set of first edition novels—the very ones Kinsey and Merry had gifted to Amelia.

Above them, a brass plaque read:

**"The Kinsey Bonneville Collection—In Loving Memory.
A gift from Amelia Levingston Bonneville,
for the world to share."**

Amelia stood beside the display; the crowd gathered before her. She took a deep breath, her notes trembling slightly in her hands. Arthur caught her eye from across the room, nodding encouragement. Rosie, Lady Edith, Charlie, Eloise, and even Gran were there—all watching with love. Merry, of course, stood front and center, still holding Kinsey proudly like a small royal.

Amelia began softly.

"Thank you all for being here today. These books once belonged to my dearest friend, Kinsey Bonneville. He believed, as I do, that stories can heal, that they can connect us across time, love, and loss. He gifted them to me, and through them, I learned what it truly means to hold history in your hands."

She paused, her eyes glistening.

"Today, I return them—not as something to keep, but as something to share. Kinsey loved Jane Austen's words because they were honest, clever, and full of hope. And hope, I've learned, is the greatest inheritance we can ever pass on. This is what he would have wanted—to give these stories back to the world."

The room was silent for a heartbeat, and then came a wave of applause—warm, genuine, alive. Merry dabbed at his eyes with a silk handkerchief. "I told you I'd cry," he muttered to Lady Edith, who patted his arm fondly.

Arthur slipped an arm around Amelia's waist and kissed her forehead. "He'd be so proud of you," he whispered.

"I hope so," she said again, smiling through tears.

After the dedication, champagne flowed freely. Glasses clinked, laughter echoed, and even the museum staff couldn't help but smile at the spectacle that was Merry—holding baby Kinsey like a jeweled treasure, refusing to let anyone else take him.

"Merry, I think it's time I fed him," Amelia said gently.

"Oh, nonsense, he's fine! We're bonding!" Merry insisted, bouncing the baby gently. "Uncle Merry is telling him all about love, art, and proper wardrobe choices!"

Arthur laughed. "He's going to need a whole new vocabulary by the time you're done."

Rosie poured herself another glass of champagne. "This is the best christening I've ever been to that wasn't a christening."

Charlie grinned. "Merry might not give him back until he's eighteen."

"Oh hush," Merry said, planting a kiss on the baby's head. "You're just jealous of our connection."

Kinsey gurgled happily in response, and the entire room erupted in laughter.

As the evening waned, the crowd drifted out into the lamplit streets of Bath. The rain had started again—soft and rhythmic, glimmering on the cobblestones. Amelia stood under the awning with Arthur, Kinsey tucked safely in her arms now, asleep.

"Do you realize," she whispered, "that this was the same city where you proposed to me?"

Arthur smiled, brushing a raindrop from her cheek. "I do. It's where our forever began."

"And look where we are now."

He leaned down, kissing her gently, the sound of the rain wrapping them in its quiet music.

Merry, standing a few feet away beneath his oversized umbrella, sighed dreamily. "If Jane Austen were alive, she'd be clapping."

Arthur laughed. "She'd be writing us into her next novel."

Amelia smiled, gazing up into the misty night. "Maybe she already did."

They all laughed softly, the sound echoing down the street like a promise. And as they walked together—Arthur, Amelia, little Kinsey, and the family that had become their world—the lights of Bath shimmered around them, timeless and golden.

Love, after all, had written the perfect ending.

THE END

ABOUT THE AUTHOR

KACIE FOOS lives in Chattanooga, Tennessee with her husband Mike, daughter Frankie, their three dogs Winter, Loki, and Love and a white rabbit named Easter. She grew up in the Pacific Northwest in a magical little city called Spokane, Washington. At an early age she took an interest in acting, which blossomed into a career in Hollywood. She graduated from AMDA LA, but also studied film at UCLA, Shakespeare at RADA in London, and even lived in Paris, France studying French literature. While living in Hollywood, she developed a passion for writing for theater and the screen. This blossomed into a dream of writing novels. *The Park House* was her first successful release, *Kiss Me in Kotor* is her second of many more stories to come. To learn more, visit www.kaciefoos.com